BAD BIRD

Also by Chris Knopf

Elysiana

Short Squeeze

Hard Stop

Head Wounds

Two Time

The Last Refuge

CHRIS KNOPF

BAD BIRD

Vintage Canada

VINTAGE CANADA EDITION, 2011

Published in Canada by Vintage Canada, a division of Random House of Canada Limited, Toronto, in 2011. Originally published in hardcover in the United States of America by the Macmillan Publishing Group, New York, in 2011. Distributed by Random House of Canada Limited.

Vintage Canada with colophon is a registered trademark.

www.randomhouse.ca

Library and Archives Canada Cataloguing in Publication

Knopf, Chris
Bad bird / Chris Knopf.

Issued also in electronic format.

ISBN 978-0-307-35732-8

I. Title.

PS3611.N66B33 2011 813'.6 C2010-907215-4

Printed and bound in the United States of America

2 4 6 8 9 7 5 3 1

Acknowledgments

Special thanks to Steve Sullivan–Air Force pilot, Vietnam vet, and ace of a human being–for the opening flying sequence and related aeronautical instruction. Sean Cronin for weapons and editorial advice, both well-aimed. Paige Goettle for my intentionally fractured French. Cindy Courtney and Rich Orr for ongoing legal consultation. Peter Joseph for editorial wisdom. John Yeager for connecting the IT dots. Anne-Marie Regish for logistical wizardry. Randy Costello and Bob Willemin for counsel along the way, and Mary Farrell for continuing to put up with all this.

1

If I hadn't been spending so much time living in my head, I might have noticed earlier that there was something terribly wrong with the single-engine plane circling overhead.

I was leaning on the top rail of a white plastic fence that encircled a huge grazing and exercise pasture for a herd of show horses. When I was in the thrall of a certain kind of moody unease, I liked to hang there and watch the elegant creatures trot around, caress one another with their long necks, and occasionally drop to the ground and roll around on their backs. I'd made friends with a few of them, relationships reinforced by the breath mints I'd hold out in the palm of my hand, which they'd slurp up into their huge horsey mouths with surprising delicacy.

I don't remember which internal debate had driven me there that morning, but I remember it was a pretty spring day—early spring, when the grass of the pasture was in its first blush of new growth and the big maple trees planted randomly along the white fence were sporting a fresh coat of light-green fuzz. The sun was still fairly low on the horizon, but the cloudless sky was already a vivid blue, presenting a clear contrast with the white fuselage of the little plane as it passed above.

My mind suddenly became disengaged from the obsession of the moment, and my heart leaped to my throat as I realized a trail of gray-black smoke was suddenly pouring from the engine as the plane wobbled drunkenly through the air. I reached for the cell phone in the pocket of my pants and held it, along with my breath, as I watched the plane continue to circle as it lost altitude. The horses weren't as transfixed as I was, accustomed as they were to the sound of small aircraft buzzing into East Hampton Airport about five miles to the east. But I was very aware of them innocently standing or milling about directly beneath the struggling aircraft.

"Get out of there," I yelled, which alarmed only one of the breath-mint enthusiasts standing nearby. He pulled up his head, swiveled to the left, and trotted directly into harm's way.

The smoke was now gushing out of ventilation ports around the engine, leaving a thick, spiraling contrail that began to dissipate into a formless cloud. The plane was close enough for me to see numbers on the underside of the wings and to hear the irregular, angry-insect whir of the engine. The horses, which were spread out across the pasture, finally picked up on the threatening sounds from above. As if with a single mind, they immediately surged into a headlong gallop, most toward the barn up the hill, the others in a split-off herd running toward the white fence, along which they flew in a loose, frantic formation, like racehorses turning into the final stretch.

The plane continued to tighten the circle as it descended toward the ground. The dark gray smoke streaming from the engine obscured all but the propeller and the outer tips of the wings, which swung from side to side as the pilot fought to gain visibility.

With the horses now out of immediate danger, I recovered some presence of mind, flipped open my phone, and stabbed 911. I don't remember what I said, or rather shouted, at the dispatcher, but as they always do, she told me in a calm, deliberate voice to get to a safe place—wherever that would be—and stay on the line while she called in the emergency crews.

"Call everyone you know. You're gonna need it," I said.

"Have you moved to a secure location?" she asked.

I hadn't. I was too immobilized by the sight of the plane spiraling downward, ever closer, its wings seesawing and tail slashing back and forth in a desperate effort to see through the cloud of smoke. And then suddenly, it was quiet, the sound of the engine replaced by a breeze through the trees lining the road behind me. The silence snapped me out of my trance, and I ran toward my Volvo station wagon where it was parked by the side of the road. But before I could get there, I heard a steady whir as the engine caught hold again. The plane's nose lifted slightly as it regained purchase on the air and settled back into its banking descent.

The voice of the police dispatcher barked out of my phone, still steadfast and composed, asking me to report on the state of affairs.

I told her the plane was still struggling, though my voice might have been drowned out by the sound of the engine, now even closer overhead. The left wing dipped severely as the plane banked into another turn, and with the smoke temporarily diverted by the wind, I caught a glimpse of the pilot. It was a woman, with brown hair secured by a headband. She was too far away for me to make out more than that. It sounded like the engine had straightened itself out, the unsettling silence replaced by a smooth buzz. As she continued to turn left in that inexorable circle, I strained to get a better look at her face. It was a hard face, nearly attractive if not for the determined, anxious set of her jaw, and though still a distance away, I was sure she looked directly at me. I waved like mad, hoping she'd know our eyes had met.

The pilot's door abruptly opened, and out flew a large silver thing that took but a few moments to fall to earth.

It didn't take much longer for me to clamber over the fence and dash across the field to where the object lay. It was a type of aluminum case, cracked open by the fall. Inside was a 35mm camera and lens, each still safely in its own pocket carved out of cushioning foam. Some other debris—pens, lipstick, camera accessories, a local shopper's guide from Burlington, Vermont, and a few crumpled pieces of paper—was strewn nearby. I stuffed what I could back in the case, then slammed it shut.

The police dispatcher asked for another briefing. She was still calm, but slightly more insistent, her voice loud enough to hear out of the phone that I'd stuck in my pocket.

"Be right with you," I yelled, though she likely didn't hear me. The sound of the plane, which I'd almost lost track of, suddenly got a lot louder. I looked up and saw it coming straight down upon me, rotating in a slow downward spiral, what had been smoke now a roar of flames flowing from the engine, any semblance of control entirely lost.

"Please describe the current situation," yelled the dispatcher, patience and composure running out. I would have answered, but I was too busy running like hell with the aluminum case under my arm. The grassy field was a lot lumpier underfoot than it looked from the road, but that did little to slow me down until my toe caught some treacherous little tangle of vegetation and I pitched headlong to the ground. Aided by forward momentum, I almost scrambled back on my feet, but I lost my balance and ended up on my butt instead.

There was nothing left to do but watch. I held my face in my hands and moaned "Oh, God" softly to myself as the plane drove directly into the bright green grass, where it exploded into a beautiful orange ball, topped by blossoms of black smoke boiling up into the sky as if a fountain from hell had erupted into the hopeful promise of spring.

A wall of red-hot air punched me in the chest. The grass between me and the destroyed plane began to burst into flame. Still holding the camera case, and furiously sucking gulps of acrid air into my lungs, I stumbled to my feet and ran like a demon for the relative safety of the roadside and my waiting car.

I tossed the case over the fence and followed with a vault that would have brought envy to an Olympic high jumper. I landed on my back and stared gasping up at the blue sky, already beginning to haze over from the smoke of the plane.

A few years before, I'd been blown nearly to smithereens by a car bomb, resulting in months of painful convalescence and plastic surgery. As I looked up, I asked the cloudy heavens why all the exploding vehicles, but no answer was forthcoming.

In some ways, the worse the calamity, the less there is for first responders to do. As requested, every ambulance and fire truck from Hampton Bays to Montauk showed up on the scene, along with a half dozen black-and-white Southampton Town Police patrol cars and every available cop from adjacent villages.

The real work would be done by the National Transportation Safety Board Go Team, whom my cop friends told me would be swooping in within the hour. Meanwhile, the fire was in the hands of the emergency squad from East Hampton Airport, who were the only ones with the foamy chemicals capable of putting it out. The regular volunteer firemen could only stand around in their heavy boots and suits and watch. I, in turn, watched them, noting for some perverse reason that half of them were smoking cigarettes.

Thus engaged, I nearly jumped when Joe Sullivan, one of the Southampton Town cops, put his hand on my shoulder.

"Erin said you were the one who put in the call," he said.

"The dispatcher? How did she know it was me?"

"She recognized your voice."

"Everyone's a detective."

"You're all right?" he said, in the way people do when they really want you to say yes.

"Yes. I think."

"Should I get the paramedics?"

"Only if they can pour me a cocktail."

Sullivan pulled his archaic little casebook out of a special pouch that hung from his belt. Around Southampton Town Police headquarters he was called a plainclothesman, which for Sullivan meant he had to look like a cop in some other way than by wearing the official patrolman's navy blue uniform. That day he wore a T-shirt under a nylon Windbreaker and army fatigues tucked into a pair of paratrooper's boots. His head sat on his shoulders without the benefit of a neck and was covered in buzz-cut blond fur. Wraparound sunglasses ensured that you'd know this was a cop even if he didn't have his badge hanging from a chain around his neck.

Sullivan and I had been through a lot of things together as the result of my bourgeoning career as an underpaid defense attorney. Some of those things had been pretty traumatic, at least for me. We also had a few people we cared about in common, so even though I was a defense lawyer and he was a cop, we had a kind of genuine friendship. Anyway, that's what I wanted to believe.

"It looks like you're the only witness," he said.

"There goes the investigation."

"You know that's not true, counselor," said Sullivan. "There's no witness I'd rather have."

"You're being nice to me."

"I'm trying to be sympathetic. If it'll make you feel better, I'll slap you around a little, then we can do the interview."

Actually, I wasn't feeling that good. I felt the way normal people feel after witnessing a horrible accident. Somewhere between numb and on the verge of barfing up breakfast.

"Maybe I ought to lie down," I said, dropping to the grass.

"You sure you're okay?" he asked again, squatting down next to me.

I lied and said I was fine.

"No paramedics. I just need to collect myself."

I gave him my statement. I'd handled enough criminal cases to know that eyewitness accounts had a shelf life of about five minutes. And even then they weren't all that reliable, contrary to common misconception reinforced by cop shows and other popular forms of disinformation in which the investigators knock on the door of an old lady who says something like, "Oh, yes, I was out watering my garden and I noticed this young blond man with a slight limp and a tattoo of a rose on his left hand leaving the victim's home looking rather furtive. I think it was at three forty-five P.M., though it might have been three forty-six."

So I gave my statement while I lay there looking up at the sky, now a deep blue behind a smear of dark gray smoke that reflected the strobing yellow, white, and blue lights of the emergency vehicles crowded onto the scene.

My statement was dramatic but not very long. It came down to a fairly simple story of a plane with its engine on fire, laboring to clear a place to land, and ultimately failing to do so. Except for the odd detail of the lady pilot heaving a camera case out the door a few moments before crashing.

"Is that the case?" Sullivan asked, pointing to the only aluminum case within view.

"Could be," I said.

He frowned and asked if I'd handled the contents. He knew me better than that.

"The case was open when I found it. It holds a camera with a detached lens. Also a few incidental items, like cosmetics and pen and paper, though there used to be more."

"What do you mean, 'used to be'?"

"I saved what I could. There wasn't a lot of time."

"Any film in it?" he asked.

"I don't know," I said, honestly, since I hadn't thought to look.

"You want to stay with that answer, counselor, or reconsider?" he asked.

And there it was, the eternally unresolved conflict between a cop with a reflex devotion to proper procedure and a defense attorney with anything but.

"What are we, a half hour into this and you're already impugning my integrity?" I asked.

"Half hour into what?" he asked.

"This."

"Don't start," he said, pointing at me. I knew exactly what he meant.

"I don't know what you mean," I said.

He picked the camera case off the ground like he was afraid I'd snatch it up myself and run away. Then he pressed me to recall additional details of the crash, but I swore I'd done my best.

"I'm just getting you ready for the NTSB," he said. "The National Transportation Safety Board. They'll be here soon."

"I can't wait for them. I have to get to the office," I said.

He shook his head.

"Stay put and get it over with. They do not want you to leave, and they do not screw around. Try to be a cooperative member of society, just this once."

"What the hell does that mean?"

I did what he told me to do, despite impulses to the contrary. I soothed my impatience by lying on the grass and looking up at the sky. I did this from time to time anyway, when I was in the same kind of mood that drove me to stand at a plastic fence and talk to horses. This mood was usually contemplative and introspective. Sometimes pensive, more often self-flagellating. Or more likely, lazy and good-for-nothing.

It was from this vantage point that I turned my head and saw a man in a blue-and-gray herringbone jumpsuit leaning against the front fender of a pickup truck and staring at the fire. He had his hands in his pockets and one heel braced against a tire, like he was trying to get comfortable for a long stretch of disaster watching. Everything about the pose was ordinary, except I noticed he was crying.

I rolled up on one shoulder to get a better look. His eyes were fixed on the flames, and he didn't see me looking at him. When I was sure I was seeing what I thought I was seeing, I stood up and walked over to him.

"You okay, sir?" I asked.

He turned his head toward me. The wet lines running down his cheeks didn't seem to fit. His hair was a slicked-back brown, his nose a busted lump in the middle of his face. His complexion was the color of wheat dough and cratered by the scars of ancient acne, a deformity nearly disguised by thick black stubble.

"No. Not okay," he said, and turned back toward the fire.

This should have been a cue for me to back away and leave him alone.

"Can I get you some help?" I asked.

He gave a mirthless little laugh.

"Nothing nobody can do now. 'Cept maybe leave me alone," he said, which I was in the process of doing when he added, "Or else arrest me, I guess."

I turned around and walked back.

"Arrest you for what?"

He looked like he was listening to a private joke inside his head.

"Isn't that what they do in these situations? Just arrest everybody that coulda had anything to do with it? Then let the lawyers and God sort it out?"

I didn't think that was exactly how it worked, and I told him so.

"I doubt that, sir," I said. "You have something to do with the crash?"

His face went blank–if it showed anything, maybe a little bewilderment.

"Shit, yeah. My wife was flying that thing."

2

I earned my law degree against the wishes of my father. He never gave me a decent explanation for why doing this bothered him so much. He was an educated man himself. A civil engineer, though the title always made me laugh. My father was anything but civil. I guess he had to settle for what they offered. Nowadays you could probably get certified as an uncivil engineer. A Master of the Son-of-a-Bitch Arts.

I revere the law, no matter what my behavior might suggest. You have to revere something, I think, or else you become a toxic ball of cynicism and disappointment, which shows on your face, and I have enough trouble holding my looks together.

Along with a reverence for the law comes a general regard for due process, which means you go by the book as much as possible, with some faith that the book will treat you more fairly than some random schmuck who might be having a bad day. Like, for example, the jerk from the NTSB who interviewed me about the plane crash.

It was bad enough they took an hour to get there. I was so itchy from waiting I almost started to vibrate. So when the guy reached out his hand to shake, I probably squeezed tighter than I should have.

He squeezed back, and I relented a second before the small bones in my hand turned to powder.

"Give me your statement," he said, pulling out a small notebook while simultaneously wiping his forehead, which looked pretty dry to me, with the back of his forearm.

"Please," I said.

"Pardon me?" he asked, looking up from his book.

"You meant to say, 'Please give me your statement.' "

If I had to describe him, I'd have to say he looked like a self-satisfied, imperious prig. About my age and handsome, in the traditional sense, which held no appeal for me at all. I like them odd. I wanted to tell him that–to quell his sense of superiority–but he didn't give me the opening.

"Give me your statement," he said again.

I shook my head.

"Not without the magic word. If you can't say it, get me someone who can."

He looked at me like I'd told him to go pee on his shoes.

"This is a crash scene investigation," he said.

"Exactly. People are dead here. Be polite or I leave. And if you try to stop me, you'll have a habeas corpus on your desk before you get back to the office."

He stared at me for a few moments, taking it all in. I smiled, with my fists on my hips, a gesture so ridden with cliché I'd be embarrassed if it hadn't had the appropriate effect.

"Please," he said, flatly.

So I gave him my statement, one more thorough and precise than he deserved. I pulled out everything I could remember, including the metal camera case and my brief encounter with the husband of the woman flying the plane. I reported that I'd told the guy to stay put, then ran off to find Joe Sullivan, but when we got back, he was gone. All I could do was describe his appearance and recount our brief conversation.

I didn't know how helpful it would be ultimately, but it was the best eyewitness testimony he'd get. I assumed it wasn't the last time I'd have to talk to him, so I gave him a card and said I'd be available anytime for follow-ups. I waited until he gave me his card and said "Thank you," then I left the schmuck and the smoky, surrealist's accident scene and went back to my office in Water Mill so I could spend the rest of the day pretending to work.

My office was a converted apartment on the second floor above a row of storefronts and a Japanese restaurant that faced Montauk Highway, the main east-west thoroughfare stringing together the villages that make up the Hamptons. I'd shared the floor for two years with a group of surveyors who had yet to say hello to me, something you can already guess I took as an affront to common decency. Since a piece of my law practice was still related to real estate, I was in a position to recommend surveyors to well-paying clients. I could understand the surveyors ignoring me during the boom times, but now you'd think self-interest would have forced a modicum of cordiality.

I reciprocated by pretending they were all invisible. Of course, the only one actually suffering from this standoff was me, feeling tense every time I walked past their door, anticipating another failed opportunity to break the silence.

Self-inflicted pain over absolutely nothing. One of my specialties.

Once safe inside my office, however, my mood always caught an updraft. What others might describe as a madhouse jumble of paper, aging computer equipment, and broken-down furniture, I saw only as paradise, well-lit and ventilated by windows on two sides, which also afforded a perfect view of a giant windmill out on the village green and the stately Beaux Arts architecture of what used to be a convent. Its purpose now was to provide an ideal landscape for long periods of gazing out the window when I should have been applying myself to one of the tedious assignments demanded as penance for choosing the law as a living.

I loved my house in Bridgehampton mostly out of habit, but there was something about my office that made me feel transcendently sheltered and secure, as if outside time and space, alone with only what was familiar and important to me.

To get the full effect of that environment, I made a cup of coffee, lit a cigarette, and cleared a stack of last winter's case folders so I could plop down on the sofa. I slumped down, enveloped in smoke and steam with my legs propped up on the ottoman. I was wearing men's khakis, which I thought looked great with a pair of brown leather wing-tipped shoes. As I admired the look, I wiggled deeper into the sofa and stuffed my hands in my pockets, which is when I felt a wad of paper. I pulled it out and puzzled over how it had gotten there. Then I remembered how I'd crammed most of the dumped-out debris back into the camera case. Except what I'd crammed into my pocket.

When I sat up and untangled the crumpled paper, a clump of grass and a little piece of blue plastic fell out. It was a memory card for a digital camera. I remembered Sullivan asking me if there was film in the lady pilot's camera. I had the answer in my hand. There might have been photos, but they wouldn't be on film.

This confirmed that hiding in my office would do nothing to purge my mind of the sight of that woman's face, immediately followed by the black-and-orange plume billowing up from the horse pasture. So I stubbed out the butt, climbed out of the sofa, and fired up my slick, new, silvery laptop.

I Googled "Pilots, small aircraft, female, East Hampton, NY." Of the 52,000 hits that popped up, the only one that seemed useful was from an article in the *Southampton Chronicle* on how locals escape the tidal wave of summer people that washed in every Memorial Day.

"Eugenie Birkson has the quickest way to scram out of town: her own Cessna air taxi. The only female pilot based out of East Hampton Airport in Wainscott, Eugenie spends most of the summer transporting impatient wheeler-dealers to and from regional airports in

Westchester and Fairfield counties, but likes to fly with her husband, Ed, to remote parts of Vermont and New Hampshire whenever she can.

" 'Nothin' but cows and pine trees, and big old lakes you can swim in without gettin' salt up your nose,' says Eugenie. 'My own version of the anti-Hamptons.' "

I focused on Eugenie Birkson and pulled up two more hits, one a report on a softball game in which she played second base, and the other a listing on a site called "Pilot's Reference Network" that added little to the newspaper story. A look into Ed Birkson drew a blank.

I checked all the social media sites I belonged to but never participated in, and found nothing on either Birkson. I also ran the names through the ultra-double-secret, certainly illegal software given to me by a friend named Randall Dodge who used to be in naval cyber intelligence. The software's talent was aggregating databases containing personal information–basic stuff like address, phone number, date and place of birth, education, employment, and medical history–with little regard for the niceties of privacy law. This for me was a genuine guilty pleasure, in that I enjoyed the hell out of it and it made me feel guilty as sin. But not enough to delete the software and go back to regular people searches.

I turned up a half dozen Birksons who'd lived at some point on the East End, but none named Eugenie or Ed. Eugenie did turn up, however, as a professional pilot with a Part 135 flight certification, trained in a program operating out of MacArthur Airport in Islip, a town an hour to the west of Southampton. From this report, I linked her to a pair of local Birksons–Matthew and Matthew Jr.–through an address in Springs, a section of East Hampton best known for Bonackers and Abstract Expressionism.

To confirm the hunch, I picked up the phone to call Joe Sullivan, then thought better of it. It was unlikely he'd want to share the name of any victim or victims before they were released to the public, which meant I'd have to finagle it, which would spark his suspicious nature, and I'd have him on my back before I hardly got started.

Which made me ask myself, Got started with what?

Instead of answering that, I shut down the computer and left the office. The sky above the fields of Bridgehampton was clear of smoke. Traffic on Montauk Highway was monotonously bumper-to-bumper, as it would be from May until some indistinct moment in late fall, before it got busy again over the holidays. The best shortcuts around the traffic were north of the highway but involved a more circuitous trip to the airport. So I took a southern route that zigzagged through planned neighborhoods of colossal houses and around the remnants of potato fields that were once the only use people had for oceanfront property.

Those people included my late husband's family, who sold one of the area's largest potato farms for what stood for huge money back in the 1990s. Following in the fine tradition of the *nouveau* and wholly unprepared *riche,* they blew the proceeds in fairly short order on things like the new Porsche my husband flew at about a hundred miles an hour into an old oak tree.

To get to East Hampton Airport, I had to get back on Montauk Highway for a brief stretch, then head north through a forest of rangy scrub oaks and pines stunted by the type of impoverished sandy soil common Up Island and also found in the northern reaches of East Hampton.

Though I was familiar with the sound of aircraft heading to and from the airport, I'd never actually been to the place myself. I was surprised to see it was a pretty well-developed place, with modern-looking signage, lots of buildings, and tarmacs thick with little prop planes and slim, fiercely expensive–looking private jets.

I parked my car and walked toward what looked like the main terminal, judging by a pair of black Crown Victoria limos pulled up to the curb.

According to the guy manning a car rental counter, airport

management worked behind an unmarked door, which in turn was behind another counter. He told me the main man was Ralph Toomey. I breached the counter and knocked on the door, then opened it up. The office was filled to capacity with desks piloted by a diverse group of women, whose only common denominators were a pencil-thin waist and a diminutive stature. There was a white-haired white woman, a young blond woman, an African-American woman, and an Asian woman. I imagined the employment ad: "Wanted: Women to work in cramped office environment. Minimum clerical skills required, though must be no bigger than an elf. An equal opportunity employer."

"Hello," I said to the group at large. "Is Mr. Toomey in?"

None of them leaped for the ball, so I asked the tiny Asian lady directly.

"Would you know?" I asked her.

She held my gaze as she reached for the phone on her desk. Her face was perfectly round, as if drawn by a cartoonist.

"There's someone here to see you," she said into the phone. Then she looked up to ask who I was, a first step that hadn't occurred to her on her own.

"Jacqueline Swaitkowski. I'm a lawyer and an officer of the court," I said, my all-time favorite fiddle. It's technically true, since I'm a practicing trial attorney, and completely meaningless, since anyone not being tried and hung by the legal system has privilege to the same title. Including tattooed bail bondsmen and the tricky bastards who deliver divorce papers to recalcitrant spouses.

The Asian lady took the bait and reported the gravity of the moment in hushed tones. Without being asked, I stepped away from the desk and took a seat, assuming all I had to do was wait for my audience. I was right.

"Ms. Swaitkowski," said Ralph Toomey as he emerged from an inside office. He was a medium-sized guy with medium brown hair and medium Caucasian features, wearing a white shirt, gray pants, and a bland, striped tie, probably sporting the team colors of Middling University.

I stood and nodded, taking his dry, fleshy hand.

"Mr. Toomey. Sorry for interrupting you. I'm looking into Eugenie Birkson."

"Oh, of course. The crash."

And with those words, Mr. Toomey redeemed himself of all my preconceived assumptions. He was now both personable and brilliant.

"You've given a statement to the NTSB," I said matter-of-factly as I dug a ballpoint pen and a small notebook out of my purse.

"Of course."

"I'm not here for you to repeat all that; I just want to know what else you can tell me about Mrs. Birkson."

I clicked the pen and stood with it poised above the notebook.

"Let's go to the conference room, where we can sit," said Toomey. "Who did you say you were representing again?" he added as he guided me toward one of the many closed and unidentified doors that lined the domain of the diminutive women.

"The NTSB is charged with determining the cause of the crash," I said, handing him a version of my card on which I'd prominently included the seal of the State of New York and the words, in bold italics, ***Officer of the Court.*** "Local authorities are focusing on the pilot."

Again, a truthful, albeit entirely misleading, statement I hoped would stand. It did.

"So, what can I tell you?" he asked, settling in at the conference table as he studied my card, holding it with both hands so it wouldn't be blown away by a sudden breeze.

"Did you know Eugenie?"

He nodded.

"Sure. She's been around the airport longer than me, running an air taxi between here and FBOs outside the city, mostly Westchester and Fairfield County."

"FBOs?"

"Fixed-base operations. What we usually call general aviation airports, like us. The little ones. Not JFK."

"So what's your opinion? On the crash," I said.

He thought about that with the kind of deliberate expression I often saw on expert witnesses at criminal trials. The kind I never quite believed were genuine.

"You probably know some colorful characters," he said.

You don't know the half of it, buster, I thought, but said instead, "This is the Hamptons."

Toomey smiled a knowing smile.

"Eugenie broke the mold. Tough gal, you know, like Tugboat Annie in a slimmer package. Chewed tobacco, wore a set of keys on her belt, you know, like the biker chick she was. Used to drive one of those big hog things. Harley. But warm, when you talked to her. Would tear up at the drop of a hat. I liked her. Couldn't help it. Sorry," he said, tearing up a bit himself.

My opinion of Toomey took another upward leap.

"I'm sorry, too, Mr. Toomey. I know this is hard."

He shook off the moment with a toss of his head and regained his professional poise.

"Eugenie was an expert pilot, with thousands of hours in the air. Something went wrong with the aircraft. Pilot error, zero probability."

"She had a husband," I said. "What do you know about him?"

He looked up from the table, which he'd been staring at.

"Ed? Good mechanic. Maintains half the planes on the field. Not much of a talker, but easygoing enough, for a Bubbie."

"Ed's a Bonacker?" I asked, referring to the ancient colony of reclusive fishermen who once held sway along the bayside coast of East Hampton, and who in all but name had essentially disappeared in the last few decades.

"Yeah, and I don't mean perhaps," he said, Bonacker style.

"Ed Birkson?"

"Ed Conklin. Eugenie was a modern girl. Kept her name. Proud of her white-trash heritage. Sorry, that was inappropriate. Is this being recorded? Will I have to repeat the same testimony? If so, I'd like to strike that last comment."

He looked up at me with a reddening, worried face. I felt bad that it was all for naught, since there was not a single thing I could do to hurt him, unless suckering him out of this information constituted a hurt.

"I don't think I heard that last part of your statement," I said, generously.

He looked appreciative.

"Thank you."

"So, Eugenie came from compromised circumstances," I said.

"You probably don't know Matt Birkson," he said. "You would if you lived in Springs. Notorious hard case, from a long line of hard cases. Lives in a busted-down unpainted house, with derelict cars, boats, and major appliances all over the property. Spent time in prison for hijacking tractor trailers and knocking off an appliance store. And that was only what they caught him for. Ran his own gang. A real charmer."

I remembered the name Matthew Birkson from my Google search, but I wrote it down again just in case.

"Did she have a brother? Matt Jr.?"

Toomey nodded.

"He split a long time ago. Another bad apple, if memory serves." Then he snapped his fingers. "That's right. Ed told me the two of them lived at an aunt's while the old man was in stir. The boy ran off before graduating high school. I don't think there was any love lost between the kids, to hear Ed tell it."

"So how long had Eugenie been working as a pilot?" I asked.

"Long time. She started out as a mechanic. That's how she met Ed, who was a widower at the time. Pilots can be pretty obsessed about flying, but Eugenie was extra obsessed. That and being a girl made her stand out."

I didn't know if that last bit should ignite my feminist zeal or not, so I just let it slide.

"So," I said, "how do you figure out what happened when everything's just a pile of burned-up rubble?"

"She didn't have a black box, like they do on commercial or military aircraft. This is an uncontrolled airport, meaning no flight tower, so radio communication isn't normally recorded. She called a mayday on the CTAF, the regular open radio frequency, that she was short of the runway and had an engine fire. My girls in the office picked that up, as did the people around the field who monitor 122.7, which is the UNICOM frequency out here, but there wasn't much we could do but roust the airport fire crews, who are all volunteers."

"You're sure it was equipment failure? Are there maintenance records?"

"Ed kept a maintenance log, of course. That'd be with the NTSB by now, but I doubt it'll tell them much. Ed kept that plane in perfect condition. And even if he didn't, logs are easy to fake. Not that Ed would do that. Not to his own wife."

"No copies?"

"You'll have to ask Ed. Though I'm sure the NTSB will share the info when they're done analyzing."

Not with me, I thought. Not willingly, anyway.

"But I'm curious," he said. "Why this interest in Eugenie? It's a tragic thing, but accidents happen."

I dodged the question, even though I had an answer. One I knew in my deepest parts from the moment I saw the careening aircraft.

This was anything but an accident.

Toomey gave me directions to the maintenance hangar where Ed Conklin worked. It was in an area well removed from where the other buildings lined the airfield. Toomey told me this was where the original airport had been built, but it was now considered a backwater, mostly serving local flying enthusiasts and humble air taxis like Eugenie's.

I thought it unlikely that Ed Conklin would be on the job the day his wife died, but I was wrong. As I felt my way through the darkness inside the yawning entrance of a battered steel building, I nearly ran into him, standing in the middle of the hangar floor wiping his hands with a greasy rose-colored cloth.

"Mr. Conklin," I said, taking a step back. "You're here."

"Where'm I supposed to be?"

"I don't know. Home grieving?"

"Not what Eugenie woulda wanted. I seen you somewheres."

"At the crash scene," I said. "Has the NTSB been out here yet?" I looked over my shoulder as if expecting to see that young charmer and his team riding across the tarmac on war steeds.

"Yep."

"They wanted your maintenance log."

"Yep. Some young prick asked a bunch of insulting questions, then left with all my paperwork. Won't tell 'em anything. I've been fixin' planes for thirty years. Only had a couple drop out of the sky, and it wasn't maintenance that did it."

"Ralph Toomey said it had to be the plane. Couldn't have been pilot error."

"He's right about that. No goddamned way it was Eugenie's flying," he said, still wiping his hands. "Closest thing to a human bird you'll ever meet. Drove her bike the same way. Like she was a part of the machine."

"Have the cops been here?"

That seemed to confuse him.

"Cops? What for?"

"It's routine," I said, half truthfully.

He shook his head, still confused, and resigned.

"So any idea what could have happened?" I asked as I looked around for a place to sit down. Ed followed my eyes and pointed to a collection of large plastic bins holding what I assumed were aircraft parts.

"Want to sit?" he asked.

"I do."

He led me over to the bins, and I sat down. He followed me, choosing a bin uncomfortably close to my personal space. Close enough for me to smell the grease and sweat on him.

Conklin was somewhere in his fifties. Could have been fifty-one or fifty-eight. His posture was straight up and down, his shoulders narrow but his arms thick as my legs. He had hands to match, which made me wonder for the hundredth time if men with large hands naturally found themselves in the manual trades or if their hands grew that way under the stress of the job.

"I'm really sorry about Eugenie," I said. "It must be a terrible shock."

"Something like that," he said.

"How did you know it was her plane that went down?"

He looked at me with a flat expression.

"I heard it on the radio. I was expecting her to call in when she got about eight miles from the airport, so everybody'd know she was about to land. I got the call, but she just wanted to know why the oil pressure gauge had pinned itself all the way down to zero. Can't say as I had a respectable explanation."

"What do you think happened?" I asked, for the second time.

"Oil was blowing out of somewhere. Shouldn't've happened. Something got fucked up," he said, clearing the air of further speculation.

I sat there looking at him. My initial surprise at seeing him at the hangar had lessened as I talked to him. This was a man in shock. He was in a daze, distant, yet there with me, on the verge. My friends, the few I have, will tell you I'm not the maternal type, but something akin to maternal instinct sprang up in my chest as I watched him continue to work on his hands with the old rose-colored rag. There was little the ragged scrap of cloth could do to clean his hands, but he kept wiping.

"Is there anyone else?" I asked him. "Anyone at home?"

He shook his head, looking straight at me, tears once again filling his eyes.

"My boy works here, but he's got his own place. Up Island. Drives all the way the hell here every day. He's on a casino trip with his buddies. I need to call him, but I haven't figured out how to put it. Eugenie's just his stepmother, but he's known her for years."

"Do you have a lawyer, Mr. Conklin?"

He shook his head.

"Not since I bought my house in '83. You had to get one to do that."

I took a card out of my purse, the real one that just said *Jacqueline Swaitkowski, Attorney* with my office phone and official e-mail address.

"I think this would be a good time to get another one," I said. "I would like to have that honor. As the only witness to your wife's crash, it would mean a lot to me."

Ed shrugged.

"Okay, whatever. I sure as hell don't know what to do with all this."

"You need to remember everything you said to the NTSB. If you have the energy, please write it down. All of us are forgetful, especially when we're shook up, so there's no shame in it. The local cops will be dropping by here or your house. The accident was in Southampton, and you're in East Hampton, so right now they're working out jurisdictional protocols. Otherwise they'd have been here already. Don't talk to them about anything. Just call me. The number's on the card."

I told him to stay put and ran back to my station wagon, where I maintained a small roving office. Not intentionally, but all that space back there cried out to be filled, and it seemed to make sense to throw in current case files along with some basic contracts, just in case. I opened the hatch and rooted around in a bankers box until I found the right paperwork, then ran back to Ed's hangar. He was sitting exactly where I told him to stay put. This was the sort of behavior I valued in a client.

"All this means is you've signed me up as your lawyer. I just need it in writing in case somebody challenges me. If you want to get out of it at any time, let me know, and it's a done deal. If you want proof of that, I can give you a few dozen people on the South Fork who can vouch for me."

People in the throes of grief tend to follow one of three paths: fury, denial, or resignation. Ed had clearly chosen the third, though I had the feeling the first might be running a close second.

He signed the contract without hesitation. I'd slipped a sheet of carbon paper beneath the signature so I could give him a copy, an old-fashioned contrivance I found useful out in the field.

I knew I was probably taking advantage of a man in a weakened state, who was obviously afflicted by emotional pain and suffering. But there was a higher purpose at stake, I argued to myself. I needed an excuse to stick my nose into something nobody would want it stuck into. This I knew from experience. In a criminal case, outsiders were less than zero. Defense attorneys, on the other hand, had a legal right to confront anyone and anything that would support the cause of the defended, even if no one wanted to live up to that constitutional imperative but the defense attorneys themselves.

This case, of course, was sort of different. There was nobody to defend, no one charged with anything; at least not yet. There was only a dead lady pilot and a grief-stricken husband. But I felt I had a stake in the proceedings. I was the one who'd seen the plane crash. More important, I saw the look on Eugenie's face as she passed overhead, filled with a combination of determined calm and anguish beyond understanding.

I knew I'd never be able to let this one go. No way, nohow.

3

I might have mentioned that I like my men odd. You would know this if you ever met Harry Goodlander, even without me telling you. Harry stands on the plus side of six foot eight in his stocking feet and has a wingspan to match. He's bald as a cue ball, but far cuter, in his own way. He used to wear a gold earring, which I never liked, and when I put his photo up to a bottle of Mr. Clean one day, that settled the issue. There was nothing he could do about the tattoo, the location of which few have had the privilege of observing, so on that I gave him a pass.

Harry moves stuff around the world for a living. The technical term is logistics, though for Harry it was more like symphonics–the orchestration of a million little details resulting in a harmonious outcome for the owners of the stuff being moved.

I would never have cared the tiniest bit about his chosen vocation if I hadn't stumbled into caring about him. That's because Harry has a way of making even the most trivial act of transportation seem like a dazzling adventure in shipping and handling. And after witnessing or hearing about dozens of these adventures, I came to realize they were just that, gaining an appreciation for people whose lives would have otherwise seemed hopelessly colorless and mundane.

But that's not the only reason I have a thing for Harry. It was also about him having a thing for me, the painfully difficult reality of me. That sealed the deal.

"What are you doing tonight besides taking me out and lavishing generosity and attention upon me?" I asked when he picked up the phone.

"For which I get in return?"

"The opportunity to repeat the whole performance at a later date. And I'll buy the first round of drinks. As long as it's under twenty dollars."

"Deals that good don't come along every day," he said.

I used to blame my inability to manage healthy romantic relationships on my parents. It's hard to imagine two people less socially adept. This, I realized much later, was their point of commonality–neither could stand other people, least of all each other. My mother expressed her repugnance by standing aloof from all human contact, contained within herself, tightly wound, suffering silently. My father was more vocal, blaming all the people on earth for what he considered our family's chronic undervalued state in the world.

They'd been dead for quite a while, and now that I was well into my thirties, I'd begun to slow down on the recriminations and take responsibility for my own manifest pathologies. I'd begun to realize that whatever feelings drew me to oddball, albeit enriching, humans like Harry Goodlander would always come with the fear that the involvement would overwhelm and subsume my own tortured, though cozily familiar, sense of self.

Which is one reason, despite Harry's manifold charms, I'd stopped short of a genuine commitment.

Be honest. Would you date a person like me?

But Harry persisted, God knows why, and I happily let him.

The other great things about Harry are his intelligence and problem-solving skills. A lot of women complain that men keep trying to fix whatever problem we're bitching about, rather than simply *listening*, empathetically.

Not me. I loved that "Okay, let's figure this out!" quality about men like Harry.

Maybe that says more about the number of problems I'm usually grappling with than my appreciation of gender differences.

I'd planned on keeping the whole outlandish day to myself, to spare Harry from the commotion already brewing inside my head. I'd lately been on a mostly successful campaign of selflessness, giving him first shot at the conversational floor and withholding as much of my compulsive fretting as humanly possible.

It's a good thing I value people's intentions over their actual performance. Especially my own.

"You won't believe what happened to me today," I said, pushing by him when he opened his front door. "Although maybe you will. You have a good imagination."

"You were captured by aliens, but once they realized you weren't representative of the human race, they let you go."

"Weirder than that. I saw a plane crash."

I gave him a full rundown while he made cocktails and plied me with his favorite snacks, tiny grilled ham and cheese sandwiches and macadamia nuts.

"So you still have the camera's memory card?" he asked, lasering in on the only act of the whole day you could construe as inappropriate. Okay, illegal. "I should turn it in, I know," I said, getting out in front of the issue. "I'll call Joe Sullivan tomorrow and tell him I just found it in my pocket inside a crumpled piece of paper."

"He won't believe you."

"Of course not. Even if it's true, mostly. Doesn't matter. He can't prove anything."

"So I guess you won't be looking to see what's on it. In the spirit of evidentiary integrity," he said, using words he'd learned from me.

"What are you, nuts?" I said, tossing the tiny chip on the table. "Get your camera and fire up the computer."

So over drinks we ran through the photos that were on the memory card. Actually, the run-through barely covered a single gin and tonic. There were only five photos. One was of a cabin on a lake surrounded by tall trees under a deep blue sky. I assumed somewhere in New England, based on the newspaper story. Another was a group shot of six people in a bar, all in customary T-shirts, denim, and baseball caps, arms laced with tattoos, scruffy sideburns and beer guts, even on the women. They looked like my typical clients, people I often bailed out and occasionally saved from jail. I didn't have to know their names to know their pickup preferences and the songs playing in the background. They were the people who built the houses, fixed the cars, paved the roads, and ran the beer tabs on the South Fork. Invisible to the people who played here, but without whom the Hamptons really would be just a mirage.

The third shot was a portrait of Eugenie's plane, which a side trip into Wikipedia showed to be a Cessna 207, a single-engine air taxi that had been around since the mid-1960s. It had the look of a sturdy, versatile workhorse, which it was.

The fourth was a familiar sight in the Hamptons—a huge party tent in the backyard of a big, shingle-style house. Not quite a mansion, but leaning in that direction. There were people in white shirts and black pants carrying trays of finger food, and bunches of already well-fed geezers in expensive summer wear drinking out of champagne glasses and trying to look engaged. In the foreground was a group portrait, a mix of older and younger well-dressed people.

Number five was a black-and-white shot of a storefront with big glass windows and a sign that read DELBERT'S BEACHWORLD DELI. It was an old sign and an old store, and even the photograph looked old. I mentioned that to Harry.

"It's a scan of a regular film print," said Harry. "You can see the edge exposed here," he added, pointing at the computer screen.

The place looked familiar. The photo was cropped too tightly to show the stores on either side, but something in my memory said there weren't any, that it was a freestanding building.

"I think I know this place," I said to Harry. "It's long gone, but I think I can find it."

"This is a pretty motley collection of photos," said Harry. "What do they mean?"

"Probably nothing. They just happened to be on a memory card that was loose in the camera case Eugenie tossed out of the plane."

"You're sure about that?" said Harry.

"No. I'm not sure of anything. Except that she saw me, because she looked at me. And she meant to throw me the case. And I'm totally positive I'm getting really hungry and could use another drink. In five minutes we could be in the Village, where both needs could be met."

The Town of Southampton is a huge place that takes up half the South Fork and includes lots of other Hamptons, like Bridgehampton and Hampton Bays, and places like Quogue and Water Mill, where I have my office. The Village of Southampton is a much smaller subset within the town, where you find streets lined with shops, restaurants, real-estate offices, and art galleries. If you drove through quickly, it would look like any pleasantly preserved small-town commercial district common to New England and Upstate New York. If you were on foot, moving slowly, you'd notice the prices in the real-estate agents' windows, the outpost offices of top-tier brokerage houses, designer labels, and the size of the rocks in some of the jewelry-store windows. There was a time, not that long ago, when you could get an ice-cream cone next door to where you bought a five-thousand-dollar handbag, but rapacious rents and a fading local population had wiped out most of the homey, small-town elements. I missed them, but I stubbornly refused to mourn. The world is a constantly changing place, I tell myself. Get over it and move on. Which I was almost able to do.

Harry had picked one of those surviving local places that had successfully attracted the city crowd–combining hometown friendliness with off-world haute cuisine. The staff knew us there, another plus. Being a regular was usually worth about 20 percent off the final tab, if you knew how to tip.

"Jack and Merlot, two of my favorite people," said the bartender, referring to us by our establishment identities: Jack Daniel's for Harry, Merlot for me.

"Fill 'er up," said Harry.

I took a gulp of Harry's Jack before pretending to nurse my wine.

"Tough day," said Harry, explaining to the bartender, a guy named Geordie who called himself a barman, being a Brit who stubbornly refused to convert to standard American English.

Geordie sweetly patted my cheek and topped off the bourbon.

"So you're going to defend the husband," said Harry.

"He's the most likely in need of defending, whether it was an accident or not. He's the guy who took care of the plane. And foul play almost always begins at home."

"What's Joe Sullivan going to think of that?" he asked, which I wished he hadn't, since I was trying to suppress the obvious answer. But it was too late; the words were out there, where the bad-luck fairies could hear them. To prove the jinx, my cell phone immediately chirped at me.

It was Joe Sullivan.

"I can't fucking believe this," he said.

"You're trying to interview Ed Conklin," I said.

"I specifically told you not to get mixed up in this."

"No you didn't," I said.

"I did. In so many words."

"Put Conklin on the phone," I said.

After some frustrated grunting, the phone went silent, then Ed Conklin came on the line.

"Did you say anything?" I asked.

"You told me not to."

"Good. Don't. You don't have to say anything without me there. Not one single, solitary thing. If they want to use your bathroom, point. Put the blond cop back on the line."

"You know when they lawyer up it only makes me more suspicious," said Sullivan.

"Give him a break, Joe. He just lost his wife. And he's totally unequipped to deal with you people."

" 'You people'? What does that mean?"

"I'll bring him in tomorrow afternoon. You and your boss and the whole squad room can have at him. Just give it a day."

He knew that wasn't only fair, it was constitutionally undeniable. So he got all magnanimous, sort of.

"Sure, Jackie. Thank you so very much. We appreciate your eagerness to cooperate."

"Yeah, yeah," I said, and hung up on him. No point in selling past the close.

"So Sullivan's loving you on this case," said Harry.

"Tickled pink."

For the rest of the night I resisted letting Harry or my own obsessive nature drag him any deeper into the Eugenie Birkson thing. I knew he was already starting to worry about me, which was a reflex in him that both charmed and irritated me. Since I hate cognitive dissonance, especially the monotonous, incurable, repetitive kind, I moved us aggressively off the subject. Which is not that hard with Harry if you're willing to ask a lot of questions and keep track of complicated answers and convoluted narratives. Which I admit I always enjoyed coming from him.

I have another surefire way to distract Harry, which I had to wait until we got home to employ, but it did a fine job of distracting us both.

I told Harry I had to wake up in my own bed the next day so I could prepare for Ed Conklin's interview with the Southampton Town Police, but that wasn't the whole truth. The moment I snapped out of the romantic euphoria, all I wanted to do was embrace the gleaming device on my back porch that had finally supplanted the good old Hewlett-Packard desktop.

I thought I'd be all sentimental about the trusty HP, and I was, until the new machine displayed a level of blazing computational speed and stunning graphics I'd barely dreamed of.

As soon as I got home from Harry's, I stripped to nothing but a terry-cloth robe, poured a glass of wine, and lit a joint, the three things I had to do when it was dark outside and I wanted to jump on the computer.

Harry had burned Eugenie's five photos to a CD, which I slid into my computer. I downloaded them, then popped the CD back out and hid it inside a copy of *Portrait of the Artist as a Young Man,* which was the closest I could get to a photographic reference among several hundred randomly arranged books on the overstuffed bookshelves in my living room.

I spent a long time looking at the buddies in the bar. I thought one of the faces would ring a bell, but nothing rang.

From there I went up about five tax brackets to the charity event under the tent. I had a bit more luck there, recognizing some of the people from local society magazines or from direct experience, on those rare occasions I'd been invited to an event I could both afford and endure without getting drunk or ending up in a worthless argument that would result in either social banishment or arrest.

So you don't get the wrong idea, I deeply admire, even love, some of the people fawned over by those magazines. It's not their fault that human beings are so enslaved by love of hierarchy, or by prurience, that some are made a public spectacle, whether they like it or not.

Two of them were in the photograph. Kirk and Emily Lavigne. Kirk had followed the standard arc of success that frequently lands people at the edge of the ocean in Southampton. The waypoints are junior overachiever on Wall Street; a rocket rise to management, followed by defection to a small, scrappy firm filled with guys just like him; eventual ownership; the rapid expansion of net worth; the sale of the firm at a head-scratchingly inflated price; and a smooth transition to the fund-raising circuit.

Kirk had a secret, and I was one of a handful of people who knew what it was. Late one windswept summer day on the balcony of his house overlooking the Atlantic, while Emily served iced tea and cucumber sandwiches, he gave away all his money. His best friend, a guy named Raj Ramaswami, would establish and run a foundation chartered to help poor kids get into college. Funding for the foundation would remain forever anonymous, and my job was to set up an irrevocable trust that would use a separate fund to pay the Lavignes' bills. They weren't insubstantial bills, but compared to the billions that went into the foundation, chump change.

I knew nothing about setting up irrevocable trusts, but I got the gig because Kirk said I was the only person he could trust to preserve complete confidentiality. Just thinking about that always makes me choke up and start to weep. Even though I immediately broke that confidence by getting Burton Lewis, my very rich tax lawyer friend and patron, who knows everything you could ever know about irrevocable trusts, to help me write it up. My conscience was fine with that, knowing that Burton was the only person on earth who could match the Lavignes for integrity and discretion.

Kirk and Emily, still assumed to be among the limitless rich, were invited to every charity event on the East End, which meant they could go out almost every night of the summer, always looking stylish and happy when the local paparazzi snapped their picture. Kirk admitted to me that he found these occasions a bit of a bore, but went along for Emily's sake.

"She also thinks they're a bit of a bore, but she likes to dress up," he told me.

Kirk and I had become close cyber pen pals, for years maintaining a lively, ridiculously entertaining e-mail exchange, so it was easy to write him and ask if he could help me on a case. Few outcomes of a humble request would be more certain.

I moved on to the portrait of Eugenie's plane. I went on Wikipedia and dug into a series of aviation sites, which contained a lot of information I didn't remotely understand, but copied anyway for future reference. I did confirm that her plane was a classic FOB air taxi warhorse, and that the 207s and the 205s and 206s that made up the bulk of that Cessna class had an excellent safety record established over decades, with no reported tendency to burst into flames midair.

The next picture I studied was the verdant New England lakefront. The only potential clue to the location was some flowers in relatively clear focus in the foreground and the species of pine lining the back of the shot. I jumped on the Southampton College site and found a botany professor with the likeable name of Dr. Johnston Johnson and sent him the shot with a challenge to pick the exact spot on the map. I offered no reward, knowing that for most college professors showing off intellectual prowess was the only reward that really mattered.

This left the old picture of Delbert's Beachworld Deli. There was no identifying this one, I decided after searching the name and reviewing a few dozen images brought up by the prompt "Old Southampton NY buildings."

I knew I had to turn over the memory card the next day. It wasn't inconceivable that certain people at police HQ might suspect a delay in delivering material evidence. This might move them to impound my computer. So I printed out all the photos, after downloading them to my cell phone, then spent an hour copying my entire hard drive to external storage, including all my personal and professional correspondence and a picture of Harry's naked butt that I sometimes used as a screen saver. I hid the device on a bookshelf behind *2001: A Space Odyssey*.

I then deleted my browsing history, all my correspondence, Eugenie's photos, and the semi-illegal search application from Randall Dodge. I knew client-attorney privilege would ultimately shield me from aggressive invasion of my professional files, but invoking it would have meant an ugly fight, and I had to live with these guys. It was easier to hand over a computer with nothing on it but a thirty-two-song iTunes library, Harry's butt, and my mother's favorite recipe for Swedish meatballs.

At that point the smart thing would have been to shut the damn thing off and go to bed, but the regulatory machinery that controls that kind of sound judgment has never performed up to specs. So I kept on browsing around innocuous sites—so much great stuff you can just know!—until I literally passed out, as I often do, with my head on the keyboard, struck dumb by all that seductive and mostly useless information.

4

I woke to the sound of a fresh e-mail.

I've awoken more than once in confusing circumstances, but few had quite the charm of my face resting on a computer keyboard, my right thumb pressed into my cheek and both legs numb from lack of circulation. The hour didn't help. I'm not an enthusiastic morning person, unlike Kirk Lavigne, who at 6:00 A.M. had just returned my e-mail of the night before.

I'd made it thus far without succumbing to reading glasses, but no one can read a computer screen after being shocked out of a deep, dream-infested sleep. I dragged myself out of the chair and stumbled to the bathroom to splash water on my face, curse at myself, and brush my teeth. Then I went back and clicked on the e-mail.

"Nice to hear from you. Of course we'll help with anything you want. Come see us. I'm authorized to extend Emily's sincere salutation as well. Kirk."

I'd arranged to meet Ed Conklin at a diner in Hampton Bays so I could prep him for our visit with the Southampton Town Police. He didn't look any better than he had the other day. In fact, he looked a lot worse, though cleaner and better dressed in a plaid sport coat, crooked tie, and synthetic white shirt.

"Can't sleep. Can't eat. Suffering is all I seem capable of doing," he said matter-of-factly when he sat down in the booth across from me. I immediately felt guilty about the bowl in front of me filled with half-eaten cereal topped with granola and raspberries and creamy yogurt. I pushed it away.

"How 'bout coffee?" I asked. "Not too nutritious, but good for the soul."

"Whatever you say," he said.

There was already a cup at his place, so I poured him some from the metal carafe they'd left on the table.

"I'm so sorry, Mr. Conklin. I can't imagine what you must be going through. Is there a funeral planned? I'd like to come."

"That's decent of you. All we get to do is a service, since there's nothing to bury. We're thinkin' of doin' it at the Community Church. Probably get a crowd. Eugenie's a popular girl. Was."

Unlike most guys his age, Conklin had all his hair, and it was still a dark brown. I immediately began to speculate. Dyed? Natural? Wig? Conklin thought I was looking over his head, not at it, so he turned around to see what was up.

"Thought I knew somebody," I said quickly. "You sure I can't interest you in a little something to eat? Toast?"

He shook his head, sadly, as if mourning the loss of his wife and his appetite in equal measure.

"Okay," I said. "Here's what you can expect at HQ. Joe Sullivan will likely do the interview, since he's the detective assigned to the case. But it's not unusual to have another detective join in so they can play what the entire world knows as good cop, bad cop. That could be Lionel Veckstrom, who's technically a good cop in that he's good at catching killers, but he's a bad cop in the sense of being a person. So the bad cop role comes naturally to him. If it's Ross Semple, the chief and a veteran homicide detective, you get something more like good cop, weird cop. Don't let it fool you. No one who works for Ross wonders why he's the chief. Including Veckstrom."

"Why would they be payin' that much attention to me?" he asked, genuinely confused.

I hated this part of the conversation.

"Mr. Conklin."

"Ed."

"Ed. Most deaths that aren't obvious accidents, that are caused by another person, happen in the family. And most of these are caused by the person closest to the one who dies. In other words, the first suspect in any investigation of a wife's death, suspicious or otherwise, is her husband."

If his look of stunned disbelief was faked, he deserved an Academy Award.

"You gotta be kiddin' me."

I've had this conversation more than once, but it never gets any easier. In fact, it keeps getting worse.

"Ed, you're not only her husband, you're the mechanic who maintained her plane. In the crudest terms, without looking at any of the facts, you have both motive and means. You're a twofer. The cops just love that."

"I'd rather kill myself than do anything to hurt Eugenie," he said, in a voice so low I barely heard what he said.

I leaned over the table to get closer to him.

"I know that, Ed. But the cops don't. So give them the benefit of the doubt. Don't let their suspicious nature and lousy social skills piss you off. Stay calm, answer every question honestly, and if they insult you, say, 'That's offensive. I'm not trying to be rude to you, why're you being rude to me?' "

"Not sure I can remember all that," he said.

I reached across the table and gripped his sport coat at the shoulder.

"Is there anything at all you can think of that might make the cops suspicious? Ever fight with Eugenie at a bar where there were witnesses? Do you have a relative who hates you and might tell the dolts at the DA's that you made your wife's life a living hell? Do you have a big life insurance policy on her? Is there anything at all that might look bad, if you think about it, to the cops or the prosecutor?"

Conklin looked like he was still grappling with the overall implications. I felt bad for him, but this had to be done. I wouldn't be doing him any favors shielding him from the reality his wife's death had thrust upon him.

"If I'm hearing you right, the police already think I had something to do with Eugenie's crash," he said, in a thick voice.

"I wouldn't put it quite that way. They're just working the odds. It's nothing personal," I added, and then immediately regretted it.

"Nothing personal about accusing me of killing my beloved baby doll? The only human being stupid enough to love a jamoke like me?"

He tossed a crumpled napkin across the table. It wasn't much of a physical display, but I could feel the latent force behind it.

"I'm sorry, Ed. I'm doing a lousy job at this. Let me start over. The cops always suspect family members. That's a fact. But these cops, at least the chief and Joe Sullivan, are smart, fair-minded people. They're not going to make it any harder on you than they have to. And once you're in the clear, you're in the clear forever. It's just I'd be a rotten lawyer if I didn't prepare you for the reality of the situation."

The rigid mask that his face had turned into softened. He looked down at his lap and shook his head.

"I know what you're saying. Everybody's just doing their job. I'm just a dumb aeronautical mechanic."

"There's an oxymoron."

He smiled.

"I get the joke, just so you know."

"Proves my point. What about the NTSB? They been in contact?"

Looking down again, he shook his head.

"If they call or come see you, give them my number. If they threaten you in any way, get the name of the threatener and write down what they said."

He finally looked up.

"You're trying to look after me," he said.

I searched around the inside of the diner for some cosmic support. An angel in charge of earthly legal affairs to come down and help me straighten this guy out.

"Christ, Ed, what the hell do you think you pay lawyers to do?"

"Not sure I can afford to pay for that kind of protection."

I waved that off.

"You can afford me to handle this. Don't worry about that," I said, seeing in my mind's eye the face of my long-suffering accountant fall into bitter disappointment.

"Okay, okay. I get it."

"Good. So eat something. Can't visit police HQ on an empty stomach. They'll make you sign an affidavit proclaiming what you've eaten in the last twenty-four hours. If they suspect deception, they'll get out the stomach pump."

This startled Ed.

"They will?"

I rolled my eyes.

"I'm kidding. For chrissakes," I said.

He looked embarrassed, but he managed a grin.

"Sorry," he said.

"Order something, or I'm doing it for you."

"Yes, ma'am," he said, and got himself a glass of water. He spent the rest of the meal chewing on the ice.

Joe Sullivan did such a good job reinforcing everything I'd said to Conklin, I almost slapped the big towheaded lump of a cop on the back.

"Thanks so much for coming in to talk to us, Mr. Conklin," he said, greeting us in the HQ lobby. "Can I get you a cup of coffee? What do you take in it?"

Conklin had no defense against such gentle concern, and thus melted like a Popsicle on a hot sidewalk.

"I'm fine, Officer. Thank you for asking."

Sullivan herded us into a room just off the lobby where suspects met with their lawyers, often me. I hated that room. It was a place where my clients were always filled with fear and I with insecurity over whether I'd be their ruin or their salvation. I hid this from Ed Conklin, of course, on whom I bestowed my best "We're all going to be fine" smile.

"I'm sorry for your loss," said Sullivan, like he meant it.

Conklin nodded his appreciation.

"Will anyone else be joining us?" I asked.

Joe looked apologetic.

"Just us, Counselor." He looked at Conklin. "I'll be taking notes, so talk slow. I know next to nothing about airplanes."

For the next several minutes Sullivan went through some standard questions, like date and place of birth, education, family members, etc. Then he asked about Conklin's repair business and how Eugenie's air taxi operation fit in.

When he moved on to their home life, he looked up from his pad.

"So, Mr. Conklin, things were going okay with you and your wife," he said.

"Far as I was concerned," said Conklin.

"Any change in her behavior lately? She ever act strange in any way?"

Conklin squinted in the struggle to understand that question.

"What's that got to do with her plane going down? Her behavin' one way or the other doesn't explain why that engine sprung an oil leak."

"So that's what you think it was," said Sullivan. "An oil leak."

"Sure sounds like it. Oil spraying onto the exhaust manifold, smokin' up a storm till it gets hot enough to ignite. A lot of oil, if the pressure gauge had dropped to zero. Big leak. That's what I told them kids from the NTSB. They didn't look all the way convinced, though I don't know how they're going to come up with a better idea. Not much of that plane left to investigate."

Sullivan wrote all that down.

"So nothing the pilot could've done," he said.

Conklin looked at me.

"Am I missin' something here?" he asked me.

I rested my hand on Conklin's forearm.

"Joe just wants to eliminate any possibility that Eugenie had a role in the accident. However far-fetched that might seem to you, it's his job to ask the question."

Sullivan gave me a neutral look, but I knew he appreciated the assist.

Conklin looked down at his hands like he'd done in the diner, nodding his head.

"Eugenie knew almost as much about the guts of that plane as I did," he said. "If she was going to wreck it on purpose there're about a million other ways she coulda done it than the way it happened. There's not much scarier than an engine fire. No point in going through all that if you're only going to stick it in the ground. Either way, you'd have to be crazy suicidal, and Eugenie was nothin' like that."

"I hear you, Mr. Conklin," said Sullivan, one of those noncommittal statements everyone always took as an endorsement. "Sounds like Eugenie was well liked. Anybody not like her so much?"

For the first time, I picked up from Conklin the scent of reticence. Subtle, but it was there.

"Nobody I can think of," said Conklin. "Nobody she ever talked about. Eugenie had a cheerful disposition, on the whole, but her temper wasn't anything to take too lightly. She's been livin' in a man's world a long time, surrounded by cocky flyboys. Was never a good idea to push her buttons."

"But some did," said Sullivan.

"I guess so, though it never amounted to much. Plus, push too hard and you end up pushing right into me."

I looked down at those massive mechanic's hands, remembering the ropy arms hidden by his inelegant sport coat. Sullivan also took a closer look, as if suddenly engaged.

"That ever happen?" he asked. "Ever have to step in and defend her?"

Conklin looked down again and shook his head, very slowly.

"Never came to that. Nobody that stupid."

Sullivan wrote on his pad.

"You get a tat in the joint?"

Conklin looked up at him, then over at me.

"I have to answer that?" he asked.

"What tat?" I asked Sullivan. "What're you talking about?"

"You haven't told her yet?" Sullivan asked Conklin.

"Told her what?" I asked.

I hadn't been in the criminal defense game as long as some others, but I'd learned to recognize a couple things. Like when I was the only one in the room who didn't know what was going on.

"What the hell, Ed," I said.

"How 'bout it, Mr. Conklin? You know the drill. Hide one thing, makes us think you're hiding something else."

"What, what?" I nearly yelled.

Conklin leaned forward in his chair and rested his elbows on the arms of the chair. Not so much to rest as to provide a launch pad.

"Maybe a person doesn't want to have to explain his past every time he runs into some bull with a hard-on for peace-minding ex-cons," he said to Sullivan in a flat, nearly inaudible voice.

Sullivan's voice dropped even lower when he said, "This isn't a duel, Mr. Conklin. If you want to turn it into one, fine. Name the time and place. Nothing official. Badge stays in the drawer. Neither of us wants that, but talk like that'll get us there in a hurry."

All the air in the room had been sucked out of secret vents and replaced by tiny electric charges that danced on the edges of the furniture and crackled in the space between the two jaded, powerful men.

Conklin thought about it, then leaned back in his chair and took off his sport jacket. He rolled his sleeves up to the elbows. They were clear.

"Better to keep 'em guessing than to label yourself. Tats just give you a false sense of security," he said. "Might make you a big man with the group you sign up with, but it's a big fuck-you to everybody else. Excuse the French."

Sullivan probably noticed the dawn of recognition spread across my face.

"Sanger medium-security prison," he said, nodding toward Conklin. "Three years. Assault."

"Goddammit," I muttered. "Thanks a lot, Ed. Jesus. Here I am giving you advice on police interrogations."

I was about to launch into my standard lecture on the profound advisability of informing your attorney of every fact and circumstance that could have even the remotest impact on your legal situation, when I thought about how I'd more or less forced myself on Conklin, providing little in the way of ground rules. I was usually the one being sold on taking a case, usually the cautious or reluctant party, careful to set the parameters, establish protocols. This was mostly my fault.

Though, still.

"Anything else you want to tell me?" I asked Sullivan, then looked over at Conklin. "What happened?"

"What do you mean?"

"You know what I mean. The charge. What happened?"

"Fistfight," he said quietly. "Nothin' more than that."

"Except the charge hung in the balance for a while–assault or manslaughter," said Sullivan. "Lucky for you the guy lived."

"That was a long time ago," said Conklin. "What's it got to do with Eugenie?"

"What should it have?" Sullivan asked.

"Nothing," I said, before Conklin could answer. "What other questions do you have for Mr. Conklin relating to the accident?"

Sullivan studied his pad, tapping it with the tip of his pen.

"Is that what it was? An accident?" he asked Conklin. "You're sure about that?"

"No," he said. "I'm not sure about anything anymore. Except Eugenie's dead and it feels like somebody's reached down my throat and pulled out all my guts. I'm as good as dead to the world myself. And there's nothing you or anybody else could do to me that would be any worse than what's already happened."

And then Conklin sat there still as a stone, staring across the table at Sullivan, but in a way that made you wonder if he was really seeing the big cop, or anything else in the room, or rather was lost in images captured by his mind's eye, beloved or profane, it was impossible to tell.

5

After packing Ed Conklin into his truck, I gave him strict instructions to speak to no one without me there, and to never, ever, ever, withhold important information from me again—which he swore was impossible since I now knew everything about him, which I acted like I believed. Then I left the overlit, choking claustrophobia of Southampton HQ and went swimming.

It was very early in the season to be jumping into the ocean, but I'd been braving the heart-stopping chill since I was a little girl. This was a ritual that bound me to many others who'd grown up on the East End of Long Island, for whom this was home turf, not merely a place to escape to from regions made lesser by their lack of mythical significance.

I'd been lucky enough to be born with a sturdy composition, one that naturally resisted the charms of physical fitness and stood defiant against persistently unhealthy habits.

It's not that I didn't believe in exercise; I just found little pleasure in the act itself. When I was in high school, there was nothing I hated more than organized sports. You knew who the best athletes were as soon as you walked into the locker room. They were the confident ones. They all knew one another and moved around like guys, and often skipped the shaving rituals most of us felt privileged to need.

I made the mistake of signing up for the swim team because I'd been paddling around the local saltwater bays and backwaters, and of course the ocean, my whole life and thought that qualified me to race other girls in a clear, chlorinated bathtub. Up until then, I'd avoided softball and basketball, and, God help me, field hockey, but for some reason I thought this would be different.

It was. The girls were like muscular seals, smooth and ferocious and indefatigable. Nothing could have prepared me for the stress of their workouts, their suicidal drive, the spit and mucous, the nauseating, monotonous lap after lap of liquid, effervescent hell.

My bigger mistake was telling my father I was going out for the team. This meant I couldn't quit, even after it became obvious that I'd consigned myself to a watery version of the Bataan Death March. He had a rule that once you started something, you had to persevere to the bitter end. No matter how bad it got. I think this rule was imposed on me because my father wasn't crazy about his job and so devoutly wanted to retire that he could taste the moment on the tip of his tongue.

But if he was going to tough it out, so was I.

So I went to practice every day and tried to avoid dying of exhaustion or drowning from holding on to a foam board and kicking, making almost no forward progress while inhaling a spray of water off the far more energetic kick of the girl in front of me.

My specialty was the fifty-yard freestyle. I discovered some aptitude for this event after realizing it involved the briefest time in the water, minimizing both the stress of competition and the resulting humiliation. All I had to do was leap off the diving block, swim as fast as I could to the other end, execute a contorted version of a flip turn, and swim back again.

I'd almost figured out how to accomplish this maneuver when the first meet of the season was upon us. There were three swimmers from each team in each heat, and I was appropriately in the outside lane, against the wall, where the water sloshed into you from the Olympic-scale wakes of the speedy girls in the middle. I was just glad it'd be over in less than a minute.

As we stood on the starting blocks, I looked down the row of competitors and was struck suddenly by something I'd stupidly overlooked until then.

They were all flat as a pancake. I was the only girl in the event who had a chest, even though it was only about half of what I have now.

Well, shit, I said to myself. No wonder.

I won that race. I beat all of them, much to everyone's surprise, especially mine. I felt like I was a hydroplane, a water bug skimming across the surface of the water. What propelled me wasn't the revelation of my physiological disadvantages so much as the giggle that swelled up in me as I bent down with my arms outstretched and my toes curled over the lip of the block.

I didn't have much chance to enjoy my success. A week later I overheard the girl in the top slot of my race call me a scuzzy slut, and I surprised myself again by backhanding her across the mouth. She was trying to pull all the hair out of my head when the coach intervened and, to my everlasting gratitude, kicked me off the team, providing the only form of escape my father would ever have found acceptable.

So I didn't swim to stay in shape. I swam to shock myself into a clearer state of mind. To soothe my jittery, jagged, oft-exhausted self in the salty ablution of the moody gray Atlantic.

After I'd cleared the breakers and swam about a quarter mile straight out, I felt acclimated enough to take a break and get my bearings. It was while floating there, looking back at the neatly dispersed mountain-sized mansions that lined the beach, that a thought jumped to mind. A thought and a memory.

It was good that the water was freezing cold. That probably numbed my emotions as much as my extremities because otherwise, I'd have hardly glanced at such a disturbing reminiscence. But there it was anyway, flushed out of the deeper crevices of my mind. The deepest, in fact.

"Damn," I said aloud. "That can't be."

I started to swim again, parallel to the surf, heading west so I could keep my eye on the shore when I raised my mouth out of the water to take a breath. I swam hard, hoping to purge the visions that had suddenly taken root inside my imagination, but it didn't work.

I kept trying anyway, over about a mile of frigid ocean, until I found myself turning north and heading back to shore. I was tired, the whole experience having pumped my veins full of adrenaline and nervous unease. Numb as I was, I knew this wasn't something that could be stuffed back into its hole unless I immediately proved to myself that it was all an unfortunate trick of the memory circuits.

When I reached the surf, I caught a wave that carried me most of the way in, an unusual event on the Long Island coastline, where the waves tended to break late or peter out well before you got much of a ride. I took it as a sign that haste was called for in resolving the matter.

I jogged back up the beach to where I'd left my towel, unneeded now that I was thoroughly air-dried. Two good-looking guys about my age were throwing a tennis ball for a lanky young Lab, his black coat slick with salt water and his muzzle sporting a sandy beard. They tried to engage me by tossing the ball in my direction. I dodged the ball and the pursuing dog, and headed straight for the cut in the dunes that led to my car, erecting behind me an impenetrable force field of anti-sociability.

When I reached the car, I dug my phone out of the glove box and called Roberta Comacho at the *Southampton Chronicle.* Roberta was a reporter I got to know several years before when I was researching the newspaper's photo archives for one of my clients. Much of real estate law, which I did almost exclusively in those days, involves border disputes. The client's home had started out in the early twentieth century as a little hotel, what we'd now call a bed and breakfast. The ancient survey of the property conflicted with the ancient survey of the house next door, and therein lay the fight. With Roberta's help, I dug out an old photograph that clearly showed my client's driveway back in 1922 traveling down the middle of the disputed territory, just as it did today. Before I could utter the words "adverse possession" the judge handed me the hoped-for decision.

As we pulled boxes down off shelves and burrowed through stacks of moldy photos and brittle negatives, I felt myself becoming infected by Roberta's pleasure in the pursuit. It wasn't her actual responsibility at the *Chronicle,* but I discovered it to be her hidden joy. So much so that she often slunk down to the basement on trumped-up missions just to relax over a box of nineteenth-century daguerreotypes.

"Good news," I told her over the phone. "I've got a building to track down."

I'd learned from my last foray into the archives that Roberta was sixty years old. She didn't look a day less than that. Though her complexion leaned toward olive, it hadn't seen a lot of sun in those sixty years. Her hair was the color and texture of number two steel wool, and her fashion sense gave me hope that I might not be the worst-dressed woman on the East End. But you couldn't fault her for lack of enthusiasm.

"Most entirely excellent," she said. "I'm working on a deadline, but I can cut it short and be done in less than half an hour. Who cares about all the background crap anyway."

"Not your average citizen," I said. "But you can have the whole hour. I've met those boys in the newsroom. I'm not showing up in a bathing suit."

"*Libertinos estúpidos.*"

I pulled a sweatshirt over my bathing suit and drove north to my house on Brick Kiln Road. It was set back a fair distance from the road on a flag lot my late husband bought with some of the potato field fortune. Unfortunately, the one area in which he and his family succumbed to parsimony was residential construction. It wasn't family pride so much as sacred ethnic doctrine that male heads of households build their own houses. Pete had his fine qualities, some of which I ached to recall, but handiness wasn't one of them. My father had a minuscule measure of Pete's good nature, but he was a civil engineer whose universe was built out of straight lines, tight joinery, and adequate load-bearing dimensions, all things that did little to entrance my husband, his father, or the endless gaggle of goofy, jovial cousins and brothers who jumped in on the project.

So you would have called the house an architectural disaster if you weren't so distracted by the shoddy construction.

But it was mine, mortgage-free, mostly weatherproof, and utterly indifferent to my failings as a housekeeper.

Contrary to some of the wisecracks I endured from my closer friends, you didn't have to follow paths to get from one room to the other. Between the various piles, a few of which rose to some prominence, there was plenty of open space. At least a few square yards or so. The biggest detraction in my mind was the wall-to-wall carpet and living room furniture, once an off-white that Pete fantasized to be the pinnacle of urban chic, now far more off than white. But like a lot of things I inherited on his death, I could no more change it out than perform my own appendectomy.

It's not exactly grief. I really didn't love him as much as I should have, about which I'm strangely less guilty than my Irish Catholic nature would lead you to believe. It's more a frail attempt at honoring his happy delusions, his blessedly obtuse view of the world.

The one feature of the house I insisted on, much to the Swaitkowskis' bemusement, was a wall of bookshelves in the living room. A huge wall of bookshelves, which held tons of books, CDs, record albums, and magazines, along with hidden photo files, external hard drives, illegal software, and drug paraphernalia. This is what I came home to every day. The rest was just a place to flop in and ignore.

I took a shower to wash off the salt and sand and climbed into clothes I'd likely wear to clean out the basement, since that was exactly the type of environment I was heading for.

I still had the memory card I'd sworn to hand over to the police, which I decided not to do after Sullivan outted Conklin's history as an ex-con. It could have been nerves, rattled as mine were by the revelations. Or some possessive impulse out of my subconscious that told me I wasn't yet done with it.

As promised, I made it to the *Chronicle* an hour after I called. Roberta was waiting for me in the lobby, also dressed in her best archive spelunking outfit–blue jeans, a sweatshirt, and sneakers.

"I went home and changed," she said. "Of all days, today I decide to wear a skirt. I don't even like skirts."

The rest of her looked about the same as when I'd last seen her. Maybe a little older, with a little more fat on an already overloaded frame. But just as cheerfully eager.

"How long have you been working here?" I asked her as we trotted down the enclosed stairwell to the basement.

She thought about it.

"Has to be about twenty years. I settled for copy editor at first. Thought I needed something to help support Pedro. I told you that story, didn't I?"

She had. Pedro Comacho had been a tennis pro working out of a tony country club in Newton, Massachusetts. He seemed to lack ambition, but he was handsome and charming and apparently nuts about the plain-Jane reporter on the *Boston Globe* city beat. Roberta found herself swept off her feet, and more than willing to chuck it all, marry Pedro at the county courthouse, and follow him back to his hometown of Southampton. But being a practical girl, she lined up the best job she could at the local paper before they arrived.

Unnecessary, as it turned out, at least for financial reasons. Pedro had neglected to mention that his father, Alejandro Comacho, owned his own international airline and enough stock in DuPont to be a frequent houseguest at various stately homes tucked away in the hills of western Delaware.

"This way I know you didn't marry me for my money," Pedro told Roberta as he helped her haul her luggage up to the entrance of the family's fifteen-thousand-square-foot cottage on Gin Lane.

She kept the job anyway and eventually worked her way back to covering her local municipality—not quite Beacon Hill, but enough to keep her busy self engaged.

When we got to the basement we stopped at the long, narrow workstation that served as a staging area for expeditionary teams assaulting the mountains of archival data. The work of cataloging and cross-referencing had begun long before computers, and management saw little advantage in digitizing the towering stacks, so you had to pore through the microfilmed records stored in cabinets above the workstation and enlarge them on a big hooded monitor that looked like something Gene Roddenberry would have put on Captain Kirk's bridge.

I pulled out Eugenie's photographs and placed the one titled "Delbert's Beachworld Deli" on top.

"That's the building in question," I said. "I think it's long gone, but it looks familiar to me. I have a theory, but I want it to be wrong."

Roberta, who was studying the photo, looked up at me.

"That's interesting," she said.

"Don't get all reporterish on me," I said. "I just want to find the building."

"'Reporterish'?"

"Curious."

"I think that's my job," she said.

I ignored that and took the photo out of her hands. I put it on the table.

"Do you recognize it?" I asked.

She picked it up again and moved it around, catching different angles of light.

"No," she said. "But judging from the condition of the façade, the junky trees showing here above the roof, and the potholes in the parking area in front, I'm thinking Hampton Bays, North Sea, or Springs."

"Really," I said, taking the photo out of her hands to get a closer look.

"I'm not criticizing those places," she said. "In fact, I love those places. For the very reason I think this building belongs to one of them. It's funky. A little worn. A natural, regular place."

"Let's see if it's in there," I said, going to the "D" drawer and looking up "Delbert's Beachworld Deli." Of course, it wasn't. "How old do you think this photo is?" I asked.

Roberta studied it again.

"Pre-digital by a healthy margin. Say early eighties. Though taken with a decent camera–a thirty-five millimeter, not a disposable or some piece of crap your mom used to take snapshots."

I asked that question because the archives were organized by title and number code, but you could also search by basic categories, such as geographical location (e.g., Hampton Bays), people/politicians, landscapes, fund-raisers (by far the largest category), fatal car crashes, residences, commercial buildings, missing cats and dogs, etc. These in turn were organized by date, so we started with commercial buildings/retail, Hampton Bays, 1985 to 2000.

I wish I could say it was fun to operate the archaic technology, but it wasn't. In fact, it really sucked. Before we sat down in front of the thing, Roberta warned me not to mutter "O Google, wherefore art thou?" every few moments like I had the last time.

The process was to write down all the ID numbers within that search category, then go to the stacks and pull boxes down off the shelves, trying to avoid bleeding to death from paper cuts inflicted by the razor-sharp edges of the aging manila envelopes as you extracted the photographs and, disappointed, slipped them back in, whilst sneezing and wiping your nose with your sleeve from all the dust and mold.

It was a tribute to Roberta's infectious enthusiasm that I endured all this in reasonably good humor. Most of the time.

The first hour netted nothing but a little blood and proof positive that the photo archives included nothing that looked like our subject, based on our search criteria. We pondered a change.

"I think 1985 was too late," said Roberta. "I say we go earlier."

"What else? What about the location?"

"The scientific method calls for changing only one criterion at a time," said Roberta.

"And what are we, scientists?" I asked.

Roberta liked that, though she looked a little rueful.

"Okay. How about North Sea?"

We went back to the microfilm, and a half hour later had another list of names and numbers. The subsequent search through the boxes was even more physically punishing, given the earlier vintage of the photos, but the moment it became nearly unbearable, we found something.

It was a roll of film shot in the summer of 1977, turned into strips of negatives that were slid into the slots of an 8½ × 11 plastic sheet. The title on the envelope was "Motorcycle Rally Means Hog Heaven in North Sea." Even with the sign out of the picture, and the images of bikers and their machines lined up in front of the store, you could see it was Delbert's Beachworld Deli, though an even older version. This was confirmed to the satisfaction of both of us after multiple perusals with Roberta's trusty loupe.

Seeing the store, even in the negative, brought me a lot closer to where I didn't want to go.

"What's the matter?" Roberta asked. "You look like you're ready to hurl."

"I am."

"When are you going to tell me what's going on?"

"What are the chances of me borrowing these negatives?" I asked.

"Officially? None."

"Unofficially."

"Excellent. But only if you tell me what's going on."

"How about half the story, the rest to be filled in as facts are confirmed?"

"You seem to forget I'm a reporter. They pay me to report the news. It's a fiduciary responsibility, counselor."

"I could argue the fiduciary part, but I understand," I said. "Did you hear about the plane crash in Bridgehampton?"

"Uh, yeah. We here at the newspaper and the rest of the world, both at about the same time."

"This has to do with that. And that's only the start."

"That's supposed to make me less curious?"

"Let me take this sheet of negs and I promise that as soon as I have the whole story worked out, and I can let it out, I'll give it all to you. Only you. And I'll buy the drinks."

"No way."

"I don't need the negatives to confirm my story," I said, suddenly realizing that myself and feeling stupid for overlooking the obvious. "They'll just help seal the deal."

I dropped the sheet on the table and stood up.

"I'm not trying to be an asshole," I said to her. "I appreciate all you've done for me. You're great." I turned to walk back up the stairs.

"I hate that," she called after me. I stopped. "Just say you want to keep things loose till you've ironed out a few wrinkles," she said. "That's good enough for me."

"No it's not."

"No it's not. But it preserves a person's dignity."

I walked back and picked up the sheet of negatives.

"You're still great," I said.

"You don't know the half of it," she said as I vaulted up the basement stairs and burst out a side door into the spring air.

A few minutes later I was knocking on the glass door of my friend Randall Dodge's computer repair shop, Good to the Last Byte, off the big parking lot in the middle of Southampton Village. The sign on the door said, "Absent without leave," but I knew he was in there somewhere. He almost never left.

A few moments later his rangy shape filled the space on the other side of the door.

"I assumed it was you," he said, opening the door with one hand and munching a slice of pizza with the other. "Who else takes 'not here' as an invitation to knock."

"I bet you can turn a photographic negative into a regular print in about five seconds," I said, handing him the manila envelope.

"Not as easily as a photo developer," he said.

"Don't know any of them," I said. "But I know you. I just need this one here," I said, pointing to the one that showed the clearest view of the storefront. "How long will it take?"

"About five seconds. With no interruptions."

I sat down on a nearby chair, folded my arms, and gave him a tight-lipped not-saying-another-word smile.

It was more than five seconds, actually about five minutes, before he emerged from some hidden space deep in his electronics-crammed cave holding an eight-by-ten print. He handed it to me.

It was an older, run-down version of Delbert's. The print was clear enough to show paint chipping off the trim around the door and the two big display windows on either side. Some local kids were gawking at the motorcycles while the bikers stood around looking ferocious and drinking beer from bottles held at the neck. The scene didn't quite fit the cheerful innocence of the headline labeling the sleeve of negs, but I wasn't paying much attention to that. Instead, I was staring at the sign that ran across the front of the building above the windows and the door. Most of the name was sliced off, but it was definitely not "Delbert's."

"Shit," I said.

Randall looked unhappy.

"Sorry, Jackie. That's the best I could do on short notice."

"Not your work, Randall. Something else. Can I use your computer?"

Randall was enough Shinnecock Indian to qualify for a spot on the reservation in Southampton, but he was just as much African-American and Caucasian, by way of an Irish Catholic grandfather, which he never tired of reminding me. Every St. Patrick's Day we'd tie one on at O'Malleys, starting the night with Irish brogues that either improved or disintegrated depending on which side of the conversation you were on.

But true to the stereotype of the reticent Indian, he never smiled with his mouth, a deficiency that was amply compensated for by his gray-green eyes, which were always alight.

"You may use anything I have in this world, Jackie. Because I know you would do the same for me."

"You're a doll, Randall."

"Just leave the Volvo in the lot when you go. Big date tonight."

Those sparkly eyes could have lit Yankee Stadium.

"Deal," I said, tossing him my keys.

He snatched them out of the air and led me down a canyon formed by towering shelving units stuffed with computer hardware and tangled cords to a cramped workstation equipped with the gleaming desktop version of my new laptop. I think I let out a little cry of delight, though I hope I didn't.

Since real estate is the principal industry in the Hamptons, few lawyers in the region do anything but. I was no exception when I started out. There are a few things I could do really well, and there are a small number of things I can do as well or better than anyone. One of those is title searches. Not unlike Roberta Comacho, there was a time when I lost myself digging around the mildewed records in the basement of Southampton Town Hall, following conveyances from buyer to seller sometimes all the way back to the mid-seventeenth century.

Sometimes in the course of a title search I'd come across a name or a property that looked sort of interesting and then find myself following transactions that had nothing to do with my clients. I know it's more than a little voyeuristic, and not even close to ethical, but it's that damn curiosity of mine.

Imagine a hound sniffing around the woods, with only a minor objective in mind, and a rabbit runs by. It was like that.

So it didn't take very long to narrow in on Delbert's physical location, which I already knew was somewhere in North Sea, and from there, cross-reference the number on the lot with the prior owner of the property.

I took that information and went into the archives of the *Southampton Chronicle,* this time of the editorial pages, which the paper had taken the effort to digitize and put online, and did another cross-reference.

And that's how I nailed it down. Clinton Andrews, the owner of the Peconic Pantry, which had hosted the motorcycle rally in 1977, had sold the property to Delbert J. Johannson after coming out of a coma caused by the severe beating he received during the course of an armed robbery at the store.

This event had been somewhat of a sensation back in 1978, a time when Southampton was less accustomed to the types of crime then common in the big city at the other end of Long Island. Especially since the perpetrator was a local kid who'd been caught when he tried to cash the only check the owner had left under the tray in the register. Both the arrest and subsequent trial held at the criminal court in Riverhead made for a minor media frenzy. I was only seven years old at the time, and didn't remember specific news coverage. Probably because my parents did everything they could to keep the story away from me. An understandable impulse for any set of parents, but particularly for mine. The last thing they wanted was for me to read the name of the accused splashed all over the local papers.

Billy O'Dwyer. My brother.

6

Like most people, the first time I heard the term "elephant in the living room" was from a shrink. I liked it then, and I still do. It perfectly explains what it's like to have the most important thing that ever happened to a family remain completely and forever unrecognized.

An elephant is a big thing, with a powerful gravitational pull. Like gravity, the ones grazing around a living room are invisible, but the pull is relentless, affecting everything and everyone, all the time.

It was like a sudden death, only worse. The visit from the cops in the middle of the night (they were hoping to catch my brother at a vulnerable moment, but he wasn't there). My parents speaking to them in urgent, hushed tones. My mother crying, my father cursing. The shock waves of fear and incredulity permeating the walls of my bedroom, where I'd been told in the harshest terms to stay put.

Billy wasn't just dead to us. It was as if he'd never existed.

I don't remember the last time I saw him, what I said to him or what he said to me. I do remember never seeing him again after that night. His name never again passed my parents' lips. If I'd been older, I'd have forced the issue, but I was blasted into compliance by the scale of their heartbreak.

It's hard to gauge the relative effects this kind of thing can have on people, but I believe it was worse for my father. I was a late, probably somewhat unwelcome, arrival, though I knew he loved me, in the way you love an irritating house pet. Billy, on the other hand, he adored. An only child for eleven years, until I came along, Billy was the archetypal golden boy. Handsome, whip-smart, and athletic. Ready to head off that fall to his freshman year at Notre Dame.

It's not a surprise that my father became so embittered. More the surprise that he lived out the rest of his life as well as he did. His heart in shreds, though his sanity reasonably intact.

The elephant concept explained a lot about why the remainder of my childhood played out as it did. I was lucky to have a smart psychiatrist, who laid it all out in logical terms. But luckier to have a priest named Father Dent who reminded me of why God put such a high premium on forgiveness, once I had something substantial to forgive.

Forgiveness was something I could manage with my parents, though only after they died. But never with Billy. Wherever I went, I took that elephant along with me. We had a deal. I kept him healthy and well-fed and he kept all memory of my brother and what he'd done to our family locked away in the deepest, darkest corner of my heart.

It's good to have wise, compassionate friends like Randall Dodge standing by at the moment you break into uncontrollable tears. He knew to simply place a broad hand on my shoulder and gently squeeze while patiently waiting out the torrent.

"Bad news?" he asked when I finally got control of myself.

"Old news, but yes, bad."

"I'll get something to mop you up."

While he was gone I brought up my e-mail program and between sobs sent myself a message with all the links to the title records and the press stories attached. For my sake and Randall's, I thought it was best not to research the thing any further. But I knew I had to do it sometime, so why not be prepared.

"You okay?" Randall asked, handing me a roll of paper towels.

I nodded.

"Sorry about that," I said.

"Tell me if I can help."

"You did already. I'll never forget it."

"Same here."

I got to know Randall when I defended him in a drug case that he'd been innocently swept into because of the foolish behavior of his own sibling, a younger brother who hardly deserved Randall's gallantry. That I pulled him out of the fire without making things worse for young Alexander had put me on Randall's eternal gratitude list.

Of course, thinking about that in the context of the moment almost triggered another gusher, but I got past it by thanking him again, insisting he take my car for the evening, and getting the hell out of his shop.

So now what? I thought as I felt myself being drawn to the place a few doors down that had an outdoor bar looking over the big parking lot behind the storefronts.

It was an interesting dilemma. Any number of people could have driven me home, including the Southampton Village Police, but that wasn't my real problem. I had this thing I never thought about, much less talked about, simmering in my mind. Most people would say this would be a great time for one's patient and understanding boyfriend to come out and provide comfort. But instead, my keenest desire was to have my irritating, often thoughtless, and usually frustrating male friend handle this particular duty.

First off, Sam Acquillo had a lot more experience with criminal behavior than Harry, who had virtually none. I knew that from the many times I'd defended Sam against criminal charges, the definition of a thankless task. Secondly, his very lack of sentimentality was what I needed right then. And I needed his brain, which was better than any I knew, and I knew some very brainy people.

"I'm busted up, Sam. And sober, but not for long," I told him when he answered his cell phone.

"Sobriety's way overrated."

"You have about ten minutes to get here before things get dangerous."

"Where's 'here'?"

I told him the place, one we'd made dangerous on more than one occasion.

"I'm on a job only five minutes away," he said. "Order me a double."

Sam had been in R & D and the head of a huge division at an oil and gas company until he ran afoul of some corporate politics. These he tried to handle the way he did opponents as a young professional boxer, with less than stellar results. When I met him, his big-time career, fancy marriage, and glorious prospects had collapsed into a beat-up cottage on the banks of the Little Peconic Bay in Southampton, where his main pursuits were hitting golf balls for his dog and consuming enough Absolut vodka to materially affect the Swedish balance of trade.

That and drawing the attention of criminal justice, which is where I came in.

Somewhat happier times have ensued for Sam, which have done little to moderate his habits. That's why I knew the offer of a free drink was the proper motivation.

It was about three o'clock in the afternoon, early for most carpenters to knock off for the day, but Sam had an easy relationship with Frank Entwhistle, the contractor he usually worked for. Sam not only did finish carpentry, but also custom cabinetmaking and architectural detail in a shop in the basement of his cottage. He made every oddball thing Frank asked him to and never missed a deadline. In return, Frank paid him by the week, gave him as much latitude as each project would allow, and ignored his personality.

True to his word, Sam appeared almost immediately, though not soon enough to see me down my first martini. Luckily, the second was on its way.

"What's with the red face?" he asked as he sat next to me at the bar and gathered up his drink in one of his gnarled, chewed-up hands. "Fall asleep in the sun?"

"So I cried a little. I'm a woman. Get used to it."

"That bad?"

"That complicated. You ever have something happen in your life so terrible that you just pretend it never did?" I asked him.

"Denial? Is that what you're talking about? It's my specialty. Almost as good as repression, about on par with avoidance."

"Where does drunkenness fit in?" I asked.

"I don't know. Let's drink these and find out."

"You only drink. You never get drunk."

"What's life without a goal?"

"I do get drunk," I said, "so let me get this out while my tongue can still form words."

So I did, haltingly at first, then gaining momentum as the narrative unfolded, telling the story like it had happened to someone else. I started with the horse pasture and went all the way to the police interview with Ed Conklin, and on to the trip through the photo archives and what the subsequent research had revealed. Sam listened without comment or change in expression, two gifts I'd devoutly hoped for and he blessedly delivered.

"Is Billy dead or alive?" he asked me when I stopped to take a breath.

"I don't know."

"What happened to him after he went to jail?"

"I don't know."

"What *do* you know?" he asked.

"Nothing. That's the point. I know absolutely nothing."

"What do you want to know?"

"I would have said nothing two days ago. Now it's not so easy," I said.

"Why do you think Eugenie had a picture of Delbert's, which Billy knocked off back when it was the Peconic Pantry?"

I hoped the look I gave him adequately conveyed the words, "You've got to be shitting me."

"Didn't I just say I don't know anything?" I asked. "That would include why Eugenie had a picture of the store Billy knocked off on that memory card."

"What are you going to do?" he asked.

"What I always do. Run down leads until they send me into a brick wall or over a cliff."

"Maybe this time you could do that without pissing off the entire legal establishment."

"Nice lecture coming from you," I said.

He liked that.

"I'm with you, Jackie. I'll do whatever you want me to do," he said.

This is what I wanted to hear, what I expected to hear, but it still made me start to tear up, a response I jumped on like a cat on a mouse, so nobody, not even Sam, saw it happen.

"I hate all this emotional shit flying around. It makes me feel vulnerable. I can't afford that right now. Do you hear what I'm telling you?"

Sam didn't react to that. He just stared into his drink as if there was an insult written on the bottom of the glass.

"You know, a second ago there was vodka in this thing. Where does it go?"

I waved the bartender over.

"So I need a plan," I said, after ordering another round.

"No you don't. You need to decide what to do next. That'll tell you what to do after that. And so on."

"Like you never plan," I said.

"Not if I can help it."

"So what do I do next?"

"Drink some more. It'll come to you."

"Fabulous help you've been here."

He set down his drink and used both hands to rub his curly-haired head.

"Come on, Jackie. You know what you need to do. What's with all this validation shit women always want? How many times have I put my life in your hands? You think I'd do that if I didn't trust you? You've got a fucking head on your shoulders. Use it."

Ah, that finely tuned sensitivity you can always count on with Sam.

"It's the brother thing. It's thrown me," I said.

"That's where you need to go. Or else drop the whole thing and go back to handling zoning variances for Muffy and Biff."

"Don't drag the Biffster into this. He's stupid, but cute."

By this time I was thoroughly and happily buzzed, meaning I was anesthetized against further blows to the heart. Which had been my plan from the start. There are times that call for prompt remedial action, and this was one of them.

A few martinis, a brutally honest pep talk, a little easing up on the psychic pressure valve, a ride home in Sam's ridiculous old car, and in the end, the thing he said he didn't want to give me, but invariably did.

Validation shit.

After Sam dropped me off, I thought it was a really good idea to pour a glass of wine, light a joint, strip down to a floppy tank top and gym shorts, and go sit on the mildewed outdoor furniture on the patio.

The sky was moonless and brilliant with stars. The woods rustled, buzzed, and faintly crackled around me as it always did when the warm seasons returned. The winds were from the south, so the ocean breeze had stripped the land of annoying bugs. It was cool, the air not entirely dry, but tolerably gentle to the touch.

After a few hours of brooding and more than my share of Chardonnay, I passed out on the picnic table, bolstered and resolute.

7

It's not easy to pick out the perfect outfit for a visit to the police. Not for lawyers, anyway. I don't know what the issues are for suspects or bail bondsmen.

You want to be professional and serious, but not completely unapproachable. Since you're entering a seriously male environment, you have to be modest, but a little bit of girl goes a long way. Though not so much that you attract the ire of lady cops and administrative workers, who can ruin your prospects of a successful relationship with the squad room.

All women fret over decisions like this, but for me it's agony on a Wagnerian scale.

I blame it all on my mother, who had only one look. Dowdy. I know this isn't fair, since there are plenty of women whose mothers had similar failings who still look like they just stepped off a runway.

I chose a light wool suit and silk blouse with a strategically placed top button and a pair of sensible flats. I knew I was on safe ground, since this was the only outfit that ever drew a compliment from Edith Madison, the Suffolk County district attorney. This was no mean trick, which you'd know if you ever saw Edith Madison.

I called ahead to make sure Joe Sullivan was in the office.

"Were there any photos in that camera?" I asked as soon as he got on the phone.

"Why?" he asked, all suspicious right off the bat.

"Just tell me."

"No. It's digital. No memory card in the camera or in the case."

"I have something for you," I said.

"You gotta be kidding me."

"The memory card. I found it in my pants pocket. Balled up in a piece of paper I must have snatched off the ground."

I was never very good at long silences. Especially over the phone.

"Still there, Joe?" I asked.

"Bring it in now," he said, and hung up the phone.

"Excellent," I said into the dead line.

My Volvo was waiting for me in the driveway with the keys under the floor mat. It didn't surprise me that Randall had managed the trick without me knowing it. I'd later have to hear him extol the Native craft of moving about the earth unnoticed by humans, wildlife, or police officers, like the ones I was headed out to see.

Southampton Town Police headquarters is in a white, single-story building surrounded by scrub pine and pin oaks in the north end of Hampton Bays. The front desk was run by a short-haired Tasmanian devil named Janet Orlovsky, who was nicer to me than she was to most people, though not what you'd actually call nice.

"You have an appointment?" she asked when I told her I was there to see Joe Sullivan.

"Yes. He told me he wanted to see me immediately."

"He didn't tell me," she said.

I just smiled at her sympathetically, refusing to let her draw me into a contest. I looked at her phone through the slab of bulletproof glass she sat behind. She frowned and dialed Joe's number. A few moments later the door to the reception area opened, but it wasn't Sullivan. It was his boss, Ross Semple, the chief of police.

"Hello, Ms. Swaitkowski," he said, offering his hand with the sort of antique flourish you see in corny old movies. "Terribly glad to see you."

I took his hand, but kept a safe distance. Not that Ross was lecherous in any way, but his movements were so impetuous and awkward, I was afraid he'd smack me by mistake.

"Nice to see you, too. I have a meeting with Joe Sullivan."

"You do? Isn't that capital."

Ross was in his mid-fifties, with a minimum of his iron gray hair intact, which he flaunted by keeping it long and disarrayed. He had a square jaw and high cheekbones, which sounds attractive, but somehow wasn't on Ross's face. Which might have been the fault of his glasses, which were thick as bottle bottoms and set in heavy black frames.

He'd spent the first half of his career in homicide, first in Manhattan, then in the South Bronx. He'd seen more dead bodies and tracked down more killers than Southampton had seen in three centuries. Born and raised here, he'd applied for a detective's job when he started having kids. No one who ever worked with Ross thought he was running from the carnage. And if they did, they'd likely wait until Ross was dead and buried before giving voice to that opinion.

"You knew I was coming in, didn't you, Ross."

"Of course I did, Jackie. I'm omniscient. It's why they made me chief of police." He gave another dopey flourish, bowed, and held the door to the squad room open for me. "If you'll do me the greatest of privileges and accompany me to my office, I would greatly appreciate it."

Orlovsky looked my way with more than a little satisfaction. Sadist.

None of the cops or administrative people made eye contact as I walked through the squad room to Ross's office in the back. Except for Joe Sullivan, who gave me a look that was impossible to misinterpret.

"Listen, Ross," I said as I took one of the chairs in front of his desk, "it can happen that people find evidence after the fact."

"Absolutely they can. I have myself."

I took the memory card out of the inside pocket of my suit jacket and tossed it on his desk.

"What's on it?" he asked without looking down.

"If I knew that, it would mean I'd taken the trouble to download the pictures before I brought it to you."

He dug a crumpled pack of cigarettes out of the top drawer of his desk and lit one. He threw me the pack, which I caught with one hand. Then a little beanbag ashtray and a Bic lighter, which I almost fumbled. Years before, the Town of Southampton had instituted fines for smoking in municipal buildings, but so far no one had volunteered to serve one on the chief.

"Do you have them with you? The printouts?" he asked.

I took the duplicate copies out of the other inside pocket and threw them on his desk next to the memory card. I felt like we were playing a weird form of tennis.

"How many photos and what are they of?" he asked, his head enshrouded in cigarette smoke. I told him as I lit one of my own. "What do they mean?" he asked.

"I have no idea," I said, which was mostly true.

He leaned back in his wreck of an office chair and put his feet up on the desk, right on top of a stack of papers. His office was a mess, which should have made me comfortable, but I'm too much of a hypocrite. I really don't like other people's messes. It's too easy to hide dangerous things. I like a nice clear space with everything in view.

"We've been down this road before, haven't we, Jackie."

"Which road?"

"The one where you involve yourself in matters that lie outside your professional responsibilities."

"That's a matter of interpretation, Ross. And even if there were an occasion or two when I might have accidently strayed into ambiguous territory, that isn't the case here, since I'm acting to uphold my professional responsibilities."

"As a witness?"

"As a defense attorney. Ed Conklin's."

"Why does he need defending?"

"Why are you interviewing him?"

His peculiar face relaxed into a wide grin.

"There's something you don't know? How novel."

Goddammit, I thought. Cat and mouse with Ross Semple. My least favorite thing.

"Okay, you know something I don't," I said. "The bidding's open. What'll it take to find out?"

"What's the meaning of these photos?"

I described each of them in as much detail as I could remember, including the physical details of Delbert's Beachworld Deli, though that's as far as I went.

"And these are the only photos discovered at the scene?" said Ross.

"The only memory card I'm aware of. You have the camera."

"It would break my heart if you weren't in full disclosure," said Ross, and I knew he meant it.

"Never happen. I'm an officer of the court."

"Hm," he said, pulling his feet off the desk and dropping them down to the floor. He picked up the stack of photos and leafed through them.

"They could mean nothing at all," he said.

"That's what I think. Just happened to be in the camera case. Random occurrence." I watched him study the photos for a few minutes. "Hey, Ross," I said. "What do *you* care?"

"Huh?" he said, looking up.

"Why the interest in those photos? Wasn't this just a plane crash? Why all the interest in Conklin? What don't I know?"

He liked that.

"So now you're giving *me* the third degree. I like that."

"Well, of course I am, Ross. Who wouldn't? You're omniscient. You know everything."

He put his elbows on his desk and rubbed his face with both hands, reaching up under his glasses, which almost made them fall off his head.

"So how come I'm not rich?" he asked in a muffled voice.

"Your wealth is in your friends. Like me."

"We're friends?" he asked. "That's a pretty thought."

"We are. And friends don't let friends defend clients without all the information she needs to do her job."

His cigarette had burned down to the filter, but he still held it in his hand like a tiny pointer. He pointed it at me.

"Here's the problem, Jackie. I've got an ongoing investigation and you've got a client to defend. What would happen to our friendship if these things happen to conflict?"

"Cut the crap, Ross. They already have," I said, digging out another of his cigarettes and lighting it, then using the smoldering end to point back at him. "You don't have to tell me anything at all. I'll just wait for the charge, if one's coming. Then we'll play it from there."

"What happens when you deposit more than ten thousand dollars in cash?"

"The bank reports it to the government," I said.

"Excellent. What happens when you deposit lesser amounts of cash with some frequency in more than one bank over a longish period of time, say three years?"

"The banks report it to the government?"

"Bingo."

"Ed Conklin?" I asked.

"Close."

"Eugenie?"

I'd handled these cases before. There were only two reasons people tried to sneak cash deposits past officialdom. Tax evasion or drug deals. Or both. Hiding cash in a bank was never an easy thing to do, but after 9/11, it was nearly impossible. Professional criminals knew this and had a dozen ways to run their cash through the laundry. So the people I defended over dirty money were uniformly amateurish, or at least naïve.

"You're thinking drugs," I said. "Flown in from wherever for distribution in the Hamptons."

"Either flown in or out. We only uncovered her little enterprise a few months ago. Your lady pilot's been a very bad bird. A local bank president gave me the tip-off that the FBI had come to call about the deposits. He knows I don't like the feds poking around my town without me in on it."

"He does? A bank president knows this?" I asked, trying to imagine the conversation.

"He's my cousin," said Ross. "His mother's my father's sister. Pompous little fink, but richer'n all of us put together, so there you go."

"Since Conklin's an ex-con, you're making the assumption that he got her into this. Used connections made in the joint."

"The commonsense assumption. You know as well as I do that the obvious is almost always the truth," he said. "*Numquam ponenda est pluralitas sine necessitate.*"

"That's right. Anyone can see that the sun goes around the earth, which is flat as a pancake, by the way."

"*Exceptio probat regulam in casibus non exceptis.*"

"So what do you do now? And say it in English. I feel like I'm back in catechism."

"We do what they pay us to do around here. Investigate your client."

"Why tell me?" I asked. "Sort of takes away the element of surprise."

He laughed one of those weird little half laughs that always sound contrived. Not without humor, just not exactly genuine.

"I wouldn't normally, Jackie, but you messed me up with the memory card caper. Pulling a stunt like that again could finally get you that obstruction of justice rap we both know you richly deserve."

My heart raced at that, partly from outrage and partly from the truth of it. The effort to calm myself down was well spent, since it kept my mouth in check just long enough for me to get my better judgment back in control.

"So, if I'm hearing you properly, now that I'm on notice that there's an ongoing investigation of Mr. Conklin, there's a higher standard of evidentiary integrity at issue."

"Don't get all lawyerish on me, Jackie. I'm just looking after you."

"Just as long as you understand that Mr. Conklin's my client. And therefore matters between us are protected under attorney-client privilege."

"Unless that privilege is used to perpetrate a crime or fraud. Supreme Court, *Clark v. United States,* 1933."

It didn't seem fair that the chief of police in the town of my birth—the town in which I'd chosen to undertake a career in real estate law, now tragically morphing into defending the poor, the corrupt, the cynical, criminal, and sometimes sociopathic, to say nothing of occasional innocent—would have to be Ross Semple. The foreign languages and command of philosophy I could take. The command of constitutional law, not so much.

I sighed and said, "Almost never invoked, though I'm sure you know that."

Ross jumped up out of his chair and stretched, his arms held high above his head and his face straining with the effort.

"I'm glad we got that out of the way," he forced out.

"Me, too," I said, jumping up myself, more than eager to vacate the premises.

"Hey, Jackie," he said to my retreating back. I turned.

"Yeah?"

"The guy's dirty. I know it in my bones."

I tried to work out "You mean up your ass" in Latin, but I couldn't do it fast enough, so instead I just muttered it in English as I turned again and left his office.

8

Scrambled eggs. That's how I imagine my brains under certain circumstances. All lumpy and clumpy and incapable of coherent thought.

I have no cure for the condition, but I do have a coping strategy. I start doing things. It doesn't matter what it is, I just do. I fix things, buy things, puzzle over things, remember things, organize things, and toss things in the trash (albeit reluctantly).

I also make up for things I haven't done, but really should have, like returning an e-mail from a forgotten high school friend who tracked me down over the Internet. Throwing away run-filled panty hose and socks that permanently and mysteriously lost their partners decades ago. Transferring hand cream from the store bottle to a lovely glass container given to me by who-knows-who. Cancelling the expensive cable TV package I bought the night the sales rep called me after I'd already had half a bottle of wine and was weeping over the late-night loss of Johnny Carson and Ed McMahon. Or washing the hand towel hanging in the guest bathroom that smelled like a wet sheepdog (for naught, since I rarely had a guest).

Somehow, all this doing begins the process of focusing my chaotically unfocused mind, cauterizing the jagged nerve endings and calming the tempest often raging inside my skull.

Only then can rational thought commence, strategy be divined, or planning put in place.

After meeting with Ross, I committed myself to an orgy of doing, until I exhausted both myself and the strategy itself. Though still at my wit's end, I stopped the whirling dervish thing and poured a glass of wine like I should have done in the first place.

That was when I finally knew what I had to do next.

O'Dwyer isn't that common a name, which helped. Sitting at my office computer and using Randall Dodge's semi-illegal, database-aggregating, privacy-violating software, I had a dozen William O'Dwyers that fit my brother's vital statistics in a matter of minutes. Five were in Ireland, where they belonged; one was in Canada, one in Argentina, the rest in the United States. Of these five, two lived in the New York metropolitan area, one born in a pizza parlor in Brooklyn, the other in Southampton Hospital.

I hate to admit that something as statistically daunting as tracking down one person in 300 million can be this easy, but it is, if you know what you're doing and you have the right tools. Welcome to the world as we now know it.

I had no proof that this was my brother, but the circumstantial evidence was overwhelming. In addition to the place of birth, there was the fourteen-year stay at Sanger medium-security prison on the banks of the St. Lawrence River in seriously Upstate New York.

I had a phone number and an address in Port Jefferson, a town on the north shore of Long Island and about an hour from Southampton. I also had a firm conviction that I was not going to do this alone.

"Ever been to Port Jeff?" I asked Harry when he answered the phone.

"No, but I bet I'm going."

"I'll drive."

"Let me. You navigate."

"You don't like the way I drive," I said.

"You don't drive. You approximate. It's exciting, in small doses. What's in Port Jeff?" he asked.

"Emotional havoc brought on by bizarre coincidence."

"When, and what's the dress code?"

"Tomorrow afternoon. I want to get there by six. Wear something empathetic. With a tie. But nonrestricting, just in case."

"In case of what?"

"I'll explain in the car," I said. "When I do you'll see why I have to go in person."

"No explanation necessary, Jackie. I'm simply honored to be your driver," he said, which from anyone else would have sounded vaguely sarcastic, but Harry said things like that all the time, and after knowing him for a few years, I realized he meant just what he said.

"You're a wonderfully patient and understanding man, Harry Goodlander. As well as handsome in an atypical way and a reasonably good dancer for a guy the size of the Empire State Building."

"Though too easily swayed by flattery."

I don't know what accident of divinity, fertility, or dumb happenstance caused my parents to produce me eleven years after my brother, but that's what they did. My father was already in his forties, my mother not much younger. They'd already settled into their lives as a classic American family unit, my father engineering bland office buildings Up Island, my mother looking after the house, and the two of them raising young Mr. Wonderful.

I didn't fully appreciate the impact I must have had until I found some 8mm movies in a closet when I was clearing out the house after my mother died. I thought converting them to DVD was a good idea. Here's a tip for the hypersensitive: don't do this.

It was a backyard barbecue. My father was talking to a guy who looked a lot like him. Each had a cocktail glass in one hand and a pocket stuffed with the other. The scene was relatively static until a little girl with fuzzy reddish blond hair leaped into view, hopped about in a crazy sort of dance, then zipped back out of the picture. This happened two or three more times, until the cameraperson, I assume my mother, sought more promising subject matter.

I didn't remember the specific event, but I thought it conveyed the central truth of my childhood—that I spewed out far more riotous energy than the family could ever absorb. You can see in those movies my father suffering through the imposition. He tried to look like the parent of a lively kid, but the best he could muster was a weary tolerance, laced with irritation.

So imagine what it must have been like to lose a beloved son the way he lost Billy, and then to realize that all he had left was me.

On the way to Port Jefferson, I gave Harry a full rundown of the facts of the case, treading lightly over the emotional terrain. Anyone could see this was tough stuff. He didn't need the gory details.

Port Jeff was a mixed bag of a town on the North Shore of Long Island. It had a lot of nice-looking buildings around the harbor. You could eat fried seafood or buy T-shirts and kitsch. Motorcycle clubs passed through so frequently they had their own parking section. On the water was a grand old hotel that had a good view of the dock that received giant ferries running back and forth between Port Jefferson and Bridgeport, Connecticut.

None of which Harry got to see on this trip. My brother's apartment was officially in Port Jeff, but about as far from the coastline as the town's borders would allow.

It was in an old three-story house with a wraparound porch. There were three buzzers next to the front door. The one I wanted buzzed on the third floor. A woman's voice came out of the speaker.

"Who's there?"

"My name's Jacqueline Swaitkowski. I'm an attorney. I'm here to see William O'Dwyer."

"What's it about?"

"I need to discuss that with Mr. O'Dwyer. If you don't mind coming to the door, I can show you my identification."

The speaker went silent, and we waited. Now that I was about to actually confront the situation, I was strangely unmoved. Maybe that was it. The situation was too strange to feel real.

"You didn't tell her who you are," said Harry. "The sister part."

"One thing at a time. I don't even know for sure he's my brother."

The door had a large single pane of glass, through which I saw a young woman come down the stairs. She had thin brown hair parted in the middle and a small face, with a small nose but eyes that were disproportionately large. She wore a cotton dress that could have come out of my mother's closet, and black exercise sneakers that would never find their way into mine. She looked concerned but opened the door, not all the way.

I handed her my card. She read it carefully, as if the entire explanation for my visit was printed there.

"I'm investigating an accident," I said to her. "Mr. O'Dwyer is not directly connected in any way. But he might have some information that would be valuable. It should only take a few minutes." I looked over at some dusty wicker chairs loosely arranged around a coffee table. "We can talk out here."

She looked in the grip of manifold uncertainties, as if any response had its unique hazards.

"I'll go see," she said, finally, taking my card and leaving us to wait on the porch.

"I wonder if she knows," I said to Harry.

"Knows what?"

"About the prison time. Not the first wife to be left in the dark."

"Or girlfriend," said Harry. "No wedding ring."

"Was that brilliant detection, or do you always look?"

"I'm brilliant enough not to answer that one."

Almost ten minutes went by, and I was starting to think I should either push the buzzer again or pack it in and go home when the woman came back down the steps, this time with a guy walking behind her. She stepped out of his way when they reached the door, and he swung it open.

My heart clenched.

It was my father. A fleshier, paler version, but with the same curly orange hair and big, cartoon ears. He wore rimless glasses, behind which his eyes squinted at me, as if trying to read an explanation on my face.

"Mr. O'Dwyer?" I asked, or more likely croaked.

"What's this about?" he asked, looking at Harry, like men always do. Don't ask the woman standing right there, who's actually the one you're supposed to be asking.

"As I told your wife," I said, "I'm investigating an accident. A plane crash, to be more accurate. You might be able to shed some light on our investigation."

The suspicion in his face matched the woman's uncertainty. For both of them, no choice seemed easy.

"I don't know anything about a plane crash," he said.

"Can we sit down?" I asked, pointing again at the ratty wicker chairs.

Harry did just that, drawing the rest of us in his wake. Billy sat; the woman continued to stand. On guard.

I described Eugenie's crash with most of the detail intact, including the flying camera case and the photos in the memory card. I saw no point in withholding anything. Especially since I was withholding the biggest fact of all–that Billy's estranged little sister was telling the story.

I carefully watched his face as I talked, looking for involuntary reactions, but his only expression was of pained confusion. I was not too worried that he'd identify me. I was a little kid when he went away, never to return. It was possible that a person in his situation would try to keep remote tabs on his lost family, but I doubted he'd be one of them. I had nothing to base this on, but judging by his reactions on the porch, I thought I was right.

Plus, I didn't exactly look like me anymore. The aforementioned car bomb didn't kill me, but it thoroughly smashed up my face. The plastic surgeons not only put everything back together again, they improved on the product. Most of their clients were Upper East Side dowagers trying to look like Marilyn Monroe, so some of that got mixed into my native Irish cheeks. If he hadn't checked up on me recently, he might not realize who he was talking to. Though in this Alice in Wonderland moment, I realized that it wasn't only my father who looked back at me through my brother's eyes. My mother was there, too. And a little of me, including the bits of me that no longer existed.

For all that, I still didn't have admissible evidence that this guy who looked like me and had my old last name was who I thought he was. Until I got to the part in my story about Delbert's Beachworld Deli, formerly the Peconic Pantry. When I dropped the black-and-white photo on the table, brilliant red blossoms ignited on Billy's pale cheeks. The woman put the back of her hand to her mouth. Two mysteries solved at once.

I tried to continue my narrative, but he cut me off.

"I have no idea what this has to do with me," he said.

I took the photo off the table and put it back in my pocket.

"Do you want to talk about this in private?" I asked, looking over at the woman, who still had her hand over her mouth. Her eyes darted at me, and widened. Then she looked at Billy and shook her head.

"Don't say anything, baby. Not without Ivan." She looked back at me. "His lawyer."

I sat back in the wicker chair.

"Did you know Eugenie Birkson?" I asked.

Billy shook his head.

"Bill," said the woman, part warning, part plea.

"The Peconic Pantry was pretty popular in the old days," he said, ignoring her. "Lots of people would have photos of the place. What happened there was a long time ago. Can't have anything to do with a plane crash. That's a little cracked."

When he said that, I not only saw my father, I heard him. I hoped it didn't show on my face.

"I can't help you," he said. "Not because I don't want to. I don't know anything. I'd cooperate if I could."

That time I heard the words of a guy in the interrogation room, like the one back in Hampton Bays. The ex-con, the former perp, the one who didn't do it, though there was plenty else he'd actually done.

"Bill's got a good sales job. Had the same one since he got out. He's home every night," said the woman, which the uninformed would think a non sequitur. I knew different. The whole dreary history was self-evident. Plenty of official types had shown up at their door. Asking questions about people and things Billy may or may not have known anything about. Submitting to unspoken threats, knowing he was doomed to the status of an ex-con, forever cursed.

"No accusation here, ma'am. Just trying to get some information."

"He doesn't have any. You heard him."

"Kathy," said Billy, as if finally noticing her. "It's okay."

I wanted to say, Be nice to her. She's trying to protect your worthless ass. But I decided it didn't matter. He didn't matter.

I stood up and flicked another of my business cards into his lap.

"Just in case you actually remember anything, call the number on my card. Meanwhile, have a nice day," I said, then walked off the porch, after giving the shoulder of Harry's suit a sharp yank.

I knew Harry was behind me because I could hear the crunch of his shoes as he walked across the gritty sidewalk that led to where we'd parked the Volvo. I could also feel the disapproval, even before I heard it in his voice.

"Geez, that was a little weird," he said as he opened the car door for me.

"I need to get out of here."

We drove in silence through the ranch-house-and-shopping-center landscape of Eastern Suffolk County. When we were safely on Sunrise Highway heading back to the Hamptons, I apologized.

"Sorry, Harry. That wasn't me at my best."

"How come you didn't tell him you're his sister?" he asked.

I didn't know. Not exactly. Part of me thought I'd get more information out of him if he thought I was more of a threat. Another part didn't know how to broach the subject, since I hadn't right from the start. "Oh, and by the way . . ." Neither of which was the true answer, as I thought about it. The fact was I didn't want it to get personal. After all those years denying his existence, I didn't know how to kick off a new relationship. Mostly because I didn't know what flavor it would turn out to be–good, bad, or indifferent. I felt like all three were possibilities. Maybe not good, but maybe not so bitter.

"It's too complicated," I said to Harry.

"Is that why you didn't push him very hard for information?"

"I didn't?"

"Hardly at all," he said. "I was trying to figure out what you were thinking."

This was the closest Harry usually came to criticizing me. Even in the days leading up to me tossing him out, which ended our first go-round together, he was relentlessly considerate and nonconfrontational.

At the time, this only pissed me off that much more. But that was just Harry being Harry, which took a second time around to sink in.

"I'm not thinking. That's the problem. This thing with Billy just jumbles everything up. He doesn't know anything about this. It's just a creepy coincidence. I should've left well enough alone. Now I've got his goddamned face stuck in my head for the rest of my life."

He drove along without commenting. But I knew what he was thinking. If only his girlfriend could learn a little impulse control. I agreed with him. I decided I'd work on that, right after I dragged my boyfriend through another interview, this one sure to be considerably more pleasant.

9

It was nearly sunset when we reached Kirk and Emily's place on Gin Lane. But it was still light enough to see the shingle-style mansion standing hard against the dunes at the end of a long, open lawn. It was built in the 1920s when the fashion was to call houses like that cottages. This to me is a nice example of how to confirm pretense by trying to hide it. Though with Kirk and Emily, you nearly bought the label. The giant house was so warm and comfortably broken in, you could almost call it unassuming. Almost.

Kirk greeted us at the front door. He wore a baby blue sweater over a yellow shirt, which seemed to suit his natty white hair, and blue and white seersucker pants. He earned Harry's instant esteem by letting Harry's room-filling proportions go entirely unnoted.

"Emily asked me to report on your relative state of hunger," he said as he led us up to the enclosed porch on the ocean side of the second floor. "She's poised at the refrigerator and won't budge until I do."

"We're all set. Don't want to impose."

"Nonsense." He spoke into a small black device unclipped from his belt. "I think we're on with the fruit bowl and chocolate chip cookies."

"Roger that," we heard Emily say through the trebly speaker.

"Walkie-talkie," said Kirk. "Comes in handy around here."

The porch filled an area between two exposed balconies, where it was still a little too chilly to sit in the evening. The Lavignes had bought the place furnished, seeing no reason to replace the lovingly cared-for belongings, none of which was less than fifty years old, left by the prior owners. I particularly liked the seating–art deco bamboo with cushions you could sink into up to your neck.

I listened to the breakers down below while Kirk rustled drinks behind the matching bamboo wet bar.

"Glad to finally meet you, Harry," he said as he handed over a scotch on the rocks. "Jackie likes to talk about you."

"She quotes you," said Emily, arriving with the promised fruit bowl and bag of locally baked cookies. "You and her criminal friend."

"She means Sam," I said. "Never convicted, I might add."

"Thanks to you," said Kirk.

Emily matched her husband perfectly. Same hair, same blue eyes, same preppy clothes and tidy stature. They were the type of couple who seemed of a piece, a single unit with two complementary parts. They spoke in alternating sentences, as if they'd rehearsed their lines beforehand.

"I'm intrigued," said Kirk, after food and beverages had been thoroughly distributed. "Your e-mail was so cryptic."

"I didn't mean it to be," I said. "There's just too much to put in writing."

"So put it in words," said Emily.

So I did. Harry by now had heard the story enough to add in things I forgot, along with a few observations of his own. By prior agreement, we left out Billy and the Peconic Pantry. No need to muddle things with that sideshow.

I pulled out Eugenie's photo of the fund-raiser and gave it to Emily. Kirk moved closer to her on the bamboo settee and tilted his head back to get a clear view of the print through his bifocals.

"We look great," he said.

"Though look at that dress. What was I thinking?" said Emily.

"This is the Children's Relief Fund summer drive," said Kirk. "Two years ago, maybe? I'm going by the lapel pin. Remember?"

"We were pushing the pins. I have mine on a chain. You can see it."

Kirk looked up at me.

"Is this helping?"

"Immensely. So you think it was about two years ago, and the event was for the Children's Relief Fund? Can you identify the other people in the photo? Here." I handed them a pen and a notepad to write down the names, left to right. Kirk took the pad and pen, then both he and Emily arched back to focus on the shot. I could have sworn their lips pursed at the same time, in the same way.

"Archie Milenthal, of course," said Emily.

"Of course. Lizzy Witherspoon. Real name, no joke."

"Judge Andrews, Felicity Hunt."

"Akim Sharadze, Benson MacAvoy."

"Decker Daggit, Janie Wilson."

"Peaches the Pomeranian."

"No."

"Yes, right there, peeking out from under the table."

"Cute."

They looked up at me.

"How'd we do?" asked Kirk.

"Brilliant. Can you write all that down?"

We spent the rest of the evening listening to the Lavignes present the biographies of the people in the photo, to the best of their knowledge. Most of the commentary revolved around the usual vacuous and, for me, skin-crawling society conventions of boarding schools, trust funds, and stints in rehab. Kirk and Emily were able to deliver it all like anthropologists–observant, but with no particular allegiance to the observed. They had grown up together in a town just beyond the suburbs of Philadelphia, married after graduating from high school, put themselves through college on ROTC scholarships, and survived the Vietnam War–Kirk as an infantry officer and Emily with the Army Nurse Corps.

People unlikely to be impressed by the fancies of the seaside gentry.

By the end of the evening I'd begun to focus on two of the people in the photo, Janie Wilson and Benson MacAvoy. The criterion was simple. Both lived in Southampton year-round. Which meant I didn't have to go into New York City to talk to them. I loved the city, but I just didn't have the time. My secret investigative technique: expediency.

Janie was part of a family who'd run a nursery business in Bridgehampton for several generations. She'd acquired some modest fame by hosting a gardening show on the local public radio station. Enough to earn the dubious honor of an invitation to the Children's Relief Fund charity event.

I should have identified Benson MacAvoy long before the Lavignes pointed him out. We'd had a moment a few years before at a political rally in support of a doomed knucklehead running for Congress against the lucky and, in my opinion, thoroughly corrupt knucklehead who eventually won. I'm in no way a political girl, but I had nothing else to do that night. MacAvoy was the master of ceremonies, meaning he had the mic most of the evening, and though I'd heard about his compelling antics for years, I was unprepared for just how compelling those antics could be.

So when the night was winding down, I made the mistake of approaching him at the cash bar. I remembered his large face, with a deep scar that distorted his upper lip and prominent chin. His hair was dirty blond, long and wavy and thick, flowing back from his temples like a flag in the wind. His fingers were meaty, but manicured, unlike Sam's or Ed Conklin's; their hands looked like they'd been stored at the bottom of a toolbox.

I remembered the exchange of a drink or two, or three, a fair amount of banter, which I recalled as witty though it was probably ridiculous, some gazing into each other's eyes, an attempt on his part to extract a phone number by asking to borrow my cell, and on mine, a successful, yet somewhat reluctant, withdrawal.

"So no interest in Peaches the Pomeranian?" asked Harry.

"I'll get to her in due course."

Kirk and Emily escorted us to the door when it was time to leave. Hugs and kisses and handshakes were passed around, ending with Kirk slapping Harry on the shoulder, which took some extension of his right arm to achieve.

"You caught a good one," he said.

"I know, sir," said Harry.

"Just keep an open mind."

"I do, sir," said Harry.

By then I'd had enough wine and good company to let that one just pass on by.

I drove home after picking up my car where I'd left it at Harry's, after doing as much as I could to express my appreciation for his having kept me company that day (shy of staying the night, which greatly expanded my repertoire of ways to show appreciation).

When I got there, a pickup was parked halfway in the woods and Ed Conklin was sitting on my doorstep.

Poor impulse control or not, I knew better than to just leap out of the car. My house is deep enough in the woods that in summer the only lights I see are in the sky. I'm a single woman and there was a convicted felon who'd almost killed a guy with his fists sitting in the dark, waiting for me. Most people would say the prudent thing would be to back out of the driveway and go spend the night somewhere else.

I considered that for a moment, then I leaped out of the car.

"Hey, Ed. What's up?" I asked, standing behind the open car door with one foot on the floor mat and one hand on the wheel.

He squinted into the bright headlights.

"Miss Swaitkowski? Got a minute to talk?"

"I'm pretty flex on most stuff, Ed, but it's better you call ahead. This is my house. I see clients in my office."

"Sorry. I just wandered over here. I know I shoulda called."

"How'd you know where I lived?" I asked.

"I got a computer. Tells you everything."

Live by the sword, die by the sword.

"Have you been drinking?" I asked, though I knew the answer.

"A little."

"Here's the thing, Ed. I can't be okay with this as it currently stands. But if you're willing to sit there for a bit, and agree to another person being present, we can talk. About anything you want. Otherwise, we're done here. We all have our rules. My number one rule is the house is off-limits. You dig?"

My front stoop is low to the ground, so he wasn't very comfortable sitting there, his knees up in the air and his hands in the pockets of a baggy Windbreaker. Pockets big enough to hold anything, lethal or otherwise.

"I need to talk," he said, moving his face away from the Volvo's headlights. "Do it any way you want."

I dropped back into my car, closed the door, and flicked on the door locks. I slipped the shifter into reverse and put my foot on the brakes to hold the car in place. Then I called Sam.

"Yeah?" he said, in the charming way he usually answered the phone.

"I need you at my house. Now. Come prepared. No time to talk."

The phone went dead.

I flicked my cell phone shut and settled in to wait, one hand on the shifter and the other on the wheel, my foot on the accelerator.

A few minutes later I started to think about cigarettes. I've been able to hold my intake to three or four a day, but times like this were designed for something far more engaged. I wondered about the glove box. Was there a pack in there, or was that just my hungering imagination?

This is how I occupied myself until Sam showed up, a few minutes after I remembered there were three Marlboro Lights in the console beneath my elbow, stuck there last month for a reason I couldn't explain until now.

Just in case.

The meager orange glow from the headlights of Sam's '67 Grand Prix did little to illuminate the scene. I didn't care, I was so vastly relieved to see that absurd land yacht sail down my driveway. I left the Volvo and waited for him to pull up behind me so I could jump into the passenger seat.

"Scary client," I said to Sam, as fast as I could get it out. "Husband of the dead girl pilot. Sitting on my doorstep."

"Guns?" he asked.

"Not that I'm aware of."

"So we haven't called Sullivan," said Sam, rolling down his window to get a better look at the situation. "We don't want the dope busted. We just don't want to be killed for our kindness."

"In a nutshell, yes."

I tossed him one of the Marlboro Lights I'd brought along and lit up both of us with a very shaky hand.

"You're worried about this," said Sam.

"You think?" I said, sucking down half the cigarette with a single draw.

"Okay," he said.

Before I could stop him, he opened the door of the big car and walked over to where Ed was sitting on my doorstep. I was too far away to hear what they were saying, but I could read the body language, more or less. Sam was presenting the organizational chart to Ed, and Ed was showing enough resistance to cause Sam to settle into that pose I'd seen before—the one immediately preceding an explosion of lunatic violence.

Though, thank God, none of that happened. I saw Conklin's shoulders sag, giving up the fight, resigned. I saw him stand so Sam could frisk him. When Sam waved to me, I got out of the car and strolled across my gravel driveway, loose and unconcerned, like this particular scene played out here on Brick Kiln Road every day.

"So, Ed," I said, "what's the deal?"

"I'm goin' a little crazy."

"That's evident."

"Can we talk?" He looked over at Sam. "You and your friend?"

"Let's go back here," I said, leading them around the side of the house to the brick patio where I'd recently spent some contemplative time. I wasn't going to let Conklin into my house, but he was still my client, and I needed to hear him out. We sat at the picnic table under the harsh downward light that came from a pair of security floods tucked under the eaves. Sam sat next to Conklin; I sat across the table.

"I'm sorry about the prison thing," said Conklin. "Keepin' all that a secret gets to be a habit. I know I shoulda spoke up."

"You shoulda," I said.

He put his elbows on the table and rubbed his hands together.

"Whatever I tell you is private between us, right? Attorney-client thing?" He looked over at Sam.

"Yes. Completely confidential. That includes Sam, who's my investigator, and therefore covered under the same privilege."

Sam didn't know that what I'd said was approximately true, but he played along anyway.

"Lips are sealed, pal," he said.

Conklin closed his eyes, as if that made it easier to squeeze out the information.

"Eugenie'd been acting odd lately, in ways she'd never acted before." He opened his eyes again. "Tense and kind of fussy. When I tried to talk to her about it, she told me I was full of crap and to lay off. That wasn't like her, either. We've had our go-rounds, but at least the reasons would be there out in the open. This time there was something secretive going on. Husbands can always tell these things. The wives just think we're too dumb to notice," he added, looking at Sam.

Who said, "You got that right."

"How long had you been feeling these things?" I asked.

"Six months, maybe. Maybe a little more. It came on gradual. I didn't want to say anything to the cops about it. I mean, she's dead and all, but I couldn't help being protective."

"So you're assuming Eugenie was up to something she shouldn't have been?" Sam asked.

Conklin looked even more pained.

"That's the problem with this. I did. She was hidin' something. I still have that ex-con's radar. Of course, any husband might be imaginin' all sorts of things. Even if you don't want to. But that's not where I was going with this. If she was steppin' out on me, she was drinkin' the greatest love potion in history, 'cause that part ain't never been better."

I could have told him it wouldn't be the first time a cheating spouse discovered renewed ardor back home, but no purpose would be served.

"So now you're wondering if there's a connection to her death," I said.

"That's the torment," said Conklin. "Even if I spill the goods, the only proof I got is a feeling. They'd think I was nuts."

"Nothing else?" I asked.

He thought about it.

"Fuel consumption," he said. "I started noticing the Cessna was burning more fuel than usual. More than what she'd normally need to get from, say, East Hampton to Sikorsky in Connecticut. I asked her about it, but she'd say, You're the mechanic; you figure it out. I'd check that plane from prop to tail, and never found a thing."

"Like an unscheduled diversion to some other landing field," said Sam. "Where she couldn't refuel."

"Yeah, something like that," he said, quietly. "Sometimes she burned less fuel than she should've. Might lead you to the same conclusion."

"So there's no record of where she went."

"Not official. Just our logs, which she kept."

I knew what Sullivan would be asking right about now, if he was there. I could hear him ask it.

"So how's the money situation been with you two?" I asked. "Things going all right?"

"Not bad," he said, without hesitating. "Never what you want, but enough to get by."

"Did Eugenie have any expensive habits?" Sam asked. "Handbags, ponies, blow?"

This time it took Conklin a little more time to answer. He was trying to decipher the question. When he finally did, he almost laughed.

"Hell no. Are you kidding? She dressed like a slob, so forget the pocketbooks. Didn't even like to shop. Bought everything out of a catalog. If she'd picked up a gambling or drug thing, she hid it pretty good. I guess it's possible, but I just can't imagine it. Wouldn't be the Eugenie I knew."

Most addictions, almost by definition, were secret. The spouse is often the last to know.

But again, I kept that thought to myself and moved off in another direction.

"What about your father-in-law?" I asked. "Matt Birkson. I hear he did a little time himself."

"Nice family Eugenie's got, eh?" He gave a little shrug. "The guy's a grade A son of a bitch, I'll grant you that, but he never bothered me. Raised Eugenie on his own after the wife abandoned them. Can't say she had much feeling for the old man, but can't say she was abused or anything either. She lived with her aunt part of the time, when Matt was in stir. I think that balanced things out. But as far as I know, she hadn't had much to do with either of them for years."

I couldn't see Conklin all that well in the glare of the floodlights, but what I saw didn't tell me much one way or the other. I pushed a bit more on the older Birkson, but that was all I got.

"So no ideas," I said. "You just knew something was up, but you didn't know what."

"That's about it."

We talked for a little while longer, but nothing of further substance emerged. However tipsy Conklin might have been before, he seemed perfectly sober now. More sheepish than anything. Sam gave him one more bit of advice on staying away from my house, then we walked him back around to the driveway in front of the house and watched him drive away.

"What do you think?" I asked Sam.

"That you still have some vodka left from the last time I was here."

"Excellent chance of that. I have better use for lighter fluid than drinking it on the rocks."

Once I had him settled on the couch with the drink and an ashtray, he told me what he thought.

"Never trust a con," he said.

"That's what I'm thinking. But do you believe him?"

"Almost. The guy's pretty busted up, that's for sure. Could be the shock of it, could be guilt. For doing something, or not doing something."

"That's exactly what I'm thinking," I said.

"Well, good. You were paying attention."

"Like I usually don't?"

"I'm not up on my light aircraft, but internal combustion's the same for everything. You got oil under pressure, contained at dozens of different points around an engine. Gaskets and seals, pumps, lines. Plenty of opportunities for something to go wrong on its own, or for someone to engineer a leak. The incidence of pure mechanical failure that drastic is so low you can hardly measure it. But it happens. Planes usually crash because of a combination of events no one has anticipated. People don't want to know this, but it's impossible to anticipate all the possible combinations. The fact is, planes hardly ever go down, which is the good news. It's just so scary when they do."

"So you don't think it was sabotage," I said.

"Didn't say that. I don't know much about airplanes, but I can think of a hundred ways I could cause an airplane engine to fail, where and when I wanted it to."

"Keep 'em to yourself."

"I intend to."

"So, all we know is that the plane crashed," I said. "But we don't know why and likely never will."

"That's it in a nutshell."

The next morning Sullivan woke me up with news that the NTSB was planning to declare the crash an accident.

"You're fucking kidding me," I said eloquently, my first words of the day.

"I'm fucking not. They're still ass-deep in the rubble, but the head guy told me he saw nothing that said it wasn't a simple mechanical breakdown. Happens in a car, you pull over. Happens in a plane, you die. Any reason why I shouldn't let it stand at that?"

"I don't know, you tell me. You're handling the investigation."

"I am. Me and my shadow."

As his shadow crawled all the way out of a deep sleep, she found herself splitting in half. One part of me was relieved for my client Ed

Conklin, who would now be totally in the clear. No prosecutor would bother with a case already settled by the NTSB. As his defense attorney, this made me happy. On the other, without a client to defend, I had no legitimate standing to pursue my own suspicions, only made stronger by Ed Conklin's nocturnal admissions.

"I love it when I'm damned if I do, damned if I don't," I said.

"How would I feel if I knew what you were talking about?" Sullivan asked.

"Equally conflicted."

"So why don't you just tell me. I'll give you immunity from further hassle."

So I did, more or less. I told him I'd been following the photo trail, for no other reason than it felt right. The very randomness suggested something to me—that it really wasn't random. That it was a collection, with specific meaning. I told him about challenging Dr. Johnson's skills at regional botany, likewise Kirk and Emily on the subject of society fauna and flora, and, after negotiating an expansion of his amnesty offer, about Ed Conklin's unscheduled visit to my house.

Though I hated to reinforce his theory of Eugenie the drug runner, I thought Conklin's story might help set the hook.

"I knew it," said Sullivan.

I pulled myself up into a sitting position and tried to scratch the night out of my eyes.

"You don't know anything other than her husband had suspicions," I said. "Everything else is supposition."

"Oh, sure. Give me something, then take it away."

"Sorry. You're right."

"What's it to you anyway, counselor? For that matter, what's it to me? Apparently, we got no crime here, so no perp. We have theories of a drug operation, but even if they're true, that operation's gone up in smoke. I don't know about you, but I have plenty of real live crimes with honest-to-God criminals to deal with."

I wanted to say, Because you didn't see Eugenie's face seconds before she died a terrible death. You didn't see her elbow open her side window and toss out that camera case. You didn't track a piece of evidence back to your brother, who'd basically sent a missile into the heart of your childhood. You're not invested in this. You're not the obsessive-compulsive who not only chews the bone, but also rips the hand off anyone who tries to take it away.

"I understand, Joe," I said. "It makes sense to let this one go. I'm just gonna poke around a little more. And you won't have to worry about busting me for interfering in an investigation, since now there isn't any. I'm sure that's a great comfort to you."

I didn't know if that would irritate him, but it was still too early in the morning to completely care.

"Stay in touch," was all he said. Part offer, part threat. Then he hung up.

Two hours later I was driving east from Bridgehampton to East Hampton Village, and from there toward Springs, a place I hadn't seen since I helped the daughter of a famous novelist force her next-door neighbor to move a stockade fence that he'd run through the middle of her garden.

I was going unarmed and unescorted into hostile territory. This wasn't because I was brave, or foolhardy. It was a rational calculation: I wouldn't be able to ply my trade as a defense attorney if I was afraid to talk to people connected to the case at hand. No matter how intimidating. And I wouldn't be able to preserve my sense of self if I depended on others, mostly formidable men like Harry and Sam, to keep my butt out of trouble.

On the other hand, sometimes I like to have them along anyway.

They're my best friends, and sometimes my butt needs to be kept out of trouble.

Matt Birkson's house was easy to identify. It was a two-story colonial box covered in those oversized asbestos shingles that were all the rage right after World War II. Ugly as hell, but whatever promise of durability was made by the asbestos shingle salesmen had proven to be understated. Their presence disguised the actual age of the house, but I thought it could be a hundred years plus. To get to the place you had to wend your way through several rusted-out auto bodies, heaps of brush and rotting piles of firewood, a bulldozer, lawn chairs, a clothes dryer, other heaps covered by blue plastic tarps, a thirty-gallon drum (which I guessed was used to burn things), a crumbling vine-entangled pergola, and the one thing I really hated seeing in that type of environment. A doghouse.

I got as close as I could to the front door and waited in my car. I didn't know if Birkson was home, since I never call ahead. Calling ahead usually cuts the odds that you're going to see the person by about 50 percent. Much better to just show up and knock on the door. It's harder to tell someone to go away when you're standing there face-to-face.

Since the sound of my car pulling into the driveway hadn't roused any slobbering, rabid people killers, I decided to get out of the car, walk up the dirt path, and ring the doorbell. Which I did, and that's when I heard the bark.

It was a deep bark, the kind you hear partly through the soles of your feet. I backed away and was about to make a quick dash to the car when the door swung open.

"What," said a tall old guy with a thin ball of curly white hair and the kind of beer belly I always think looks better on pregnant women. He wore black jeans and a flannel shirt. His cheeks were round and red as apples, dwarfing a nose far too small for his face. His eyebrows were in keeping with the white coif, and nicely accented a pair of half-lidded, bloodshot eyes. I'd seen that face before, but not in person. It took a second to realize that he was one of the people in Eugenie's photographs, the one taken in the hard-luck bar.

Grappling with that recollection slowed me down, so when I finally held up my card and gave him the good old officer of the court routine, the effect was less than hoped for.

"Get the hell out of here," he said.

Right then a large black nose poked between his knees. Based on the bark, it should have been at his torso. You can't tell a whole lot from a dog's expression, but I usually know the difference between "I want to rip out your throat" and "Let's play!" This one clearly expressed the latter.

I pointed at the dog.

"That's it? Heck of a bark on that one."

Birkson reached down and got his hand under the dog's collar, then stepped aside so it could move further into the doorway. It was all head, perched on a long body supported by stubby legs and covered in long reddish brown fur.

"Got a lot of mutt in him," said Birkson. "Including shepherd, I'm thinking from the bark. Must've been a shepherd that sang bass in the choir."

Without asking I squatted down and used both hands to scratch the dog's face. He liked it well enough, based on how he tried to lick the skin off my face.

"Do you sing bass?" I asked the dog. "I think you do. I think you sing and play a little guitar when your daddy's not looking. What's his name?" I asked, looking up at Birkson.

"Guthrie. Wasn't up to me. That's what the tag said when he showed up at my door, half starved. That's all the tag said, so that's why he's still here."

I stood up.

"Couldn't be because you like dogs," I said.

"Dumb furballs," he said, but didn't really argue the point.

"Mr. Birkson, I'm investigating your daughter's accident," I said.

"Ah, shit. I've had enough of that," he said, and reached for the door.

I put my hand on his, always a risky gesture, but usually effective. He looked at me, both confused and annoyed.

"I know how hard this is for you," I said, "but if you could give me a few minutes, I'd really appreciate it."

"I already told the local bulls everything I could think of. And then a bunch of dickheads from out of town show up and I got to do it all over again. None of it worth shit for their purposes."

He didn't reach for the door again, but he looked like he was ready to.

"I don't care about all that," I said. "I want to know what you didn't tell those other guys. I don't want any facts. I got 'em already." A lie. "I want to know what you think in your gut."

You wouldn't call Matt Birkson a handsome man, but he had a presence, something hard to pin down. He was too ugly for it to be charisma, but it wasn't hard to imagine him running a criminal gang. You could sense the executive skills, if you could look past the long stares and lack of affect.

"Wasn't an accident," he said, finally.

"Why do you say that?"

"Who the hell are you again?"

"Don't you want to know what happened?" I asked him.

He reached for the doorknob, this time with determination, and I expected him to shut the door in my face, but he just used it to steady himself. He let go of Guthrie, who leaped out onto the landing and rubbed up against my leg. I reached down and stroked his side.

"When Eugenie was a kid, she tried to use a sheet to fly off the roof of the house," said Birkson. "Flying is what she wanted to do. That and racing motorcycles, which for her was pretty much the same thing. This is what she knew how to do."

"You two were okay?" I said.

"I hadn't talked to her much in the last few years. But we were okay; she just had a lot going on," he said, moving an inch or two closer to where I stood than I usually preferred.

"What do you think of Ed Conklin?" I asked, stepping forward myself, thus violating some of his own personal DMZ. He stepped back.

"Ed's okay. She coulda done worse."

"So no marital conflict," I said.

"What's that mean?"

"They weren't fighting."

He looked at me like I was an idiot.

"Them two? Jesus Christ, they was like fucking teenagers. No"–he looked up at the sky, trying to get the words right–"they was like a two-sided coin. Different, but equally the same as each other. Like I said, she coulda done a lot worse. There was some respect there between me and Ed. That's what I told those other assholes that come 'round. And I'm not going against it."

"I'm not asking you to," I said, letting it go unacknowledged that he'd just implied I was also an asshole.

"Was she in any trouble that you knew of?" I asked. "Mixed up with people she shouldn't have been?"

His expression, which had been an uneasy blend of hostility and nervous fear, shifted all the way to hostile. The air around us dropped about ten degrees.

"Hear this," he said, sticking his face about an inch from mine. "Eugenie weren't no princess. That's probably my fault. Her and her brother didn't have much of an upbringing, not havin' a mother through most of it. But I'm here to tell you, when it came to flying, the girl was a straight line. No hanky-panky, no bullshit. That's all there is," he said, and after wrenching Guthrie back inside the house, he finally shut the door.

Okay, I said to myself, that went well. I'm not bit, I'm not shot, nor am I raped, murdered, or eviscerated. All in all, a good interview.

10

I look great in my funeral outfit. The black pencil skirt and black jacket with a bit of extra shoulder, the cream-colored camisole and plain black pumps feel like the simplest yet most flattering combination conceivable for a woman with my shape and hair.

However, since I now associate this ensemble with funerals, I can't allow myself to trot it out for cocktail parties or nights in the city. Typical.

On the other hand, when a funeral is in the offing, a little part of me says, Oh goodie, the outfit.

The notice of Eugenie's funeral was a computer printout on an 8½ × 11 piece of paper stuck in my front screen door. The production values were much less surprising than the hand delivery. And after Ed Conklin's escapade, a little creepy. But I was very happy to be invited. I never knew the woman, but it's rare I go to one of these things genuinely wanting to pay my respects. No matter what she might have done along the way, I couldn't quell that feminist surge of feeling over any brave, tough, and flawed female desperado. This one daring to fly above the clouds.

And I was, after all, the last woman to look into her tragic eyes before she was consumed in a giant ball of flame.

The invitation didn't say you could bring a date, but tough luck. No way Harry wasn't going to see the funeral outfit.

"What do you got in black?" I asked him over the phone.

"My Nike cold-weather jogging suit."

"Perfect. Does it come with a tie?" I asked. "We're going to a funeral."

"I have a charcoal gray gabardine. Worked okay for the last dozen or so funerals. No push back from family members."

"Sold. You drive. It's hard to work the pedals with my knees sewn together."

"You'll explain that, I'm sure."

"Just you wait."

The Presbyterian church where the service was held was an appropriately restrained expression of Calvinist impulses. Beautiful, simple, stolid, and brilliantly white. The clapboard exterior, not the funeral-goers. At least a third were either black or Hispanic or somewhere in between. The rest were a lively mix of white people—lots of workingmen and -women, but not exclusively. After we pulled into the parking lot, Harry parked between two German luxury cars. I was careful not to ding any door panels when I got out of the Volvo.

We were sort of late; my fault, as usual. The church was a lot bigger on the inside than it looked on the outside and was nearly filled to the rafters. From the rear pews I could scan the crowd, which is when I recorded the diverse demographics. I was impressed by how many people knew Eugenie, how different they all were, and most of all, how they were summoned. If my experience was universal.

I was ill prepared for the brevity and modesty of the service. Catholics, especially Irish Catholics, like a meaty funeral process. We think, Somebody just died; the least we can do is spend a little time and make a bit of a fuss over them, even if we rarely did so when they were alive. This service felt a lot more matter-of-fact and perfunctory, even though I could see by people's faces and body language it was anything but insincere.

On the way out the door, we shook hands with Eugenie's family. I sort of shocked Ed Conklin by ignoring his hand and giving him a big hug. He didn't quite get his arms around me, but I could feel the rock-hard torso under his suit. Next to him was a young man about Ed's height with an approximation of Ed's build and features but completely different coloring. In fact, virtually no coloring at all. I've met albinos who are all the way white. This guy was close, with platinum hair, see-through skin, and pale blue eyes. He was meaty, but he lacked Ed's ramrod posture. His shoulders were thick but slightly turned down, which forced his head forward, reminding me of a buzzard. His left arm hung at his side, and when he shook hands, he only moved his right at the elbow. Though the handshake itself was surprisingly strong.

"I'm Brian. Stepson," he said.

"I'm terribly sorry," I said.

"Yeah. Major bummer."

I wanted to talk to him more, but his attention had been drawn by Harry, who was explaining his presence to Ed. So I moved on to Matt Birkson, whom I didn't hug, though he had the good manners to shake my hand and thank me for coming.

"Where's Guthrie?" I asked.

"Didn't bring him. Hates funerals. Too depressing."

The only other family member was Matt's sister, Ida, who looked exactly like an Ida should look. She had her brother's nose, meaning small and upturned, and his hair, frizzy gray, but none of his outgoing charm. She didn't even look at me when we shook hands, and showed no curiosity about who I was.

"I'm terribly sorry," I repeated for the fourth time.

"Very well," she said, dropping my hand as soon as she could. I was happy to pass her along to Harry, who actually had an effect, as he usually does.

"Mercy," said Ida.

Luckily, after that we all retired to one of those old regular guy joints—a clubbish but nonexclusive resort with a big open restaurant area full of worn and slightly beat-up furniture, a huge bar, and plenty of bar stools. In addition to the main building, which had a great view of Gardiner's Bay, there were cabins arrayed around the premises that you could rent for a week in the summer or for an afternoon off-season for, you know, whatever.

It was warmer than usual that night, warm enough for people to stand around outside, which they did in large groups in an area within the embrace of the club that included the still-empty swimming pool and a cabana bar.

It was lit well enough for me to make a solid ID of people I knew who weren't relevant, and those who were. I patted Harry's arm to let him know I was taking off, then made a beeline to the most prominent of the latter.

"Benson MacAvoy," I said, reaching out my hand.

He swung around, grabbed my hand, and launched his giant, ragged grin.

"Jackie S," he said.

"Swaitkowski."

"Easy for you to say. What the hell's the latest and greatest?"

MacAvoy was one of those people whose face nearly always expressed some form of smile. Even when his mouth settled down to get in line with the occasion, say a funeral, the corners of his eyes curved upward. His eyes were a brilliant blue, nicely accented by deep crow's-feet. He wore a navy blue blazer, a red pinstriped shirt, and a polka-dot bow tie. Based on how he usually dressed, this must have been as somber an outfit as he could muster.

"I can't answer open-ended questions," I said.

"Okay then, how's the grind?"

"Keeping me alive. I'd ask you the same thing, but I've never understood exactly what you do."

He twisted around and looked at the bar, which was about twenty feet away.

"Don't we only speak to each other over a glass of wine?" he asked.

I let him get me a Merlot; white wine seemed too festive. He got a scotch on the rocks, which he swirled around with vigor, seemingly oblivious to the booze cascading over the rim.

"I'm a political adviser," he said, after a big gulp. "I advise corporations and individuals, and political people."

"Advise them on what?"

"Whatever they want. I'm nonsectarian. Liberal pinkos, conservative cavemen, fringe kooks, I take them all. I'm a skill guy. Hired gun. Pro from Dover. I thought I told you. You probably don't remember."

Since I'd met him at a political fund-raiser, I guessed my recollection of the evening wasn't as crisp as it should have been. I told him that.

"I remember you looked fabulous," he said, then stood back a pace and ran his eyes from sternum to pumps and back again. "Though not this fabulous. Black's *so* your color."

Then he held my blue eyes with his in a way that signaled the sincerity of the compliment. I tried to remember what I didn't like about him, if there was anything. Then I decided the only reason things hadn't gotten started is because they'd already started over again with Harry.

"So you knew Eugenie," I said.

His smile dialed down a notch.

"I was a regular. She flew me up to Westchester and New England, sometimes Upstate New York, probably two or three times a month. Loved her. Tough-ass broad that she was."

"Explains all the expensive cars," I said. "Didn't think that was her natural crowd."

"Watch it there, Jackie. My progressive clients would consider that a highly classist remark."

"You'd advise me to forego common sense?"

"Let's discuss it when you run for governor."

He took a sip of scotch and used his hand to comb back his wavy hair, which didn't need combing. Made me think that's how it came to look like that–constant hand combing. I thought of my own hair, equally dense and in the same general color spectrum. I started to wonder what our children would look like, then suddenly had to shake free the subsequent gush of mental images.

"Do you know Janie Wilson?" I asked.

He nodded.

"Plant Girl? You bet. Love Plant Girl."

"I think her show's called *The Merry Gardener.* And don't let your progressives hear you call her a girl."

He liked that.

"I don't know her socially, exactly, but she's a regular on the fund-raising circuit. Local star power."

"Like the Children's Relief Fund?"

"You mean last summer? Were you there?"

I pulled my cell phone out of my jacket pocket and scrolled through Eugenie's photos until I came to the one taken at the event. I handed MacAvoy the phone.

"Do you know any of these people?" I asked.

He looked at me with cheerful curiosity.

"Am I allowed to ask why?" he asked as he studied the shot.

"You're totally allowed to ask, but I totally can't tell you. Client confidentiality. But you'd be a total ace if you helped anyway."

"I'm already a total ace, but what the hell."

He cocked his head, trying to get the tiny image into focus.

"Akim Sharadze is hanging there with one of his best buds, the handsome and charming Benson MacAvoy," he said. "Another best bud, the distinguished and dedicated Decker Daggit, is probably hitting on the aforementioned Janie Wilson, who doesn't seem to mind."

"She's married with two kids."

"And?"

So now there was something for me to not like about him. Took care of the image of crazed children with enormous manes of wavy orange hair running around the yard. He must have seen the shift on my face.

"Sorry, bad joke. I meant him. I love the guy, but we're talking serious hound dog."

One of the blond kids came back into view, but my internal skeptic had taken note.

"Don't know this guy," he said, pointing at the little screen.

"Archie Milenthal."

"Still don't know him, but the name rings a bell. Kirk and Emily Lavigne, of course. You must've know that," he said, looking up at me.

I nodded. "How about Lizzy Witherspoon?"

"Know her well. A little too well."

"Bad date?"

"You don't date her, she dates you. The whole time you're out you can hear little boxes getting checked off. I'm a person, Lizzy, not a profile," he said, jabbing himself in the chest to punctuate the point. He looked back at the phone. "My dad helped get the judge elected to the Court of Appeals back when you could buy and sell judges on the open market. Now it's all insider trading. Kidding. Don't know the slinky blond, but I like the look."

"Felicity Hunt."

"Do you think she's hunting for happiness, or has already found it?"

I didn't make him ID Peaches the Pomeranian.

"Did any of them know Eugenie?" I asked.

He puzzled on that.

"I don't know. I guess any of them could have flown in her plane. You got the right socioeconomic demographic there. She was cost-effective, but a private plane's a private plane."

"So she didn't take the photo."

That really puzzled him.

"Eugenie? Our Eugenie? At a fund-raiser? Think of a tit on a bull. Not bloody likely. So you really can't tell me what this is all about? You're killing me."

"You'll survive. So who took it, do you think?"

He looked at it again.

"I'm guessing either Pat Eberson or Skitch."

"Skitch?"

"Sue Kichner. Society photog. Pat's a guy, by the way. They both freelance this stuff and dish it out to the highest bidder. Not exactly paparazzi-ism, since who doesn't want to be in a party pic?"

Me, I thought, though I guess if it ever happened I might change my mind. Especially if I was in my funeral outfit.

When he handed back the phone I looked over his shoulder and saw Harry at the other end of the bar, not hard to do when a person's head and shoulders are at the highest elevation in the room. I asked MacAvoy if he wanted to meet my boyfriend.

"Wow, there's a way to take the wind out of the old sails," he said, disappointed, but cheerfully so. "At least you didn't say 'husband.' Hope can keep springing."

I put my arm through his and pulled him through the crowd. When we'd almost reached Harry, I heard MacAvoy mutter, "Don't tell me."

"Harry Goodlander, meet Benson MacAvoy. Political adviser."

I knew Harry would remember the name. He never forgot a detail. It's one of the ways he'd become a Ph.D. of Logistical Science, as he'd put it. But he was also smart enough to not let the recollection show.

"Pleased to meet you," he said to MacAvoy.

MacAvoy demonstrated his political acumen by ignoring Harry's size. As it had when the Lavignes did it, this quickly captured Harry's affections. It moved him to buy MacAvoy another scotch, which had a similar effect. I left the two of them to cement the bond.

I tried to track down Matt Birkson, but I was told he'd left right after the service. As had his sister, Ida. So I had to settle for Brian

Conklin, who was standing alone, his ghostly skin nearly glowing out of a shadowy corner, drinking a Budweiser held by the neck of the bottle.

"Hi, Brian. Jackie Swaitkowski. We met on the receiving line. I want to tell you again how sorry I am about your stepmother."

He took a pull of the beer.

"Thanks. It was pretty uncool what happened to her."

"You work at your dad's shop, right?"

He nodded.

"Oh, yeah. Grew up with that shit. Wouldn't know what else to do."

"He told me the plane was in tip-top shape."

"You got that right. My dad checked everything I did, twice sometimes." He pointed at me with the neck of the beer bottle. "And I checked him. And Eugenie checked the both of us. She was a mechanic, you know, before gettin' into flying. Awesome mechanic. Anybody'll tell you that Conklin Maintenance and Repair is the sickest, most serious grease head outfit on the field. Fanatical overkill on that shit. Goddamn right."

He nodded, in agreement with himself.

"So what the hell happened?" I asked.

He shook his head.

"Don't know. Can't figure it. It's shitty for me, but it's truly fucked up for the old man. Worse'n when my mom died, and that was pretty bad."

"Sorry about that, too. Been there myself, only a lot older than you were."

He seemed to appreciate that. He nodded again, which I began to realize was a gesture more of habit than affirmation. A tic.

"My dad was in the slammer when it happened. It got him out, based on me being, like, twelve years old. Got him away from all those faggots. Not that any of them dared fuck with my old man. Just good to get away from there. Hate those faggots," he added, his voice falling away until I could barely make it out.

He looked at me over the beer as he took a swig, as if he wasn't sure he should have said what he'd said.

"If you're talking about prison rapists, I'm with you," I said.

"Yeah, that," he said. "That's what I mean. Those guys."

An awkward silence formed between us.

"Look after your dad," I said, covering my escape. "He's a good man."

Brian nodded.

"You got that right."

Then I left him there, alone, because I was afraid I'd start in on him, and the guy didn't need that. I veered back toward the bar, where I ordered a big-girl drink–a martini on the rocks without olives in a glass I could walk around with, and went off to find Harry. Which I did, talking to a young woman in a black dress with a scoop neck that in my opinion was way over-scooped. She held her wine in front of her with both hands, which I hoped obscured Harry's view of that deep valley, though it probably didn't. Harry's face lit up when I approached, which would likely spare him future repercussions.

"Hey, Jackie. We've been talking about you," he said.

"Oh?"

The girl nodded in agreement.

"This is Shawna. She wants to be a lawyer."

I shook her hand with lawyerly authority. She lifted her shoulders up to her ears and smiled a nervous smile.

"I'm pre-law. I'm so into it," she said.

"Good," I said. "We need all the female lawyers we can get. Need to kick some male ass."

This probably wasn't the mentorly encouragement she was hoping for, but it actually was what I most wanted to say. She looked down at the cocktail in my hand and registered a thought on her face that I had no trouble deciphering, and no interest in correcting. Instead, I wished her the best of luck and swept Harry away.

"So, learn anything?" he asked.

"Yeah, but not sure what. How about you?"

"Eugenie was a popular girl. With everybody. But nobody thought her untroubled. By what, nobody knew."

"Or would admit?"

"Or would admit."

We mingled for another half hour to no worthy end, then with strong consensus decided to make a break for it. We tracked down Ed Conklin to pay our final respects. He was in Brian's corner in deep, sub-audible conversation with his son. I had to clear my throat to get their attention.

They both looked at Harry before they looked at me. I took it as the usual man thing. Assess the threat before you engage in contact.

"Thanks again for the invite," I said to Ed. "I didn't know Eugenie, but it meant a lot to me to see her off."

He took my outstretched hand in two of his. I would have enjoyed the added intimacy more if I hadn't seen him weave a little, clearly half in the bag. He tried to put together a coherent good-bye, but it was too much of a challenge. So all he could do was say thanks and pump my hand.

Brian just stood there and watched, one eye on Harry.

We left them and got out of there without incident. Harry suggested we stop in some brightly lit, fun-filled joint on the way home, just to recalibrate our moods, which were slightly dinged by that last encounter with the fresh widower and his son. I was all in favor.

Rightly so, because by the time we reached my house, most of the gloom had been washed away. So much so that I jumped out of the car, ran around to the driver's side, and pulled Harry out of his seat, whispering suggestive things in his ear as I did.

Once in the house, I changed into my ratty bathrobe, turned down the lights, lit up the stinky candles, poured wine, put on the Mary McPartlan, and pulled off Harry's size-twenty boots. I was about to coast pleasantly from there when I heard the little electronic incoming e-mail ping from the computer out on the porch that I'd unfortunately left running before going to the funeral. The mood took a dip, but I felt resilient enough to bear a quick peek at what had just come in.

Harry smiled at me and told me to go look, then please turn the damn thing off. I brought up the e-mail screen with a few taps on the keyboard. There was one new message, from someone named "yourfriend." More important, the subject line was "RE: plane crash."

I clicked on the message, hoping for the best. What I got was simple and to the point:

Back off or die, bitch.

11

I was waiting for Randall Dodge when he showed up for work the next day. I was sitting on his front stoop with my laptop and a big cup of coffee to keep me company. When he walked up, his lanky frame blocked the sun, which was a relief.

"Trouble?" he asked, pointing at my laptop.

"Not with the computer. With what's on it."

"Let's take a look-see."

I gave him the ten minutes he needed to fire up various machines, check their screens, and eat half a bagel, the other half eaten at his insistence by me. When he was ready, I put my laptop on a table where we could both see the screen and opened the e-mail from the night before. After he read it, I said, "One question. Where did this come from?"

"I have no idea."

"Ah, come on. You're always saying that and then you do stuff. You mess around on the keyboard, mumble to yourself, then come up with the answer. Just do that. That thing you do."

He looked over at me.

"You're missing the part where I tell you to go away so I can concentrate."

I pushed myself back from the table.

"Fine, no prob. I can do that."

"You don't have to leave your laptop. Just forward me the e-mail."

"Roger that."

Back outside, I noticed it was already a warm day. Not quite summer-like, but warm enough to unzip my jacket and drive with the windows down. Randall's shop is off the parking lot behind the storefronts that line Main Street in Southampton Village. From there it was a fifteen-minute drive up into North Sea, where Sam had his cottage with a wood shop in the basement where he built architectural details for Frank Entwhistle. He'd told me the week before that he had a mantel and a pair of built-ins to fabricate, so I was pretty sure I'd find him down in the shop, which you could access by pounding on the basement hatch and rousing the dog.

It's always a good idea to show up at Sam's with something to drink, which in the morning means coffee from the corner place in the Village. I was thus prepared when the hatch door opened. I thrust a large cup in his irritated face before he could start gritching at me.

"Black and still slightly warm, the way you like it," I said.

"Jesus Christ."

He took the cup but kept the frown. Eddie bounded up the basement steps and almost knocked me over in his eagerness to say hello. I rumpled his head and told him his roommate was a grouch and a pain in the ass undeserving of the kinship of pleasant and well-intentioned people like the two of us.

Then we all walked out on the front lawn to a set of Adirondack chairs perched on the edge of a breakwater, beyond which was the Little Peconic Bay. Sam and I sat, and Eddie disappeared off the breakwater, presumably to scour the pebble beach for tasty saltwater detritus.

The sun had risen high enough by now to light up the bay, turning it into a shimmering gray-blue piece of slate. A sailboat moved along the southern coast of the North Fork, its sails a brilliant white against the green hills.

"So what's the problem," said Sam, after downing most of the coffee.

"I only visit when there's a problem?"

"Mostly."

"I got a death threat."

I brought him up to speed on the Eugenie thing, laying out as much detail as I could remember–since I knew he'd want that–ending with the e-mail from *yourfriend*, now under the analytical gaze of Randall Dodge.

"Even the NSA can have trouble tracking down an e-mail address if the sender knows what they're doing," he said.

"You always say not to get defeatist."

"True. Let Randall tell us if we should be."

"So what do you think?"

"It's great news," he said.

"That somebody wants me dead?"

"That it's not all your imagination."

"Dandy."

Eddie startled me by coming up to the side of my chair and dropping a sandy flip-flop in my lap. He stood there for a moment, then trotted away again.

"That yours?" Sam asked.

I picked it up with two fingers, then dropped it again.

"Don't think so."

"You'll offend him if you don't take it home."

"See if you can teach him the word 'Gucci.' "

"You can stay here if you want," he said.

"I could also stay with Harry, but I'm not ready for that either."

"Okay."

"Any theories?" I asked.

He rested his head on the back of the Adirondack and closed his eyes. The sunlight coming in over our shoulders did nice things with his curly gray hair, but not much for the lines in his face or his busted nose.

"In the absence of other evidence, you have to assume the most obvious interpretation," he said.

"I know that. Thanks to Ross, I can even say it in Latin."

"You have a pilot whose husband and father are both ex-cons. She was probably running drugs and got into trouble with somebody—a supplier, a customer, a competitor. This somebody sabotaged her plane, killing her. You have no proof of this and neither does the NTSB, since they're about to call it an accident. But that's not the whole story."

"The camera case," I said.

"Thrown to you."

"With an empty camera. And a few photos on a memory card."

"The photos have no significance," said Sam. "It's pure luck that you know of their existence."

"Is it? She threw me the case. Which is pretty heavy and reasonably indestructible. The memory card was probably in the camera. It was ejected by the force of the hard landing. When I picked up the case, all this stuff fell out, and the card landed in my cuff."

"The photos are just random shots," said Sam.

I swatted his arm.

"Exactly. Even a heartless brute like you has to have saved at least a few photographs from your past, if only for historical purposes. How would they look to someone who doesn't know you?"

"Random."

"Exactly. The fact that they appear random and were the only shots on the camera tells me they were intentionally saved, and that's because they were valuable to her. I'll bet you a million dollars there are prints of the same photos somewhere, maybe in Ed Conklin's house."

He swatted me on the arm.

"Still hypothetical, but credible."

"What've I been doing since I got ahold of those photographs?" I asked.

"Stirring up trouble?"

"You bet, but with whom? Unless Randall traces that e-mail back to the Southampton Town Police, most of the people who know I'm interested in Eugenie's death are in those photos."

"Hm."

"Hm?"

"You're right," he said. "The e-mail sender doesn't have to be one of them, but it's more likely that they are. Or someone connected to that group."

"*Ipso facto,* the photos are significant."

"*Ad utrumque paratus.*"

"What the hell does that mean?"

"Loosely? Brace yourself. It could go either way."

I called Randall on the way back to my office. He said he'd nailed the IP address–the location from which the e-mail was sent–in the time it took me to get to my car. It was an Internet café in Queens where everyone paid cash and the screens faced the wall so you could watch porn or play online poker in complete privacy. He said the next thing was to penetrate the e-mail account at the access provider, which would take a bit more effort.

"Unless the FBI owes you a few favors," he said.

"Do what you can."

It was still relatively early when I got to my office, so I was able to put in serious time writing briefs and e-mails in support of my once lucrative, now waning real estate practice. How had that happened? For about five hours it was all about well-paying clients, but then I made the mistake of writing to Mr. Charming at the NTSB. I asked him if it was true they were planning to declare the crash an accident. I could have shared my grave suspicions, but since the most likely scenario involved drug running, it would surely blunt his interest. Also, there was so little of the plane left after the crash and fire I couldn't imagine what they'd investigate.

After I clicked the Send button, the magnetic pull of the Eugenie case forced my cursor into the Google search box, and before I knew it I was down the rabbit hole.

My first search was for Skitch the photographer. That took a few seconds. Because I'd confused Skitch with her subject matter, I imagined some blond, whippet-thin, high-cheekboned society nymph. The reality was just the opposite—overweight, with heavily permed black hair and what looked like a big mole next to her crooked nose. Though she had a nice smile. Personality plays an important role with party shooters. If you're not cute or famous, you'd better be fun.

I clicked on her gallery button and was rewarded by hundreds of options—parties, events, and fund-raisers going back at least ten years. She had a generous policy on downloading her work: you could take anything you wanted as long as you gave her credit and didn't try to resell the images. She posted only unpurchased photos and only after the event was well over, protecting paying media. It was on the honor system, but I could see what she was doing. Even if a quarter of the downloaders actually gave her photo credit, that was a lot of publicity.

I wanted to invite her to dinner so I could gush over her business acumen, but I was already deep in search mode, tracking down the Children's Relief Fund event of last year. Didn't take too long. In another few seconds, there was the shot saved on Eugenie's memory card. I rolled my cursor over it, and the familiar little icons asked me if I wanted to e-mail, save to disk, copy, or print. I saved it to my hard drive just for the hell of it, since I could.

Then I jumped into e-mail and wrote Dr. Johnston Johnson at Southampton College, since I hadn't heard from him about that photo of the cabin. I used various extravagant euphemisms that added up to an apology for giving him a task apparently beyond his intellectual powers. Inspired by my chat with Sam, I tossed in some Latin, what little I knew, just to seal the deal.

I pulled up the other shots in the Eugenie collection and went through them all over again, for the millionth time. That was the problem, I thought. I'm looking at everything the same way every time, so I'm seeing the same things. Be different.

Nevertheless, by then I was getting bleary-eyed and it was almost closing time at Jackie Swaitkowski Enterprises. So I shut down the computer and packed up to go home. Out in the hall I saw one of the surveyors slipping out the door. A surge of impetuosity overcame me, as it often does.

"Looks like a beautiful evening," I said.

"Not to me," he said, without looking at me, then stuck his hands in his pockets and rushed down the stairs to the parking lot below.

Just go home, Jackie, I said to myself, and let it go.

Home wasn't much, I admit. But it did have a shower, which I used, and my ancient, and therefore extremely comfy, terry-cloth robe, marijuana that I bought at usurious prices because it came in tidy pre-rolled joints (you pay more, but think of the convenience), wine, leftovers, broadband, and a fireplace. It took about an hour to assemble all these vital ingredients, but it was worth it.

I sunk into the ratty sofa in front of the smoky snapping fire, surrounded by sinful indulgences, in particular my laptop, perched on my lap, where it was designed to live.

I started with the lakefront cabin shot, because it was first in the series. My prodding of Dr. Johnson aside, I didn't think he'd be able to narrow the location any closer than, say, southern New Hampshire, which covered a lot of territory. It was a high-resolution image, so I used the little magnifying glass feature on the computer to zoom in on the cabin, which didn't tell me much. It was a generic cabin, as if on a movie set, taken from about fifty feet away.

I moved on to the bar scene, which I thought more promising. This was also in high resolution, which I made good use of, cropping out and copying square-ups of each person's face, for future identification. Two were simple—Matt Birkson and his sister, Ida. The others might have been at the funeral; I kicked myself for not searching them out. They were much younger, but no less hardened and roughly composed. One guy had a goatee, tattoos on his forearms, and the beginnings of a Matt Birkson–gauge gut. The woman with her arm around his waist was heavy, with deep bags under her eyes and too much hair clumped above her forehead. The other two were in full denim regalia—shirts, pants, and jackets, all in varying shades of blue so you could barely tell where one article of clothing stopped and the other started.

I skipped over the Cessna and went to Delbert's Deli. This was the first time I'd lingered over the image at its full size on my own computer. I popped in the disk Randall had given me with a complete set of the *Southampton Chronicle*'s photo coverage of the motorcycle rally. I picked a shot that most closely resembled Eugenie's later image in angle and perspective, and put them side by side.

Then I lit a joint and drank a little wine, just to sharpen my visual acuity. I looked at the two photos until I started getting bored and let my mind wander off into other corridors, where I could access things like gentle fantasies of me and Benson MacAvoy trapped in an elevator in midwinter and needing to cuddle to stay warm, which shifted to worry about who was going to plow my driveway next year, since I'd fired the dope who took out the only line of healthy shrubs on the property, thoughts that were suddenly intruded upon by the memory of the last time I balanced my checkbook, which a rough calculation put at over six weeks ago.

At this point, I realized my eyes were closing as relentlessly as my anxieties were opening up. I drank a little more wine, sucked down a little more pot, then shook my head, resolved to take one more solid look at the two pictures.

And that's when I saw it.

I shook my head again, then ran into the kitchen and splashed cold water on my face, dabbed it dry with paper towels, and ran back to the computer. It was still there.

It was a trick of the eye. In Eugenie's photo the storefront window had what I'd thought was an odd wrinkle in the glass, but was actually the reflection of a man looking at the store and a second with a camera up to his face, taking the picture. It depended on how you interpreted the shapes, like seeing a person smoking a pipe in a cloud formation, or a woman with a pile of clothes on her head in a Rorschach test. Only the more I looked at the photo, the less I saw alternate visions. It was definitely two people, one clearly snapping the shot.

I reached for the phone that sat on a table at the end of the couch, then caught myself. What the hell was I doing? Who was I going to call and what was I going to tell them?

Randall once told me you can't extract greater clarity from a low-resolution image than what was already there in the first place, despite what you saw on TV shows. All you could do was ask the computer to give you options as to what those big, fat, pixilated blobs might be saying, and for that you needed very expensive software, which he owned. That meant another trip to Randall's, so for now I'd have to move on.

I don't remember what I did after that, because I'd finally passed out all the way, which was inevitable. As always, I woke up disoriented in the middle of the night, and had to drag myself out of the gooey slop of interrupted sleep before heading for the bedroom.

I flicked out the light in the living room, leaving the house in darkness. I stumbled over to where another switch lit up the hall that led to the staircase. I patted around the wall, found the switch, and went from there. This is how I normally did things in this state. One pool of light at a time.

I made it all the way to the bathroom, where I cleaned my teeth, halfheartedly brushed out my ridiculous ball of hair, put cream on my hands, searched my ruddy face for incipient signs of skin cancer, and staggered off to bed. This was my favorite approach to getting a good night's sleep–be essentially asleep before you hit the mattress.

Some nights, like that one, I'm so zonked I forget to take off my bathrobe and just flop down on top of the covers. I'd achieved the flopped-down part and was about to slide into oblivion when I heard the noise.

Everyone knows what it's like when you hear a sound at night you're not used to hearing. When you live alone in the middle of the woods, you know it with every cell of your body. And at that moment, every cell in mine woke up.

I held my breath and listened as well as I could over the white noise exploding in my head. Then I heard it again.

Someone was moving through my house.

I let out a muffled cry and leaped out of bed. I sleep in one bedroom and keep my clothes in another, for reasons too embarrassing to explain. That meant I had to cross the hall, which I did at a dead run. I gently shut the door of the clothes bedroom and fumbled for a lock that wasn't there. I scooped a pair of jeans off the floor and wriggled into them, then searched the piles for a top, coming up with a loose cotton sweater, which I pulled over my head before I had my bathrobe completely off. The two articles of clothing fought it out till the sweater won.

Shoes were easy. My cowboy boots were right within reach. Now all I needed was a gun, which I didn't have, never had, and, until that moment, wasn't sure I needed.

I heard footsteps in the hallway, then the sound of doors being opened and shut. I looked around in the dark, trying to remember what in the room would adapt to a decent weapon.

The crystal lamp. It had been my grandmother's and had a slim top, a curvaceous mid section, and a square base with four sharp corners. I ripped off the shade, unscrewed the lightbulb, and tore the cord out of the middle of the base. An easily handled, lightweight club, and far better than nothing.

I opened the window and looked down. At two stories plus it was a serious drop, more than I'd likely survive with all limbs intact. But still a better risk than getting cornered in the house. Tucking the slender lamp into the waistband of my jeans, I stuck one leg, then the other, through the window until I was sitting on the sill. Then I twisted around so I was resting on my belly, my legs dangling below. With great effort, I switched the crystal lamp from the front to the rear waistband of my jeans. My next move was to slide through the window, grip for a moment with my fingers, then drop to the ground. But before I had a chance to do this, the door opened and a light went on in the room.

It was Fred Flintstone. Or more accurately, a guy in a Fred Flintstone mask, a hooded sweatshirt, Levi's, black leather gloves, and motorcycle boots. I screamed and lost my grip on the frame, causing me to slip uncontrollably through the window. I saw Fred leap toward me, but only for a second, because the next moment I was falling through the air.

The landing was such a piece of cake, I felt like a complete fool. When I hit, I tumbled backward–aided by the angled heels of my cowboy boots–and rolled into a cluster of spindly azaleas. The lamp dug into my back, but no nerves were severed and no crystal shattered.

I stood up, gripped the lamp, and rubbed the inflamed part of my back, furiously considering my next move. I was at the back of the house. My car was around the front, but no good to me without the keys. Behind me were acres of woodlands, but difficult to run through without the sound of dry leaves giving me away.

I only had an instant to decide, knowing that Fred would be there in the next few seconds. Instead of bounding into the woods, I ran to the house and squeezed myself inside the casement surrounding a door that opened on a stairwell leading down into the basement. Then I waited.

Everything about the plan was good until the moment Fred walked in front of me and I was supposed to club him over the head. I stepped out of the doorway and swung the lamp, but instead of hitting his skull, I hit the top of his back with the edge of my hand and the lamp merely clipped the side of his hoodie.

Before I could entirely take stock of the situation, he'd spun around with one hand darting out to grab me by the throat, the other gripping my wrist and shaking loose the lamp. In an instant, I was helpless.

I heard him chuckle. At times like this, I would always prefer an angry word over a chuckle, because I know what comes next. And it did. No sooner was I pinned inside the doorway than I felt his hand running up the inside of my sweater toward my unfettered boobs. So I did what I'd done before in these situations. I kneed him in the balls.

I've learned that most guys find this to be a serious distraction. He doubled over and turned away, though without losing his grip on my sweater. I was pulled out of the doorway and knocked to the ground, which freed his grip. As I tried to scramble up again, my hand grazed the shapely form of the crystal lamp. Fred was hunched over, leaning against the house. He was breathing heavily and, I thought, with his head bent toward the ground. But I'd been confused by the Flintstone mask, so when I took another swing with the lamp he caught my hand again, pulled me into him, and stuck a hard fist right in my stomach.

He pulled me by the hair almost all the way to the front of the house before I was able to get a breath of air in my lungs. I was barely conscious from lack of oxygen and the shock of the blow, but I knew enough to realize this was heading the wrong way. I grabbed his wrist and tried to wriggle out of his grasp, but he held on and yanked me through the front door. I stumbled and dropped to my knees on the living room floor. Then the guy dove on top of me, pushing my face into the rug and pinning my wrists to the floor, using his far greater weight to hold down the rest of me.

I could hear the hollow sound of his breathing behind the plastic mask.

"What are you doing?" I yelled at him.

He just breathed. I tried to squirm back up to my knees, but it was impossible. I felt him move his hips, rubbing his crotch against my backside. I struggled some more, for naught. I'm not a small woman, but he was very strong. And for all I knew he was jacked up on something, like a lot of the evil bastards I'd defended liked to do, just to get in the mood. I had to think of something else.

"I'm gonna spit up," I said, more calmly, my voice muffled by the way my mouth was pressed against the rug. "Let me at least get up on my elbows."

He stopped moving. I waited, limp, hoping that would signal my willingness to cooperate.

"Please," I said, the word punctuated by a gagging sound. "I'll choke to death."

"Who cares," he whispered behind the mask.

I turned my head slightly up off the floor.

"It'll get on your arm."

Who knows why in the midst of all that mayhem such a trivial hazard would bother him, but I didn't have much else to go with.

I felt him shift slightly, then pull in my wrists, which gave me just enough leeway to turn in my elbows and lift myself up. The shift brought more pressure down on my lower half, but my head was now free. I could tell by the echoey breathing that Fred's face was now directly behind me and about four inches away.

As noted, I didn't have a lot to go with, but I took what I had.

I dipped my forehead toward the floor, then snapped back my head with as much force as the angle would allow. Even through the cushion of my thick hair I could feel the plastic mask collapse into the face behind. Probably more startled than injured, the guy let out a little grunt and loosened the grip on my wrists. I banged him again with the back of my head, hard, this time getting some shoulder into the effort. I could feel him rear back, trying to get his face out of the way, which only further loosened his grip on my wrists. I twisted to the right, freeing my hand, which I used to push up onto my shoulder. Then I twisted at the hips, this time making it all the way over.

Even in the dark, Fred didn't look so good. Crumpled and partly pushed off to the side, the mask was now blocking the guy's sight, and though it was very dark in the living room, a little vision's better than none. As the guy tried to adjust the mask, I was able to get one cowboy boot between his legs and another in his midriff. Women can rarely match men in upper body strength, but our legs are another story. Especially the legs of a thoroughly incensed and terrified woman. I let out a kind of kung-fu yell and kicked upward as hard as I could.

Fred shot upright and tried to catch his balance as he stumbled backward, hopping on his heels and windmilling his arms. It didn't work, and he toppled over, crashing through a lamp and over a side table. I didn't see what came next because I was already up and on my way, pausing for a split second to grab my cell phone, then racing up the stairs and down the hall to a place I called the junk room, which was laughable, since the same label could be applied to any room in the house. I was keenly interested, however, in one particular piece of junk–an antique chest of drawers filled with crap, sitting just to the right of the door. Once in the room, I wedged myself into the space between the chest and the wall and, using my rapidly weakening legs, shoved the chest in front of the door. Better than any lock.

I slid down against the drawer fronts and speed dialed Southampton Town Police HQ, listening keenly for sounds of pursuit. They were faint, but I could hear the soft tread of footsteps out in the hall. Janet Orlovsky answered the phone. I whispered, "Hi," identified myself, then told her, "There's a guy right outside my door who's trying to rape me. Need the boys here pretty quick."

She said to stay on the line, then put me on hold.

I heard Fred wiggle the doorknob.

Janet came back on the line.

"Danny's less than five minutes away. Hang tight."

"Could you repeat that? But say he'll be here in three. Make it loud," I whispered, then pushed the button that turned the cell into a speakerphone. I stood up and held the phone up to the door.

"Officers Sullivan and Izard will be on the scene in three minutes," Janet squawked out of the phone, her voice a near shout. "Expect lethal force. Please seek a secure area."

She kept going on like that, but I didn't hear the next lines because I'd switched off the speaker and held the phone away from me so I could listen for Fred. The junk room's window faced the front of the house, so moments later I could hear him running down the gravel driveway. After that I heard an engine start up and the subsequent sound of tires over gravel, accelerating quickly. I put the phone back up to my ear.

"Officer Izard has his weapon drawn and is approaching the house," Janet was shouting.

"Okay, Janet. He's gone."

"Are you all right?" she asked, worry etched in her voice.

"I think so. Shook up a little," I said, but I had trouble saying more because of the wad in my throat that usually presaged a fountain of tears. I choked it back down. "Is Danny really on the way? He might catch the guy in the driveway."

"I'll tell him," said Janet, and put me on hold.

I slid back down the front of the chest of drawers. There should be a word that means relief on a galactic scale. It's not joy, it's not euphoria, it's not even gratitude. I felt all those things, but stirred in was an emotion no less deeply felt, though of an entirely opposite nature.

Pure and absolute rage.

12

Fred Flintstone had cleared the driveway by the time Danny Izard got there. I could see the roof strobes light up the trees and hear the roar of the Crown Vic's pursuit engine and the rear wheels whiplashing over loose gravel. Janet told me his first job was to clear the area around the house. He gave her a blow-by-blow of his progress, which she relayed to me.

Before he entered the house, she asked me if I was armed, and I said no. She said his weapon was drawn and to stay put until the house was cleared and we were in audible contact.

"Roger that. Happy to sit right here," I said.

I talked her through the layout of the house, which she passed along to Danny. When he reached the top of the stairs, I told her which door I was behind, which was his final stop. She said he'd tap three times when he got there.

"Jackie?" he said through the door. "You okay?"

"What's my maiden name?" I asked.

"Come on, Jackie. You know it's me."

"What is it?"

"O'Dwyer. Everybody knows that."

"Where did Ross go to school?"

"Same place we did," said Danny. "Southampton High."

"College."

"Jesus Christ. Cornell. Nobody knows that. I wouldn't know that if Sullivan hadn't told me."

"That's the point, Danny," I said, standing up. "Secret passwords are supposed to be secrets."

I was wobbly, with barely the strength to pull the chest of drawers away from the door so I could get out. Danny gently moved me behind him, stepped off to the side, and shot his flashlight into the room. Then he shot it in my face, though only for a second. I flicked on the hall light.

I'd never been so pleased to see Danny Izard's pale and earnest face, assured in his dark blue uniform festooned with armaments and communications gear. He didn't push me away when I wrapped my arms around him and stuck my face in his shirt, though it was clearly outside proper protocol.

"Oh, man, that was bad," I said.

I felt a tentative pat on my back.

"We'll get you to the hospital."

"He knocked me around a little, but he didn't do what he came to do," I said.

"We'll get you to the hospital," he repeated as he gently pulled away my arms and guided me down the hall.

"It's important you know this, Danny, because everyone's going to ask you if I'm telling the truth. I don't need that weirdness factor right now."

"I get it. I'll tell them," he said, in a way that I believed. Danny was too good and simple a man to lie and get away with it.

I had him wait for me in the hall while I changed clothes. I put what I'd been wearing in a plastic bag and brought it along with me. I also brought my laptop, my cosmetics, the external hard drive and the other stuff I'd hidden in the bookcase, the little wooden Tibetan box where I kept the joints I hadn't left half-smoked in an ashtray, my terry-cloth robe, and as many clothes as I could cram into the back of the Volvo.

"He was wearing gloves, so don't bother checking for prints," I said to the cops arriving on the scene. "The place is enough of a mess without all that dust everywhere."

Danny wanted to drive me in his cruiser, but I made him follow my Volvo. Before we reached the end of the drive, my cell phone rang. It was Joe Sullivan.

"Izard said you were okay."

"Okay enough."

"He said you fought the guy off."

"I got lucky. I'm depending on you guys to put a lid on the chatter. What could've happened didn't happen."

"Already done," he said.

"I took a sock to the gut and got a big bump on the back of my head. Otherwise, I'm okay," I said.

"You're one tough mick," he said.

"Takes one to know one. You gotta reopen the case."

"I knew you'd say that."

"This wasn't random. I've already had a death threat."

"You didn't tell me that," he said.

"I was getting around to it. It came through my e-mail. I've got Randall Dodge tracking it down. They're trying to scare me off."

Sullivan was quiet on the line. I could see him sitting somewhere in his house in his underwear, scratching his blond crew cut as he grappled with the manifold implications.

"Stay at the hospital till I get there. I'll take your statement and then we'll figure it out."

Harry got to the hospital first. I'd called him after talking to Sullivan. I told him I was okay, but I waited until Sullivan and the ER chief, Malcolm Fairchild, were there before going through the whole rigmarole. When I was finished, Malcolm shooed the boys out of the room so he could examine me.

"You sure about that rape kit, counselor?" he asked, after checking my pulse, squeezing my limbs, and shooting a little flashlight into my eyes.

"I'm not one of those who thinks there's any shame in being a rape victim. If needed, I'd be screaming for the kit."

He studied my face, then nodded. He'd seen plenty of the real deal in his time, and knew what to look for. He let Sullivan and Harry back in the room.

"Forensics will go through your place, but I'm not optimistic, based on your statement," said Sullivan. "We have your DNA on file. If we find some of this jamoke's, he might be in the system."

"Fine," I said. "What about the Birkson case?"

Sullivan frowned at me, but not too hard. There was a hint of a grin somewhere inside the frown.

"You are such a pain in the ass," he said. "Which I say with all due respect," he added, looking up at Harry.

"Duly noted," said Harry.

"I'll talk to Ross. Forward me the death threat and I'll see if our lads in forensics can get there ahead of your geek. We got that funny thing called police powers. Sometimes comes in handy."

Harry lived in a gas station, where I spent what was left of the night. A former gas station, first converted into an artist's studio, and later into the world headquarters of Goodlander GeoTransit. The artist had done a beautiful restoration job, so the living space was lovely. The bedroom had a wall of windows looking out on a brick patio, which you could drench in light with an array of brilliant flood lamps controlled by a switch next to the headboard.

As we undressed in the dark, Harry lit up the patio. We crawled into bed, where I slept well into the morning, enclosed within his gigantic, tireless embrace.

The next day Sam installed a peephole, an alarm, and a massive dead bolt on the door of my office. He also put hidden security cameras at the front entrance and in the hall leading up to my door. While he worked I cleared the sofa of legal papers and stashed half-smoked joints so the guys from the furniture store could take it away and replace it with a pull-out sofa bed. Since the office had once been an apartment, all the other living amenities were in place, including a kitchenette and a shower stall in the bathroom.

We all agreed I wasn't going back to my house anytime soon, but that didn't call for total capitulation. I'd already decided on this solution before Harry, and then Sam, had a chance to mount aggressive campaigns to have me move in with one of them or the other. Part of the deal included the loan of Harry's 40-caliber Glock automatic, a gun I hadn't known he had.

"I've lived in some pretty funky locations along the way," he said. "Don't feel the need out here, but just in case, I still have the Winchester twelve-gauge."

To his credit, I didn't have to endure that condescending don't-you-worry-your-pretty-little-head lecture I usually get from guys when a real gun enters the room, even though he didn't know my father had trained me well enough to get a pistol license on my twenty-first birthday, renewed every five years after that. At the time, I had a few self-righteous notions about the evils of gun ownership, some of which I still believe, so I never got a pistol to go with the license. Recently, after being blown up, run off the road, assaulted by a kickboxer, and threatened by any number of criminal deviants, some my own clients, I'd learned that gun evil was mostly the province of evil people. So I'd started to go with Joe Sullivan to the range, where I could shoot his service Glock and privately held .357 Colt Python, just to feel that reassuring kick.

To establish my cred with Harry, all I had to do was point the gun at the floor, tilt it sideways, flick the magazine release, and pull the mag out of the grip. Then, still holding the magazine, pull back the slide to eject the cartridge, which I caught with my left hand. I cleared the muzzle visually, slapped in the magazine, and used the slide to put the gun back into battery with a live round ready to go.

The only thing left was to twirl it around by the trigger guard, slam it into a holster, and spit on the ground.

"Alrighty then," he said. "Let's be sure we give Annie Oakley sufficient ammunition."

Sam was less accommodating when he came to my office to rig up his security array.

"I'm willing to hang with you till they splatter the son of a bitch," he said. "I've got nothing else to do."

"I'm not going to do this," I said.

"What?"

"This. You offering your help and me trying to politely demur. I appreciate the security measures. Leave it at that. And I know you've got plenty to do. Just keep gas in the Grand Prix and your cell phone in your pocket."

He acted like he didn't hear me.

"What's going on?" he asked.

"I told you. I'm okay."

"That's the problem."

"What do you mean?"

"You're not okay," he said. "You're just pretending to be."

Anger and gratitude competed for control over my mood. I compromised by speaking softly when I told him to stop fucking psychoanalyzing me. That I could do that all on my own when I could spare the time and the cost of a hotel room in a warm climate. Right then, what I needed most was to be left alone with the space I needed to get back to work. Which I did when I finally got him out of my office.

Then I surprised myself with how well I could concentrate, and how productive the day turned out to be. As did the evening, until I wore myself out enough to fall asleep on the pull-out bed, the Glock under my pillow, oft caressed throughout the night.

Ross Semple set the alarm off the next morning, which did an excellent job of waking me up. He claimed he merely tapped on the door, but that was enough to trigger the alarm. Fortunately, I didn't shoot him. Or Joe Sullivan, whom I saw standing next to Ross when I looked at the video monitor.

I shut off the alarm, told them to wait a minute, stowed the ordnance, folded up the bed, and put on my robe. Then I threw back the dead bolt and opened the door.

"Welcome to Fort O'Dwyer."

"Jesus, Jackie," said Ross. "That scared the crap out of me."

"Coffee, anyone?" I asked. "It'll take a sec. Have a seat while I pull myself together."

When I got back from the bathroom, dressed and, as promised, more or less pulled together, I found the two of them sitting uncomfortably on the hard sofa version of the pull-out bed. That's because there was nowhere else to sit, since every other chair was groaning under a massive stack of paper. I handed out coffee, rolled over my desk chair, and settled in.

"Okay, boys," I asked, "what's the occasion?"

"I didn't think it seemly to make you drive all the way to Hampton Bays to receive an apology," said Ross. "For the record, Detective Sullivan took the opposite view."

"Thanks, boss," said Sullivan.

"An apology for what?" I asked, immediately suspicious.

"The Birkson case," said Ross. "I read your statement. I think you're right. There's more going on here than meets the eye. You tried to tell me and I didn't listen. For that, I apologize."

Some situations are so transcendently weird, that even I, born and raised in the Hamptons, jaded and cynical, can be caught off-guard. This was one of those.

I tried to read the situation off Joe Sullivan's face, but he gave me nothing.

"What did I do now?" I asked.

"What do you mean what did you do? Nothing," said Ross. "It's all my fault. Enough of that. Let's talk about the Birkson case."

So I pretended I could take him at his word and told him everything I knew. As I spun out the story, I tried to stay alert for road hazards—minor details for me, but prosecutable to the cops. But besides that, I more or less gave up the goods.

"So you think she was running drugs," said Ross when I was done.

I shrugged.

"Probably. Sam's always telling me the obvious is almost always the explanation, but I'm not so sure on this one. It doesn't feel right."

"What if we told you we've had a dramatic drop-off in drugs coming into the East End for years," said Sullivan, still deadpan. "And what's here is easily traceable. If she was flying in product, it wasn't for local consumption."

Okay, I said to myself, there's another first. The cops giving me material information that I hadn't even asked for, much less launched a civil suit or invoked the Freedom of Information Act to get.

"What's up?" I asked. "Why are you telling me this?"

Sullivan reached into the inside pocket of his safari jacket and pulled out a thick, spiral-bound book. He tossed it into my lap.

"Eugenie's flight log for the past three years, not including the last few months, since she had that on the plane," he said. "Shows flight times, routes, weather conditions, destinations, passengers, and a bunch of other shit that makes no sense to anybody but a pilot. We don't know what to believe, since there's no third-party corroboration. Pilots can write anything they want; the whole thing could be a complete work of fiction. We're hoping you could take a look, and if something pops into your head, you could break precedent and actually help us do our jobs."

I was faltering but still suspicious. If past experience was any guide, I had good reason.

"So why the interest? The NTSB thinks it was an accident, or can't prove it wasn't. If that's true, like Joe keeps telling me, there's no crime here."

Ross put a hand on each knee and leaned back on the sofa. He looked up at the ceiling and took a deep breath.

"Back in the day, when I was living in Brooklyn, somebody broke into my house," he said. "My wife and I were at work and the kids were in school. The guy wasn't looking to rob us; he just wanted to look around to see what he could get on me that might help in his upcoming prosecution. Most criminals are pretty stupid, as you know. But occasionally you get the so-called criminal genius, which usually means some sociopathic shithead with above-average intelligence. This was one of those guys. For them, it isn't just the life that gets them off, it's the challenge. The chance to outsmart, outmaneuver, authority. It's a type of game.

"So the game here was to break into our house, go through our most intimate things, steal or record what he wanted, and then slip away without leaving a trace. The fantasy was that he'd find something that would be so revealing and scandalous, I'd immediately drop the case. Which was a big laugh since I doubt you'd ever find two people who are bigger squares than me and Arlene."

That he said "squares" went a long way toward proving the assertion.

"My point here, and I do have a point," Ross said, "was that the moment I walked into our apartment, I knew someone had been there. I couldn't tell you exactly why at first. My conscious brain would have been easily fooled. But my unconscious, the part that keeps track of anomalies in my environment, immediately set off alarms."

"Okay," I said. "Still waiting for the point."

"This whole thing is making me feel the same way," said Ross. "I just don't know why."

"Thanks for the logbook, Ross, but I can't help you if I don't have all the facts, which I clearly don't."

They looked at each other, exchanging some sort of sub-rosa communication. I could almost hear them calculating how much to reveal and how much to hold back. It was tiring, but this is what defense attorneys have to deal with every day. I behaved like the trained professional I was and waited them out.

Ross took a deep breath, exhaled theatrically, then said, "We got a call from Homeland Security."

The two of them sat there next to each other and waited for the vast import to set in. I think I disappointed them.

"Yeah? So what."

Sullivan frowned.

"They want to talk to us," he said. "Ross and me. And you."

"About what?" I asked.

"We don't know," said Ross.

"You didn't ask?"

"We did. They told us they'd ask the questions, we'd answer them, then they'd leave and we'd forget we had the conversation."

"Screw that," I said.

"We're talking Homeland Security," said Sullivan. "They're, like, not to be denied."

"Oh yeah?" I said, my hackles flaring. "Try me. I aced constitutional law."

Ross looked at me the way my father used to when I sat at the dinner table with my fists clenched and my face set in suicidal defiance over some disgusting pile of overcooked vegetables. It's me or the beans, you bastard. If you want me to eat that crap, you'll have to shove it down my throat.

"I told you she can be like this," said Sullivan.

Ross tried to get more comfortable on the new sofa, with little luck. On the other hand, I'd never seen Ross Semple look completely comfortable.

"We're on the same side here, Jackie," he said. "All we had to do was bring you in like they asked us to. We didn't have to tell you anything more than to show up."

I took a breath and closed my eyes.

"Sorry. I'm just a little tense."

"You have a right to be," said Ross. "If it helps, we're reopening the Birkson investigation as it relates to the death threat and assault on you. Joe's got the file. If there's anything else you can share with us, now's the time."

I had shared almost everything, except the connection to my brother. That one kept sticking in my throat. Until I figured out why, it would just have to stay lodged there.

"I'll do anything I can, shy of endangering clients," I said.

"In that case, know anyone at the FBI?" said Ross.

That stopped me.

"Sort of," I said, tentatively. "I used to date an agent named Webster Ig. Nice guy, but too normal for my tastes. The breakup was amicable, but I've never tested how amicable. Why?"

"I remember that dork," said Sullivan. "Maybe he knows why the feds want to pay us a call."

That was a good one.

"Are you kidding? Those guys won't tell you the sky's blue if they don't have to."

Ross stood up, rubbing his butt and looking down at the sofa.

"Good way to keep clients from lingering in your office."

"He'll tell you something," said Sullivan, also standing. "He had it for you bad."

I didn't dignify that, but I did shake their hands before they left. Ross told me I'd need to come in the following morning and to act surprised. He'd confirm the time.

"It gives you a day to get your head on straight," said Sullivan. "And forget the constitutional law. Things are different now."

"Not to me," I said, though I knew what he was trying to do: save me from myself, the definition of a hopeless task.

13

I spent the rest of the morning handing over my caseload to a woman named Alicia Brimbeck who worked in the Hempstead office of Burton Lewis's pro bono criminal practice. Burton was the one, along with Sam Acquillo, responsible for relentlessly converting my working life from the safe (mostly) and lucrative practice of real estate law into criminal defense, a course rarely traversed by any sane attorney.

After leaving law school, Burton opened a storefront pro bono legal office in New York City. He got into tax law a few years after that when his father died and left him his practice and the building on Wall Street that housed it. And the mansion in Southampton, etc., etc. Since then he'd tripled the family fortune and expanded the criminal practice, still free to qualified clients, throughout the five boroughs and into Nassau County, where Alicia ran the show. For the last several years, his agent in Eastern Suffolk County had been yours truly.

I loved Burton in a way I've never loved anyone else. That he was gay might have had something to do with it. That he was on the *Forbes* list of the fifty richest people in America had nothing to do with it, since so far he'd cost me a lot of money. That was because he liked to put me on the cases his team tried out of Suffolk County Court, which had become such a common event that it now represented well over half my daily time commitment, and well under half my revenue.

Real estate law isn't the same thing as criminal defense. In both cases you're called a lawyer, but that's about where the resemblance ends. In the first case, you can make a nice living without ever facing anything more threatening than a zoning appeals board. Since by definition, Burton's pro bono practice focused on the poor, the lunatic, and the most likely seriously guilty, it was like sliding into an alternative universe, a realm of fear, anger, and institutional cruelty. People who spent their days researching title claims and arguing over pyramid violations and nonconforming setbacks had no business there. And as Burton pulled me deeper into his practice, it was beginning to feel as if the reverse was also true.

Probably more than anything, my attraction to Burton had to do with his essential goodness and stunning lack of pretense. Like all the crazy rich people I knew whose families had been crazy rich for generations, he could be oblivious to the commonplace concerns of normal people, like navigating a supermarket or scoring first-tier tickets to Bruce Springsteen, but you always sensed that his empathy toward fellow humans was completely genuine, immense, and heartfelt.

And he was adorable, made more so by his unavailability, an opinion probably shared by thousands of women.

I'd called to say I needed to take a sabbatical from my current responsibilities in order to concentrate on the crisis at hand. After I had described the crisis in as much detail as I could muster, he did the predictable thing.

"Absolutely. What else can I do to help?"

"Know anyone at Homeland Security?"

He was quiet for a moment.

"I do, though not a person I could easily impose upon."

"Just kidding, Burt. I wouldn't want you to. Unless I end up in Guantánamo, in which case, impose away."

"You know their portfolio includes counternarcotics enforcement, in concert with the DEA, the DOD, the FBI, the State Department, and the CIA," he said.

"I didn't exactly, but there's a lot I don't know about the federal government. Suffolk County's byzantine enough."

"If your lady pilot was importing from across the border, they'd have a definite interest. The point with them isn't the drugs, it's what could come along with."

"Like?" I asked.

"Who knows? Matters of interest to Homeland Security."

"Tell me not to start invoking Kafka," I said.

"Nothing's perfect in an imperfect world."

"Okay. So we invoke Lao-tzu."

The upshot was that Alicia took my cases, temporarily I assured her, freeing me to neglect my real estate clients even more for a while so I could put all my attention on Eugenie Birkson, since it appeared that people attached to Eugenie Birkson had decided to direct so much of their attention toward me.

My Internet search for Clinton Andrews, the man who owned the Peconic Pantry, who was beaten nearly to death thirty years before, was gummed up a lot by references to the former president, but courtesy of Randall's illegal software–the equivalent of a digital bloodhound–I eventually turned him up.

He apparently owned and operated a fitness club up on the North Fork in the hamlet of Cutchogue. According to a deeper search, it was located on a cove next to a small marina catering to shallow keel boats that claimed itself the birthplace of the atomic bomb, since Einstein and a few of his cohorts sailed out of there and presumably cooked up the idea of a nuclear chain reaction while tacking around the Little Peconic Bay.

I took their word for it and climbed into my Volvo and headed north, without Mr. Andrews having the benefit of a courtesy warning, preparing myself for whatever fallout might result.

I'd debated bringing along Sam or Harry, but like most of my internal debates on this subject, it ended in a stalemate. So I went on my own, which I was glad for as soon as I reached the South Ferry and crossed over to Shelter Island–the scenic route to Cutchogue–and felt that illusion of safety as Southampton disappeared behind me.

The day had started out gray and foreboding, but changed its mind and turned sunny by the time I traversed Shelter Island and boarded the North Ferry. Spring was coming on slowly that year, so there was still enough chill to warrant my barn jacket with the flannel lining. To complete the ensemble, I wore cowboy boots and jeans, which I felt enhanced the expeditionary mood of the morning.

I got out of the Volvo as we crossed the channel and took in the breezy, saline air, and watched the seabirds zing around overhead. Even the occasional spray off the chop brought over the bow by the wind felt refreshingly perfect. One of the ferry guys came up and stood next to me at the gunwale. I asked him if he ever tired of being out on the water.

"I go back and forth on that," he said, which I deserved.

I drove off the ferry when we reached Greenport and headed southwest on Sound Avenue, the North Fork's version of a freeway. This was Long Island's wine country, which any average tourist knew more about than I did, having never set foot on a vineyard. I made up for it by drinking a fair amount of their product, my indiscriminate tastes allowing for a broad sampling. I also appreciated looking at the orderly rows of grapevines and the cute buildings along the side of the road where I heard you could drink for free provided you spit most of the wine out into little paper cups. A practice that likely explained my complete lack of interest.

Cutchogue was a world of inlets and shallow waterways, so it wasn't surprising that Clinton Andrews's studio had a water view. I found it easily, guided by frequent references to mushroom clouds and subatomic particles, and Clinton's sign for The Compleat Physique.

It was a single-story building with a partial roof, flat on the top and enclosed by a white railing. Nothing said I couldn't just walk in the door, so I did. Inside was a large open area almost completely covered by a continuous blue mat. There were several big Pilates balls, some large elastic bands, and a few small barbells, but no elaborate gym equipment, which I found very pleasing, since I truly hated gym equipment. In the middle of the mat was a tall man I assumed to be Clinton Andrews. He had long, white hair that flowed from his head down over his shoulders, a deep tan set off nicely by his hair, and a clear, nearly wrinkle-free complexion. He wore a tank top and shorts, displaying a lean but powerful body. Only the subtle folds around his throat and a slight looseness in his skin showed him to be an older man. By my calculations, he couldn't have been much under sixty, unless he'd opened the Peconic Pantry as a teenager.

Also on the mat was a young woman, sheathed in a nylon bodysuit that I thought you only wore when you wanted to smooth things out under a tight dress. And usually when you really needed smoothing, which this woman clearly did not. The bodysuit was a color they called nude, which I always thought should be "nude white girl." On this woman there was a fair amount of contrast, though the illusion of total nakedness was well within reach.

They were performing an exercise whereby Clinton supported her while she bent backward, lifting one leg with toes pointed and allowing her arms to dangle toward the floor. If there had been music playing I would have expected her to straighten out and launch into a pirouette, but she repeated the move several times, her lower back braced against Clinton's rigid right arm, the tips of her fingers reaching closer to the floor with each bend.

They must have heard me coming through the door, but neither looked in my direction until they completed the routine. Clinton pointed to a single chair against the wall as they flowed into the next exercise, this time standing face-to-face, arms straight out and parallel to the floor, hands clasped. Then they moved their outstretched arms forward and back, so each person's arms were either extended backward, or brought forward to assist in the other's extension. It also had the effect of mashing the woman's breasts into Clinton's chest, which neither of them seemed to take note of.

And thus things proceeded through a number of other exercises, which seemed to be an invigorating mix of resistance training, stretching, and erotic gymnastics. Watching them made the wait more than endurable.

I found myself straightening my back, loosening my neck, and wondering if Harry would appreciate a more fluid presentation, and less of the full-body impact I tended to deliver. I let my right arm drift eloquently into the air, then caught myself and pulled it back, self-conscious.

After that I just watched, and about forty-five minutes later, they wrapped things up with some running in place, then a big hug with kisses to each cheek and a toast of something odd in glass jars. After the woman disappeared through a door in the back, presumably leading to the locker room, Clinton came over to me, wiping his hands with a small towel. I stood up and offered to shake.

"Sweat doesn't bother me," I said.

"Then you're in the right place."

"Clinton Andrews?" I asked.

"The same," he said, shaking my hand with the ideal amount of pressure–not too much, not too little.

"I'm Jackie," I said.

"You picked the right time to join. I just had one of my oldest clients move back to the city. Though she promised me she'd still come out to visit."

His smile displayed teeth that were perfectly straight and brilliantly white. I wanted to say, Those can't be real, but it was too early for that, even for me.

"No gym equipment. I like that," I said, looking around the big room.

His smile went up another megawatt.

"That's the whole idea," he said. "All that hardware has nothing to do with fitness, but everything to do with enriching gym equipment manufacturers, especially since most of it sits collecting dust in people's basements. Did the ancient Greeks get those flawless bodies working out with a machine? I don't think so."

The door in the back opened and the woman came out in a sweat suit and carrying a voluminous, soft-sided gym bag. He smiled at her and she stroked his cheek as she walked by, barely giving me a glance, but what little was there told enough of the story.

"Are you two . . . ?" I asked.

He looked puzzled.

"No. She's just a client."

"Oh. So what is it you do here? Almost looks like yoga, or Pilates," I said.

"Like yoga and Pilates, but not. You probably know the fitness regimen behind Compleat Physique is of my own design?" he said, as if it were a question.

"I did not."

That seemed to make him happy, as if he relished the opportunity to explain. As he spoke, he very slowly, but noticeably, began to violate the outer periphery of my personal space. I responded by ever so slightly maintaining a consistent distance, though that involved a slow rotation to avoid getting backed into the wall. As we danced the world's most gradual dance, I listened to him describe in considerable detail his theories on health and fitness, well supported by borrowings from every established form of physical and spiritual expression. It was pretty engrossing, and eventually allowed me to tee up my true reason for being there.

"So what got you interested in all this?" I asked.

He pointed his finger at me to signal a new thought.

"You need one of my brochures. It's a lot to read, but everything you want to know is in there."

He strode over to a rack mounted to the wall and took out a thick, 8½ × 11 booklet. I followed him over there and he handed it to me. His handsome face was on the cover, a picture an advertising agency could use to sell toothpaste, hair product, face cream, or longevity pills.

"That's great," I said. "Thanks. But how 'bout the short version. I can read the details later."

He used the hand towel to wipe the back of his neck, then reached under his tank top to run it over his chest.

"Do you like wheatgrass?" he asked.

"Beg pardon?"

"It's a juice. Great source of chlorophyll."

"Okay," I said. "As long as my hair doesn't turn green."

"That'd be a pity; it's such a lovely reddy blond."

He led me through another side door that opened into a spare, starkly furnished office. In addition to a white-Formica-covered desk, there was a matching table and four shape-fitting chairs like the type you saw in the 1960s. I took one while he dug bottles of wheatgrass juice out of a compact refrigerator.

He snapped open the drinks and handed me one as he sat down next to me, again, not invading but skimming the frontier of my personal space.

"Do you know how old I am?" he asked.

"That's always a dangerous question, but I'm guessing around fifty-eight."

"Sixty-eight. You're ten years off."

"Wow," I said, sincerely.

He ran a hand through his long, silken white hair in a gesture that would have been preening on anyone else at that moment, but which on him seemed entirely genuine.

"What I'm going to say to you will sound insane, but if you let me explain, you'll see that it's completely rational."

I started to get it. This was the standard presentation, delivered at podiums, around conference room tables, in living rooms, and here in his office, each calibrated to suit the occasion.

"Sure. I've got an open mind."

"Thirty years ago I died. Then I came back to life as a completely different human being."

He paused there for dramatic effect. I respected the silence for a moment, then said, "Okay. That's cool. How'd you die?"

"It doesn't matter," he said, modestly.

"Hey, no fair. You get me hooked on the story, you gotta tell me everything that happened."

He smiled again, this time indulgently.

"If you must know, I was clubbed to death with what the police believed was a galvanized pipe, though the weapon was never recovered. I was still breathing when they got me to the hospital, but I died in the emergency room. They didn't have the technology they have now, so it took a while to bring me back, but only as far as a deep coma. At that point, any reasonable society would have pulled the plug, but the Sisters of Mercy got ahold of me and I spent a year as a vegetable. And I'd probably have stayed that way if they hadn't constantly prayed for me. On God's whim, I just woke up one day."

"Wow," I said again, only half sincerely this time, since I already knew some of the story.

" 'Woke up' is too generous a term," he said. "I opened my eyes, but it took days to know what I was seeing, and weeks to form a thought.

By then, they'd moved me into the rehab wing, where the physical therapists worked on me. The half of me that still worked."

Another stock line, but it was easy to hear. Clinton Andrews was very easy to listen to overall. His voice was deep and softly modulated, each word spoken in a calm, leisurely fashion, as if there were limitless time to share his tale. I noticed when I first saw him that he wasn't wearing a wedding ring, since I always look. I'd read in the *Chronicle*'s archives that at the time of the robbery he had a wife, but no children. Now, of course, I was dying to ask, but since this was obviously the first stage of a well-rehearsed seduction–one intended to get me either into his club or into his bed, or both–I didn't want to upset the flow.

"How long did it take to get everything working again?"

"Thirty years," he said, pleased to be handed a great setup line. "One to stand, two to walk with crutches, five to run, and the rest to go way beyond being a simple grocer with no more ambition than to pay my mortgage, watch TV, and do a little fishing. I was fat, dumb, and unhappy. I just didn't know it."

Now that I was sitting, it was harder to move away as he drifted inexorably closer. So I had to literally pick up the chair and move back a few inches. He took the hint but held his forward position.

"So, if I'm hearing you right," I said, "what should've been a tragedy turned out pretty well in the end."

Though still placid, his face tightened, almost imperceptibly.

"It was a tragedy. A horrible tragedy. You can't imagine the physical pain and despair I went through. I'm a better man than I would have been, but I would have eagerly chosen a less agonizing route to my good fortune," he said, his tranquil blue eyes slightly ablaze.

Wow, I said, this time to myself. I didn't know if I was talking to Jack LaLanne or Gandalf.

"It must have been tough on your family," I said, looking conspicuously at his left hand, as if first noticing the lack of a ring. He followed my eye, then looked back at me.

"My wife left me year one. Another gift I would have chosen from a different source."

I didn't know exactly where to take this from there. I was genuinely absorbed, but I had another agenda that seemed unfair to hide. On the other hand, if I wasn't able to reveal myself to my own brother, how would I reveal myself to Andrews as his attacker's sister? But if I didn't, how would I get the information I wanted?

Easily. I lied.

"Mr. Andrews, I'm an attorney by trade, but I've always wanted to write a book about some of the intriguing people I've met in the course of my practice. I would love to tell your story," I said, then took a deep, cleansing breath, pretending to have just cleared my conscience.

He reached over and tapped on the brochure I held in my lap.

"Start with that," he said. "I'm sure it's all there, but I'll be happy to tell you anything you want. Especially if you do me the honor of joining The Compleat Physique," he added, reaching behind himself to slide an application off the top of his desk.

"I would love to," I said, leaving off the "but" part of the sentence as I took the application out of his hand. He didn't set a very high bar for admission to The Compleat Physique. Name, address, telephone number, and a brief description of your spiritual and physical fitness goals. And a credit card number.

"We can start today, if you want," he said when I looked up.

I sighed with disappointment.

"You know, I'm just not prepared. No gym clothes."

"No need for that," he said, his voice dipping into a slightly lower register. "We keep several bodysuits on hand." He looked me up and down. "I know I have your size."

Having recently fought off a rapist, you'd think the guy's insinuations would have triggered my customary feminist outrage. But the tangled labyrinth that makes up my moral constitution made me feel an exception was in order. After all, I was there under false pretenses. And also, contrary to all good sense, it felt sort of flattering.

Still, there are limits.

"I'll stick with my workout clothes," I said, sitting back in my chair. "It's the only way I'd feel comfortable."

He also sat back, in gracious, patient retreat.

"Of course."

I opened the brochure and scanned the table of contents. I was eager to dig in, but I didn't want to lose his attention, however problematic.

"Did they catch the guy who did this to you?" I asked. "Sorry to dwell on that part, but the legal stuff is my business."

Still looking patient, he said, "They caught a guy, but that wasn't the end of it for me."

"Really."

"I steer clear of the legal stuff. It's not what people are interested in hearing about."

"I'm very interested," I said, leaning forward again. "For my book."

He paused–not to hesitate, I thought, but to form the right words.

"I remembered nothing of the attack until nearly five years after the fact. By then, the attacker was already tried, convicted, and locked away. The science on recovered memory is far from settled, and I concede that my own damaged mind could have concocted the recollection, but I maintain my belief that it wasn't a single perpetrator that night, but three. I cannot recall their faces, black or white, or the color of their hair, or how they spoke or what they said, but in my mind I see not one but three men milling around my store as if they were unknown to each other, and then suddenly acting as one. Whether all three beat me, or only two, or only one as the police maintained, I don't know. But I do know there were three. No more, no less."

"You brought this to the cops," I said.

"I did. And the DA, although the actual prosecutor had retired by then. Predictably, no one believed me, and even if they had, there wasn't a scintilla of evidence to support my testimony. Even the lawyer for the son of a bitch they caught said his client never told him there were accomplices, which if proven, could have deflected the full brunt of the prosecution, or at least helped out in his defense."

Sort of, I thought, having heard the it-was-that-other-guy-they-didn't-catch-who-did-it assertion a few hundred times. Most judges I went before had heard it a few thousand.

"So what did you do?"

He shrugged and loosened his posture, which had taken on an uncharacteristic stiffness as he recounted the experience. And the shining smile came back.

"I learned to live with it. I sublimated my feelings, as I had already learned to do. Do you know what that word means? It means to turn something evil into something sublime. That's what I've done with my life. I've sublimated with a vengeance."

Speaking of vengeance, I wondered if he knew Billy was out of prison, though I was afraid to ask. He immediately solved my problem.

"I have studied all the major religions, and a few minor ones, and all preach some form of forgiveness, though Christianity more than others. I was brought up a Catholic, which might have saved my life, since my priest was the one who brought me to the Sisters of Mercy. But I can no longer be a believer, because I will never forgive the bastard who was there that night, no matter what his role. The only reason I didn't kill him the week he got out of prison was this belief that he hadn't acted alone. My conscience can bear a loss of faith but not a murder I cannot fully justify. However much I would delight in committing it."

This comment should have been more disturbing, but while my body still sat at his table, my mind had already fled the scene and was racing back to Southampton.

"I have to go," I said. "I'm really sorry. This is fascinating, but I'm already late for an appointment."

Kindness and indulgence swept over his face as he rose from the table and offered me his hand. I took it, and he helped me to my feet.

"You must be a fine attorney," he said.

"You think so?" I asked as I gently pulled my hand from his.

"Don't you have to be skilled at getting people to talk? I just told you things I've hardly told anyone, and we've only just met."

"Shucks," I said as I let him escort me to the front door. I half expected him to bow as I made my good-byes.

"Do you have a card?" he asked. "I would love to continue the discussion when more time allows."

I pretended to search my pockets, passing over the stack of cards in the back pocket of my jeans.

"Golly, you know, I don't. But I'll e-mail you as soon as I get back to my office. Then we'll go from there."

He awarded me one final, all-embracing smile, and one more lingering handshake.

"I do consider myself a lucky man," he said, before I could turn to leave. "How many can claim that the worst thing that ever happened to them was also the best?"

14

I spent the rest of the day reading Clinton Andrews's brochure, which would be better described as a dissertation on the full realization of one's life potential, at times a little wacky, but on the whole filled with fairly decent advice, which if followed would likely make for a healthier, happier person. But unhappily, I knew that would never happen for me.

As predicted, there was almost nothing on the robbery of his store in North Sea, the Peconic Pantry, except for his noting that he'd started on his quest after suffering a serious injury.

That night I tried to dig up more information on the Web about the robbery itself, looking for any mention of more than one perpetrator, but I'd already thoroughly mined what little was there, given that it all happened long before news was automatically stored in digital files. It was a miracle anything had been scanned in at all.

It's like me to keep wringing a stone as long as I think there might be a molecule or two of blood stored inside, but I eventually gave up and went to bed, traveling the few feet from my desk to the bathroom, and then to the pull-out sofa, where once again I cuddled up to my deadly Austrian pal and slept the sleep of the conflicted and obsessed.

Ross Semple woke me up with a call to my cell phone, theatrically requesting the honor of my presence at ten that morning. The cell said it was already eight thirty, but there was time enough to ease wobbly into the day.

Hm, a surprise interrogation by Homeland Security. What to wear? I went with the most litigious-looking plain-Jane suit I'd retrieved from my house, the one that went with the blouse with the ruffled front that reminded me of the fruity things worn by judges. I went easy on the makeup, with just a tinted lip gloss, and wrestled my hair into a ponytail, which on me is more like the tail of a raccoon. I also brought along a pair of horn-rimmed glasses with clear lenses, since I still have twenty-twenty vision. I only wore them on professional occasions like this, just to round out the look of a former clerk to an originalist Supreme Court justice.

My co-interviewees were more flamboyantly attired, Sullivan in his best African mercenary outfit, Ross looking like he'd just rolled out of bed after sleeping off a two-week bender, which is actually how he usually looked. I was glad to see him smoking, since it meant I could steal one of his Winstons to go with my coffee. Sullivan sat with us stoically, trying not to breathe.

"Any thoughts before they show up?" asked Ross.

Sullivan shook his head.

"Could be anything," he said. "No sense wasting energy on speculation."

"Mind if I give you guys some friendly advice?" I asked.

They both looked like they wanted to be offended by that, but not enough not to listen.

"Is it free?" asked Sullivan.

"On the house."

"Okay."

"There are only four correct answers: Yes, no, I don't know, and I don't remember. If you have something that might help you remember, say you'll need to go through your records and get back to them."

They looked at me with blank faces. I thought Ross was smart enough to know that already, but then again, even smart people can get themselves in legal trouble when interviewed by federal agents. Just check the histories of Martha Stewart, Wall Street, and Washington, D.C.

"If it's possible to prove that you did know, or should have known, but claimed the contrary to a federal authority, they can toss you almost directly in the can for lying. If you should have known something because it was your job to know, that's also a problem. That's why you say you need to get back to them, so that we have a chance to regroup. Blowing that one is the difference between keeping the life you have and seeing it evaporate before your eyes."

They still were at a loss for words until Ross said, "She's right. Goddamned hell of a thing."

"You guys can also say, 'I think I have that information, but I'm not sure if I'm legally able to share it, even with federal authorities. I need to check with legal counsel. Is that okay?' I can say that to them too, but only if it involves the possible violation of client confidentiality, and as you know, since you routinely challenge me on this, the law there is somewhat unsettled."

They absorbed this as well as they could. It wasn't easy to be on the receiving end of a lecture after all those years of doling them out.

"And no swearing. It's in the federal penal code. And no unauthorized use of profanity in the presence of duly commissioned federal agents or their designates."

That really killed the mood.

"What the fuck?" said Sullivan.

"I'm kidding, for chrissakes. Designates? Where's your sense of humor?"

Ross looked amused. Sullivan, not so much.

"Thank you for that advice," said Ross. "It's appreciated."

A few minutes later, Janet Orlovsky's voice came through Ross's intercom.

"There are some people here to see you, sir. Should I admit them?"

United States federal government, meet your match.

Ross pressed the button.

"Bring 'em to Lawyer Room A, facing the mirror. Turn on the recorder. No coffee or water."

He looked up at us.

"Hey, home-court advantage."

We walked like a funeral procession through the squad room and to the front of the building, where the recently busted could presumably have a confidential meeting with their attorneys, one of whom was often me. I knew, like everyone, that these conversations could be recorded, but I trusted the cops to not do it, if for no other reason than it could mean the ignominious end of a career if they got caught.

In Lawyer Room A sat a tiny Asian woman who'd somehow managed to outdowdy me. Next to her was a bald white guy, about her height but easily twice her girth. And twice her age. They each had a yellow pad, unwritten on, and a Bic pen poised to remedy that. I'd seen scarier-looking people running the reference desk at the Southampton library. I tried to send telepathic messages to my colleagues: "Beware. Looks deceive."

"What's this all about?" I asked firmly as I dropped my briefcase on the table, just to break the ice.

They slid cards across the table. Anne Li, Investigator, DHS, and Jeff Fells, the same. I passed the cards to Ross and Sullivan and kept my own card in my briefcase.

"We're curious," said Sullivan. "Like the lady said."

"Ms. Swaitkowski, thank you for joining us," said Fells.

"I didn't knowingly. In fact, I'm not joining you until you tell me what this is about, or I call in my own attorney. Burton Lewis. Know him? He knows your boss."

"Please, Ms. Swaitkowski, sit down," said Fells. "We'll explain."

Ross pulled out a chair and waved me into it. I sat down.

"Chief Semple and Detective Sullivan assured us you can be trusted with confidential information," said Fells.

"Depends on who thinks it's confidential."

"Your government, in this case."

I folded my arms.

"I'm listening."

"Once I share this with you, you have implicitly agreed to the terms of confidentiality," said Fells. "This is legally binding, making any breach prosecutable to the limits of the law."

I wasn't sure about that, but bluster aside, I really wasn't up on current constitutional protections, except to know that they'd lately been seriously challenged. If he was full of shit, he sure made it seem like he wasn't. More compelling, of course, was that dangling hook–an offer to share interesting information. It caused my curiosity, always a nagging itch, to break out in hives.

"Yeah, yeah. Show me what you got. We are on the same side, right?" I looked at Sullivan, who looked only slightly less happy than Ross, who looked pretty unhappy.

"Christ, Jackie," he said. "Play along a little, will you? It won't kill you."

"Okay, I swear to keep my trap shut. As long as you aren't asking me to participate in an unlawful act," I added for the sake of the tape recorder.

"We aren't," said Investigator Fells as he magically came up with a manila folder from somewhere under the table. He placed it in front of himself.

"It's come to the attention of domestic intelligence sources that a person or persons is attempting to transfer sensitive technological information to parties who have the potential to further transfer this information to entities unfriendly to our national security."

Okay, I thought, that's not what I expected.

"Okay," I said, not knowing what else to say.

"I am going to show you four photographs. I want you to give us your opinion as to which of these individuals you believe most likely to be involved in such a transaction."

I felt my heart rate speed up and my bravado leak out of my ears. He started to open the folder, but I reached across the table and stopped him.

"Whoa, hold the phone. First tell me why you're asking me this."

Fells looked over at Li, who gave a faint nod. He looked back at me.

"The aforementioned intelligence sources place you at two out of three of the locations where these individuals were also present. On each of these occasions, coded communications were intercepted that connected one of them to this illegal enterprise. We just don't know who. We know it wasn't you; we're simply asking your opinion. As an attorney and a responsible citizen."

He started to open the folder, and I stopped him again.

"Okay, one more question. Are they in it for the politics or the money?"

"You know of a distinction?" Fells asked, then smiled. "Levity. I apologize. Money, as far as we can determine. Industrial espionage is the likely objective, but unfortunately, such activities can have wider implications. The people selling the information have no way of knowing that the buyers are free agents who merely sell to the highest bidder, be it a foreign corporation or sovereign nation. Or extranationals."

"Terrorists," I said.

"That's always a possibility. That's why we're sitting here with you," he added, with a gentle smile.

He looked down at where my hand rested on his folder. I took it away. He pulled out four photographs and placed them in front of me like a dealer laying out playing cards. My heart, already racing, almost buzzed right out of my chest.

"Where did you get that?" I asked, sticking my finger on Skitch's shot of the Children's Relief Fund summer drive.

"You find it significant?"

"I've seen it before."

Fells gently moved my hand out of the way and pointed at Kirk Lavigne.

"This is one of the individuals."

"Bullshit."

"Jackie," said Ross.

"Not Kirk. Doesn't need the money. This I know and can prove conclusively, but only after I talk to Burton Lewis."

Fells shook his head.

"Not necessary. We're here to obtain your opinion. That's what you're giving. What about this individual?" he said, pointing at someone I'd never seen before.

"I don't remember ever seeing him," I said, catching the looks from the two cops. I said the same thing about photo number three, this time a dark woman.

"That's Jud Hinkle," I said, pointing to number four. "He's mayor of Southampton. I see him all the time, though I don't know him very well. His day job is running a restaurant in the Village. If he's into industrial espionage, he's got the world's best front."

"You're certain about two and three?" asked Fells.

I looked at them hard and pushed my memory, but nothing appeared.

"Sorry. No go."

Fells didn't seem disappointed. Neither did the Asian sphinx sitting next to him.

"Does she ever say anything?" I asked him.

He looked at her.

"No," he said. "I don't believe she ever has."

"Number two is Rodney Burnham," said Ross. "He used to coach basketball at Southampton High but found he could make a lot more money dating rich old ladies. We used to call guys like that gigolos. Now they're male escorts. I've had some complaints after he dumped a few of his dates, but nothing illegal turned up, or at least nothing provable. The other's Natalie Koshi. She sells custom and imported clothing. All one of a kind. I heard she rolls with some heavy out-of-towners. Way out of town, like the Middle East. Just hearsay, but that's where I'd start. I agree with Jackie on Lavigne. Richer than stink and a serious patriot. All four of these people are big into fund-raisers; that's the common denominator," he said, looking at me. "But you knew that already," he added, looking back at Li.

"But not me," I blurted out. "I hardly ever go to those things."

"But not never," said Fells. "You were there on one of the aforementioned occasions. A call was made from that fund-raiser to a disposable, untraceable cell. A code was punched in with the keys."

"How the hell do you know that?" I asked.

Fells looked at Li again, who again gave a nod.

"Because the call to the disposable came from your phone."

I love my country, though I'm not a thoroughly trusting supporter of my country's government, even though I love our system of governance, however flawed. I think this makes me a mainstream American. I admit, I haven't had a lot of experience with big doings outside my tiny, albeit overwrought, world of the Hamptons. None, actually. But most people can sense what it feels like to be in the proximity of things much bigger than ourselves. You feel like a mouse trying to seek warmth from the side of an elephant who's about to roll into a more comfortable position.

"Is this headed where I think it's headed?" I asked the investigators from the DHS.

Fells shook his head.

"I told you. You are not a suspect. We believe you are an unwitting victim."

"And you can't tell me why you think that."

He shook his head again. He took back the photographs and put them in his folder, which disappeared again back under the table.

"Thanks for sharing your thoughts," said Fells. "It was very helpful."

Li bowed at me.

"If you say so," I said.

"I do."

"That's it?" I asked.

"For now."

Then the two of them stood up and walked out of the room. Sullivan, standing next to the door, moved out of their way, then closed the door behind them.

"Okay," he said, "how weird was that?"

"We didn't ask about the drugs," said Ross, jumping out of his chair and pacing around the room. "We should have asked about the drugs."

Sullivan and I agreed we should have asked about the drugs. And also about who killed JFK and what they actually found in Roswell, New Mexico. We'd learn as much.

"It's still a drug case to me," said Ross.

"We're not talking about the same case, boss," said Sullivan. "This is way over my pay grade. And yours, too. No offense."

Ross sat back down and lit cigarettes for the two of us. Sullivan sighed.

"Sorry, Jackie," said Ross. "I had no idea. I can't believe I've apologized to you twice in as many days. What's the fucking world coming to."

"You don't think it's a little odd that he had Eugenie's fund-raiser photo?" I asked both of them.

"Dumb luck. Got it off the Web just like she did," said Sullivan.

"Correlation doesn't equal causation," said Ross.

"That's Sam's line," I said. "And there were fifty photos of that event on Skitch's Web site."

"How many included Lavigne?" asked Sullivan.

I didn't know.

"I don't know. I'll look."

We pooled our ignorance and suspicions for another hour, till I wearied of it and left. I drove from the HQ down to the shoreline, then traveled on Montauk Highway into Southampton Village, where I turned right and drove all the way to the ocean. I parked at the end of Little Plains Road, where they had a parking lot and access to the beach for anyone lucky or rich enough to own property in the Village, and sat staring at the ocean and smoking twice my daily allotment of Marlboro Lights.

The ocean was active, with bigger-than-normal breakers that left a messy froth between the waves. The sun was behind me, soft and warm, though the air was still holding on to the hard edge of winter. A couple walking on the beach crossed in front of me. The man threw something ahead of him and a tiny dog streaked in and out of view in full-out pursuit. The woman put both arms around the man, which made it harder for them to walk, but neither seemed to care. He reached over and smoothed her hair, then used his own arm to support her as they trudged lovingly over the sand.

I wanted to get out of the car and jump in the ocean, but I didn't have a bathing suit with me. The water was still fiercely cold, and the crisp breeze on wet flesh would have felt like an arctic windstorm. I settled for getting out of the car and standing fully clothed in the wind and simply looking at the surf, and at the colossal houses perched atop the dunes, one of them Kirk and Emily Lavigne's.

Of all the shocks my nerves had borne in the last few days, this was arguably the worst. The sight of that bald agent sliding the fund-raiser photo across the table, his fingers pinning the four corners to the table, was stamped into my memory.

A person lives with what she knows, and what she believes. They're not always the same thing. Father Dent loved telling me that if I knew for sure there was a God, I wouldn't need faith.

There was almost nothing I was entirely sure about, based on knowledge, faith, or belief. But I would have to be sure about Kirk Lavigne, because otherwise there truly would be no meaning left in the world and nothing to mourn if it all just turned to dust and blew out to sea.

There was still plenty of day left when I got to my office. I hadn't done what I'd really wanted to do before leaving the Town HQ–dive into police archives to check out Clinton Andrews's story about the three men–because then I'd have to tell them about Billy, and then explain the connection to Eugenie's photos, and why I went to see Andrews in the first place. The prospect of starting that boulder rolling down the hill made my stomach clench.

Instead I killed the rest of the day on a research project for a complicated credit card fraud case I'd taken back from Alicia, which I later regretted giving up. At one point I had a question for her, but she said only Burton could answer it. So I called him on his secret direct line that goes to his desk in Manhattan, where he ran his grown-up business–a four-thousand-person firm specializing in corporate tax law. After he helped me with my original question, I asked another.

"Ever deal with industrial espionage?"

"That's a bit rarified for our criminal clientele," he said. "Peeping toms are the closest we get to spies."

"Not in the tax business, either?"

"I don't know. Perhaps. I'm not privy to every case."

Burton's never shown his face at a fund-raiser, even though he's often the principal donor, so I wasn't sure he'd ever met his neighbors on the water, a stone's throw from Burton's house if you had a really good arm. So I asked.

"Do you remember Kirk and Emily Lavigne?"

"The people for whom you wrote up the irrevocable trust?"

"With your immense help, yes."

"I've run into Kirk a few times in the city, but only to say hello. We did a fair amount of work for his investment bank."

"So what are the chances he's involved in industrial espionage?"

I told him about my lovely chat with Ms. Li and Mr. Fells. The line was quiet while Burton considered the question.

"On the face of it, zero to none. But we've learned not to trust anything on its face. People thought Bernie Madoff was a great philanthropist."

"Would the feds know that Kirk gave away most of his money to the trust?"

"Yes, if they wanted to. The Justice Department can know almost anything it wants. All it takes is a subpoena, and judges around here hand them out like penny candy."

"So presuming they know that, why look at Kirk? What could possibly be his motivation?"

"Blackmail, revenge, to protect a loved one, sociopathology, to name just a few."

"I don't believe it," I said.

"Neither do I, but you asked."

I thanked him and got off the phone, slightly miserable over the conversation, which I'd intended to be reassuring. As I went back to my research, I realized I'd just violated the tacit confidentiality agreement with the DHS by bringing up Kirk Lavigne and espionage in the same breath, which made me feel even more miserable. I continued to plug away at the research, even as my thoughts were interrupted by imagined interrogations wherein I tried a variety of defenses, none of which held any water, ending with me in solitary confinement in a basement in Azerbaijan.

Of course, if they came after me for this one little breach of confidentiality, they'd have to have tapped my phones. Landline and cell. I assumed they had. And were monitoring my e-mail and, for all I knew, following me around.

I needed to invent another word. One that blended outrage with paranoia.

Now that I was in the right mood, it seemed like a good time to call the FBI.

"Ig," he said, answering the phone.

"How many people think you're saying 'ick' when you answer like that?"

"Some do. They're quickly corrected. It's Jackie, right? Who else could it be?"

"How do you explain a name like Ig?"

"It's short for 'igloo.' "

"I gave you that joke," I said.

"I know. You have a sense of humor, which I don't."

"You do, too. Otherwise you wouldn't steal my jokes."

"That's a good point. Thank you for that."

"You're welcome."

"So what sort of confidential information can I not give you today?"

"See, that was a joke," I said. "And you did it all on our own."

"I'd call it more of an ironical statement, wry, maybe, or even sardonic. The humor is derived from the tragic truth that lies at the core of the witticism."

"Have you been reading?"

"I have. Also your fault."

"I don't only call you when I'm looking for information, you know."

"Yes you do."

"Okay, I do. But I also like to hear your voice. It lets me pretend we can still be friends."

"Another tragedy, darling. You can be friends. I just find myself on a slippery slope. Better to feel merely exploited than tempted by forbidden fruit."

"You're sounding very poetical," I said. "What's going on?"

"I'm going to night school to get a master's degree."

"In what?"

"Poetry. Nineteenth and early twentieth century. American."

"I'll be damned."

"Not by me. I owe it all to you. And your friends. I always felt like the dim bulb in the group. I don't feel that way anymore. Even though I'm no longer in the group."

"That's silly. You're a smart guy."

"Not yet, but I'm working on it. So what're you up to?"

"I need some information you probably can't give me."

"Most certainly I wouldn't, even if every call that comes into our office wasn't recorded and reviewed by internal affairs. Hello, boys. Meet Jackie Swaitkowski. She's a lawyer simply upholding her constitutionally protected responsibility to her clients. Not in any way attempting to circumvent or contravene the legal process for obtaining classified information."

"Jesus Christ."

"Amen," he said, before hanging up on me.

I flipped open my cell phone and called his.

"Ig."

"How 'bout this?" I asked.

"Better."

"Do you think Homeland Security is bugging my cell phone?"

"I have no way of knowing, and if I did, I wouldn't tell you."

"I'm not supposed to tell you what I'm about to tell you," I said. "But since you're the FBI, which also works for the federal government on matters of national security, I can't see the problem."

"DHS might take a different slant on that."

"They interviewed me, Sullivan, and Ross Semple today. Until a few hours ago we thought it was related to the investigation of a Cessna air taxi crash that we thought may or may not have involved drug smuggling. We'd been told the NTSB was going to declare the crash an accident, though as far as we knew, they weren't aware of the drug-running implications, and even if they were, it wouldn't fall within their purview, unless they thought it contributed to the crash. But then we find out it's just me they want in connection with what they think is domestic espionage. Apparently someone involved in that used my phone to call a number that must have been under surveillance, which won't be all that surprising to you, given how I'm not first rate on keeping track of my purse or my phone, which you pointed out to me numerous times, drawing on your professional expertise, which you don't have to remind me of now, though I'd forgive you if you did."

"Interesting story, but nothing I'm aware of," said Ig. "And even if I was, I wouldn't be in a position to discuss what would certainly be confidential information."

"The pilot of the Cessna was a woman named Eugenie Birkson. She was married to a guy named Ed Conklin, who did time for assault. No drug history, though she was also the daughter of Matthew Birkson"–I paused to give him time to write all this down–"who also did time on a host of charges, including theft of containers off the docks in Long Island City, hijacking tractor trailers full of cigarettes, and the distribution of controlled substances."

"I know nothing about any of this."

"Me and the boys at Southampton Town Police were just wondering if this was connected to the DHS inquiry. Just curious."

"How's your buddy Sam doing?" Ig asked. "Still boozing it up like crazy?"

"Still boozing it up, but not yet completely crazy."

"I liked his dog. Better than him."

"Eddie liked you, too. Of course, he likes everybody."

"Well, I'm sorry I can't help you. But I hope you stay in touch. And if there's information you believe would be important for the Bureau to know, anything relating to the security of our country, I know you'll want to pass it along. In complete confidence, of course."

"You know I will. Speaking for all Americans, I sleep better knowing that you, Webster Ig, are watching over us."

"That means a lot to me. Thank you."

"When you get that MA, write a poem for me."

"I will. Bye-bye, Jackie."

I looked at my cell phone after he hung up, wondering if I'd actually just had that conversation. Completely sober, in broad daylight.

15

The next day I was on my way to Randall's shop when he called to ask me to pick up some coffee beans.

"Plain beans, please. No additives." He said he had something for me, but only if I brought him a gift. "Since it's your fault I've drunk up my whole supply."

It was early afternoon, but it always felt like night at Good to the Last Byte. Entering the shop was a little like crawling into a cave where the walls were covered in spiderwebs, only these were made of cords and wires, through which the sparkle of LEDs and the glow of LCD screens provided the ambient light. Randall called from the back room when the buzzer told him I'd come through the door. I went around the counter, tiptoed over the electronic rubble strewed about the floor, and felt my way down a narrow hall.

"Ever try cleaning this place up?" I asked.

"Too late for that. The entire system is built upon interdependent variables. One false move and the cascading failures would bring down the World Wide Web."

"Where do I put the coffee?"

"In the grinder over there. Make four cups."

He waited until we were slightly caffeinated to break the news.

"Your death threat came from a semi-homeless schizophrenic in Massapequa, Nassau County, Long Island."

"Really."

"He goes by Sid Kronenberg or the Grand Khan, Archangel of the Universal Force, as prophesied by the Great Tree of Learning."

"Get out of here."

"He doesn't have a fixed address or reliable means of support, but he does have an e-mail account, which he mostly uses to communicate with his daughter in Arizona when he's not posting to the Grand Khan's blog."

"You sure about this?"

"These days, it's virtually impossible to send an untraceable e-mail. Millions are spent by intelligence services all over the world to either figure out how to circumvent Internet security measures, or to catch people who've almost figured out how. But none of it is worth a hill of beans if the Sid Kronenbergs of this world wander away from their computers without logging off."

"Ah."

"The Internet café is in Massapequa, located between a strip club and a porn shop where you can also bet on the horses, ex officio, of course. It's called the Hot Spot, and as I told you, all the monitors face the wall so you can watch porn or bet online in complete privacy. You can also pay cash, which most customers do. The kid who works the register said he doesn't even look at the people who come in and out. Just takes their money and unlocks a computer, which locks up again when the allotted time runs out. Simple business."

"You went there?"

"I called him on the phone."

"Oh."

"He did know Sid, however, mostly by smell. The kid told me it wasn't unusual for him to get up and leave after only a few minutes online. If he was on e-mail, anyone could sit down, open a new address on

Sid's account, and send out a message. A death threat, for example, to you."

"Totally untraceable."

"Totally. The only way to catch him would be to run security cameras and have an alert on the Hot Spot's IP address and Sid's account and wait for the perp to try it again. You could be waiting a long time. The *yourfriend* address hanging off Sid's account had only been used that once, so it could have been a spontaneous event, not to be repeated. You could also try a stakeout. What are the chances of that?"

"In Massapequa? Not bloody likely."

Randall shrugged his broad shoulders.

"Sorry. Best I could do."

"Don't apologize. You did a lot. How about doing one more thing?"

He gave his head a little bow.

"Why not?"

I moved him away from his computer and logged on to my e-mail account. Then I downloaded and opened Eugenie's scanned photo of Delbert's Beachworld Deli. I showed him where I thought there was a reflection of two men in the storefront window. He moved me back out of the way and started to manipulate the image, zooming in and out and fiddling with the contrast.

"Am I seeing things?" I asked.

"You're seeing two guys reflected in the window, one taking the picture itself. But I told you . . ."

"I know. What you see is all you get."

Randall started opening and shutting windows, clicking on little icons, dragging the image over grids, and doing all that other computer stuff that quickly makes me simultaneously dizzy and bored to tears. I thanked him again and asked if there was anything else I could bring him.

"I'll call if I have any luck," he said. "But keep your expectations in check."

I looked at the clock on my cell phone. Was two o'clock too early to have a drink? Not for Sam Acquillo. I pushed his speed dial button.

"Now what."

"I need to kill some time in Southampton Village," I said. "What do you suggest?"

"It's well after twelve. Time to shift from caffeine to alcohol."

"Interesting. Where would I do that?"

He picked a spot and said he'd be there in twenty minutes. It was a ten-minute walk, so I burned the extra time window-shopping, which is the only kind of shopping that gives me any pleasure, even that fleeting. Ten minutes, tops. But it was good enough to get there after Sam, who was having his regular drink poured by a bartender who'd had plenty of chances to learn what Sam's regular was.

"Just tonic water for me," I said.

Sam was in his shop clothes, as betrayed by the sawdust sprinkled on his shirt and in his hair. I tried to brush it off.

"Hey, I wanted that there."

"I'm confused, Sam. The more I learn, the less I feel I know. What does that mean?"

"Maturity."

"I don't mean about life in general, although there's that. I mean this case."

"I'm listening."

Sam was a talented cabinetmaker and finish carpenter, but that hardly provided the level of intellectual stimulation a brain like his required. So in the evenings he did what he claimed to have done his whole life–read dense and complicated books on every subject imaginable: fiction, nonfiction, scientific and academic texts, classics and the recently released, usually in English, but sometimes in the original French or Spanish. He'd often pick a subject, like celestial mapping in Mayan architecture, and study it until he knew it well enough to chair the department. So it didn't surprise me that he was well versed in the scientific, sociological, and legal issues surrounding recovered memory.

I told him about my visit with Clinton Andrews, and Clinton's three-man theory, and he gave me a general overview, then an off-the-cuff analysis of Clinton's assertion, and came to the exact conclusion I had the day before.

"There's no way to tell," he said. "He could be right, he could be wrong. In the absence of corroborating evidence, even circumstantial, you have to tilt toward the single attacker theory."

Then I told him about the interview with the DHS, but only after the bartender was down at the other end of the bar. That got his attention, as it had mine.

Having spent years managing technology development at his company, Sam had the genuine authority to address corporate espionage. He told me his former employer would only release proprietary processes after they'd been thoroughly commercialized and replicated around the world. Anything in bench test stayed in his labs under strict security.

"And we were only refining crude oil and optimizing petro-chemical plants, which has been going on for a hundred years. It's much more serious in other industries."

"Like what?"

He thought about it.

"Anything defense related. It could be communications, data processing, robotics, satellites, aerospace, that sort of thing."

"We don't make any of that stuff in the Hamptons."

"There's more to Long Island than the Hamptons. Like Brookhaven, for example. And Northrop Grumman. And all the crap that goes into things like that. Everyone thinks they make biological weapons out on Plum Island. Maybe they do. It's a cinch they study ways to counter the biological weapons that might be out there. And Connecticut's right across the Sound. They make submarines and engines for fighter jets up there. Within a hundred mile radius, you probably have the highest concentration of classified technology in the world."

So I don't know that much, I said to myself. Here's to lifetime learning. I took a sip of my drink, then put my head down on the bar.

"There's no connection to any of this. Where's the connection."

"Boxes and arrows," said Sam.

"Aw, crap, not with the Zen. Not now."

"I don't mean physical boxes and arrows. I mean the ones you draw on a pad. It's how you troubleshoot a process failure. Follow the flow, look for patterns and anomalies. Sketch out the whole thing in front of you."

He pulled a pencil out of his back pocket and used it to draw on my manila envelope. He made me list all the key facts, or assumptions, about the case. There was a lot, and it took a while and ate up the whole side of the envelope. When I felt tapped out, he flipped it over and drew several boxes, which he labeled "buckets."

"That's what I call a locus of information. In engineering it'd be a side process or a subsystem."

Then he drew lines between the boxes, on which he marked, in abbreviated language, shared characteristics or definite connections.

"This is how you start to build a relational database before you go near writing code," he said. "Figure out what goes with what and how."

I have to admit, I started to feel the way I had back in Randall's shop when he started to jigger around with the photograph. It's not that I didn't find things like this interesting; I was just more interested in the outcome than in the process itself.

"So what do we know," I said, before watching him erase and rewrite an indecipherable abbreviation in beautiful block letters for the hundredth time caused a blood vessel to burst.

"Are you familiar with attention deficit disorder?" he asked. "Do you know you're afflicted with it?"

"Yes. You told me it correlates highly with intelligence. Just cut to the chase."

"Three men and the fund-raiser photo," he said, then ordered another drink.

"Excellent. You're amazing. Case closed."

"You asked me what we know. Clinton thinks there were three men in his store that night. The DHS interviewed you, asked about three men."

"And a woman. And the reflections in the Delbert's photo, if they're real, are only two."

"Nothing's perfect. The fund-raiser photo has multiple interconnections. It was on Eugenie's memory card. It lives on the photographer's Web site. It cross-references with two people who also connect at several points, three if you count Lavigne's wife. It was one of the four photographs shown to you by the DHS."

"Who's the third?"

"Benson MacAvoy. He was at the Children's Relief Fund event where the photo was taken, and he was at the political fund-raiser you attended, as were the other people on the DHS list, including Kirk Lavigne, if you believe the DHS. He was also at Eugenie's funeral, which gives him another correlation point."

I looked at his boxes and arrows and saw, more or less, what he was getting at. It didn't really give up any answers, but at least there was a little order brought to the chaos. I pointed to one of the boxes.

"What's this?"

"Lower-order locus. People with criminal records. Conklin, Matt Birkson, and Billy O'Dwyer. By the way, three men."

"There's only one line connecting it to the other boxes," I said. "What's BV mean?"

"Benson MacAvoy. He bridges the fund-raiser photo and the excons."

"Hm. I guess I should pay a little more attention to Benson. He'd like that, attention hound that he is."

"That's what I would do," said Sam, holding up his glass so the bartender could grab it as he passed by.

"Would you flirt with him?"

"Probably not."

"He's an impossible flirt."

"That's a good thing?" he asked.

"Sometimes. I spend so much of my life around cops, cons, and thugs like you, it's nice for someone to notice you're a girl once in a while."

"You're a girl?"

"Jesus Christ."

I took the manila envelope with me when I left the bar, shocked at how sunny it was outside. I called Randall, who told me he needed more time. I offered to bring him anything he wanted, but he said the pizza had arrived and was already half-consumed. He said to stay tuned and hung up.

I finally made it back to my office after that, and found it clear of threateners, rapists, or other hostile action, if you didn't count the surveyor passing me in the hall without making eye contact. Before opening the door I bent down and checked the hair I'd stuck to the bottom of the jamb like I once saw in a James Bond movie. It was intact. I entered with confidence.

I took the Glock and my laptop out of my giant feed-bag purse and stripped off all my clothes. Then I ran through all the other rituals that ramped up to my first wine of the day, and settled in for the night in front of the computer.

This was interrupted somewhat by a decision to smoke a joint, which led to a nap on the sofa that ended after nightfall, so when I woke up I didn't know where I was for a few moments. Panic erupted as I jumped up and cleared a table of papers in search of the Glock. When my hand felt its smooth, warm, polymer-framed body, I dropped down into a corner and leveled the barrel at the door, and waited.

What happened next was a return to sanity as I remembered where I was. As consciousness reconstituted, I also remembered the dream I'd been having, one in which I lay in bed over on Brick Kiln Road and heard the sounds of footsteps moving down the hall outside my door.

"Crap," I said into the darkness, though I stayed put until I was utterly certain I was alone above a row of shops and restaurants in Water Mill.

"Sorry, I lied," I told the darkness. "I'm not okay. Not in any way."

Counting the nap, I slept over ten hours that night. I was astonished at how remarkably refreshed I felt as a consequence. I fairly bounded out of bed and dove into my morning routine, skipping the shower. Then I threw myself into the credit fraud research project for most of the day. For me, therapy comes in many forms, and demanding professional work is often the most effective, short term. Plus you get a feeling of accomplishment, and if you're lucky, you get paid for it.

Late in the afternoon, I finally took my shower and geared up for the night work. I ate a bagel while I let my hair dry enough to give the hair dryer a sporting chance, then, using a single finger, I Googled MacAvoy and Partners, saving the results to my hard drive, then jotting down the address and phone number on a piece of paper I could bury in my purse.

Choice of clothes was the main struggle. There were so many approaches I could take. The cowboy was out, as was the castrating lady lawyer I'd shared with Homeland Security. I was wearing my funeral outfit the last time I talked to Benson, but that was clearly a big not.

I decided on a blue oxford button-down shirt, a khaki skirt, and nearly sensible heels. And a brown leather flight jacket. Preppy with flair, not unlike Benson himself.

Studying myself in the mirror, I freed an extra button on my shirt, just to slightly modulate the impact.

The evening was a repeat of the one before, though noticeably warmer. I cracked the window of the Volvo and let the manufactured wind stir up the dust on the dashboard and flutter papers around on the backseat.

Contravening my established strategy, I called ahead to make sure he'd be in his office. Since he spent much of his life in airplanes, this wasn't an unreasonable precaution. I also thought he'd actually want to see me, which wasn't usually the case with other people, though that might have been an unjustified compliment to myself.

Turns out he actually did.

"Love to see you, Jackie. You've never been to my office, right? You'll love the view. I'm right on Sag Harbor Bay. I can't believe you caught me here. I just got back from D.C. Before that, Dubai. Now that's a nutty place. Nice, though, if you can take the heat. I bought a James Brown CD from a street urchin. Been listening to it on my iPod ever since. Do we love James Brown or what? Can't sing like Wilson Pickett, but had a much better band. His own boys. The Famous Flames. Maceo! You like funk? I think you do. I can tell by the way you walk. Got a good rock and roll."

I had to pretend I was losing the signal to get him off the phone. Not that I didn't want to talk to him, I just had to fortify myself after a day alone. It's hard enough to switch into social mode with normal people.

As described, his office was on the second floor of a small commercial building, like mine, only his had a balcony that overlooked the inner waterways of Sag Harbor Bay.

Before climbing the stairs I put on fresh lipstick and tried to use the rearview mirror to check my hair, which I guess worked out well enough.

"Hey, Jackie. Look at you," said Benson, swinging open the door and gathering me into a bear hug. I hugged him back.

"Look at me. I'm in your office. How 'bout that?"

It was a single room, with a seating area of big overstuffed couches anchored by a glass coffee table, a wet bar off to the left, and a desk made from a huge slab of mahogany mounted on thick black metal legs. The desk sat in front of a wall of windows and sliding glass doors that exposed the balcony and the bay beyond. The floor was stained oak, mostly covered by antique Persian rugs. The right wall was all black bookcase, composed of boxes set on the diagonal, as were the discreetly placed books inside.

Benson wore a pink shirt, open at the collar, and white pants, with a blue and gold fabric belt that should have clashed but on him looked authorized by the head buyer at Brooks Brothers. On his feet were extremely Italian yet entirely busted-up loafers worn without socks, which I caught myself admiring at the same time he was looking at my pumps.

"Espresso?" he asked. "With a twist? Or Cognac. That's all I have."

"Espresso sounds fine."

It was more like a tiny tub of thick, bitter tar, but still surprisingly good. As he worked at the espresso machine he told me how he'd fallen in love with the space, beaten the landlord into submitting to his rental offer, and done all the decorating himself with the scant help of his mother, who hadn't set foot in the place because she simply despised ticky-tacky tourist Sag Harbor, in her words.

"So what's the occasion?" he asked once we were submerged with our espressos a few feet into his soft leather couches.

"The rumor is the NTSB is going to declare Eugenie's crash an accident," I said. "Her husband, Ed, doesn't buy it, and neither does her stepson. You knew her pretty well, maybe as a customer in ways they didn't. I was wondering if you had an opinion."

"Loved Eugenie," said Benson. "And don't think I haven't thought about being in that little plane with her over a lot of miles, that I could've been there again at the wrong time, in the wrong place. Don't misunderstand me, I'm not just thinking about myself, but you got to admit, it's a little freaky."

"Did she ever get into trouble when you were on board?"

He downed his espresso and, with some effort, put the empty cup on the glass table. Then sank back into the sofa. He scratched his mane of hair with both hands.

"Not that I was aware of. I was just the passenger. Those little planes can get pretty bouncy sometimes, but she'd tell me it was SOP and to sit back and enjoy the massage. So I did. So no, I never had a moment when I felt I wasn't safe. You look great in heels, by the way. Have I told you that already?"

I wanted to get a picture of Clinton Andrews and put it side by side with Benson's and label them, respectively, smile and grin. Where Clinton was soothing, symmetrical perfection, Benson was all jagged edges, crooked incisors, and crow's-feet. The resurrected prince versus the rambunctious boy.

"I do look good in heels. Glad you noticed. You look good in pink. In a masculine way."

"I think that Cognac would be a delightful second course," said Benson.

"Agreed."

The really confusing thing was that Harry Goodlander was never far from my mind. Even though this privileged brat with the wild hair, motorized mouth, and wolfish mug had a way of flicking on little switches that I didn't even know I had.

He handed me a snifter that was only about half the size of my head. We clinked.

"How long did you know her?" I asked.

"Who?"

"Eugenie."

"Gee, a lotta years. My dad discovered her air taxi when he was looking for a faster way to get up to Boston than trudging across the sound on the ferry and driving up I-95. He's a management consultant. Makes a lot of money asking to see your watch, then telling you what time it is. Dumped my mother five years ago for a Greek slut. How do I know she's a slut? I introduced them. Is this too much information?"

It was, but how do you say that?

"Sorry," is what I came up with.

"Don't be for me. Business is great; I got a nice office, an expensive car, and zero sexually transmitted diseases. As of less than two weeks ago, and I've been a monk the whole time."

"Your dad can't be a kid," I said, eager to refocus the conversation.

"Seventy-five. Looks fifty. In great shape. Tennis, bourbon, and Viagra, I believe, is the magic formula. My mom, on the other hand, looks worse than my grandmother did at her wake. Man years are different from woman years. It's not fair. Though you'll do fine. You've got good bones. Like your brother. Pale skin, thick hide."

A tiny electric current thrilled up the back of my spine.

"You knew my brother?"

He jerked back his head and scrunched up his face like he'd just been assaulted by a foul odor.

"You pulling my leg? Best buds. I thought you knew that. You mean you talked to me just for me? I was in your house a bunch of times. I remember you sitting on the kitchen floor with your legs stuck out, playing jacks. Your mom hated me; I don't know why. Your old man wasn't much better, but he liked talking fish. I'd crewed on a shark boat out of Montauk, which he thought was pretty cool. It *was* pretty cool. Billy went out with me a few times. Geez, I can't believe you didn't know all this. Sorry."

Why would I know? I thought. That was thirty years ago. I was a little kid. I remembered lots of guys tramping through the house. They were generic older boys, more than ten years older than me. May as well have been from another planet. They had nothing to do with me. I had my own world, my own wracking fears and disappointments. Billy got to dine with royalty. I was in steerage, just trying to keep my head above water.

"I didn't know," I said, softly, looking into my snifter.

"Aren't I the insensitive shit," said Benson. "I'm really sorry. I'm sure that whole thing with Billy was wicked hard on you. And your parents. He was my best friend, but it's not the same as being related. I know that. I wanted to go to the trial, but my mother put her foot down, and I was trying to keep from flunking out of my first semester at Yale, and to be honest, I was a tad disappointed with Billy. No offense. I know about innocent till proven guilty, but he did confess, after all."

"Why would that be offensive?"

"Heard recently he was in Port Jeff selling shit over the phone."

"Who told you that?"

"Don't remember. Too much stuff to keep track of. I think I just screwed up."

Benson looked thoroughly pained. I felt a bit pained myself for whatever role I'd played in putting him there. The only way to shake it off was to throw myself back at the task at hand.

"So you can't imagine who'd want to hurt her," I said. "Eugenie, I mean."

"We didn't talk much about our private lives. She seemed nuts about her husband, Ed. Not so much about her stepson, but nothing major, not that I knew of. I'm a stepson now myself. Pretty weird. Alexandria is younger than me. I saw her drape her skirt over the head of some guy at a club in Manhattan, make out with a famous actress in the back of a limousine, and do shots of ouzo until they poured out her ears. Now she's the hostess at my dad's Thanksgiving dinner. It's a good thing she's not my type. Life's complicated enough."

The sun had dipped well behind Shelter Island, turning the light in Benson's office a dim red. I wanted to turn on a lamp, but the Cognac was starting to pin me to the leather couch, which had adhesive properties of its own.

"Benson, you've been around. Level with me," I said, though not as crisply as I wanted. "Did you ever see, or suspect, Eugenie of doing anything illicit? As in illegal shipping and receiving?"

He sat in the deep embrace of the leather couch, turning the giant snifter between his hands.

"I don't know what you mean," he said, with an uncharacteristically flat inflection.

"Drugs, Benson. I'm talking drugs."

His manner took an abrupt and lively turn for the better.

"Drugs? Could be. Did a little coke myself in the day. Okay, did a lot, but knew when to back away from the brink. I still have that little craving tickling at my nose. You too? Don't deny it. It's in your eyes."

I did have that little tickle, but I wasn't going to admit it to him, or to myself for that matter. Some things truly do need to be locked away in a very secure vault.

We sat quietly for a while, taking in the twilight and Cognac. I put my legs up on the glass coffee table, letting my pumps slip halfway off my feet. I rested the snifter on my belly. Benson did the same, mimicking me. I laughed.

"The eight hundred foot human you brought to the funeral," said Benson. "Boyfriend?"

I nodded.

"Oh," he said. "Not serious, I hope."

"Not sure."

"Good. Keep me informed on that," he said. "I want to be first in line."

"You're everybody's first in line."

"It might surprise you to know that's rarely the case. Been told often there's too much of me to take in anything but small doses. You think that's a defect?"

I looked at him, I hoped in a way that said, Are you kidding me? Who do you think you're talking to? Then I dropped my head back on the couch, closed my eyes, and thought, Decision time. Exhaustion, in all its manifestations–physical, psychological, emotional–was catching up with me. I knew this because I'd stopped obsessing over every tiny detail of the Birkson case. I'd stopped being anxious, or excited, or furious. Or even curious. All that was left was this lead blanket that lay over me, and this hopeful eagerness for oblivion to take me away.

I opened my eyes and saw Benson looking at me.

"My house is only a block away," he said. "Leftover veal medallions and Taittinger. Fireplace stocked with dry red oak. A better view of Sag Harbor Bay than this. If that isn't good enough, we can drift the Hinckley off the dock and wander further out. It's a little chilly, but the tartan blankets and Courvoisier should take care of that. Did I mention the beds I'm beta-testing for Tempur-Pedic? One for the boat, one for the house. Come with environmental music and dark chocolate. Amazing."

He smiled. I smiled back. It would be so easy.

I closed my eyes again and felt my mind at work, sorting priorities. Then I opened them so I could see what I was doing. I pulled my legs off the coffee table and stood up. Benson looked at me in anticipation.

"If things were different," I said, "they'd be different."

I walked around the table, and with a slight stagger, leaned down and kissed that tender spot right below his ear. Then I managed my way out the door, down the stairs, and into the Volvo, which I drove with the utmost of care back to Water Mill, where the only form of refuge I thought I would ever trust awaited. The one fortified by me and me alone.

16

The next day I figured it was time to check back in with Ed Conklin, who was still technically my client even though the cops had lost interest in charging him with anything. I found him in his repair hangar, with his son, both of them neck-deep in the engine compartment of a Piper Cherokee. I didn't want to startle them, so I called hello when I was still a distance away.

"Howdy, Ms. Swaitkowski," said Ed, stepping down from a short ladder. Brian stayed with the job.

"You can call me Jackie," I said, shaking his grease-covered hand. "I keep telling you that."

"Understood. Just can't make myself do it."

He led me over to the overturned bins where we'd first sat to talk. The company conference facility. I chose my regular spot.

"Have you heard from the NTSB?" I asked.

"Not really. I get a call once in a while from one of them asking a technical question about the aircraft. It's all piddling stuff, so I don't bother you with it. Is that wrong?"

"You should write down what they asked and how you answered, and then let me know. Just in case."

"Sorry. I will. They mostly want to know stuff that's already in

Eugenie's flight logs. The ones from last year back. The last four months' went down with the plane."

"You didn't keep copies."

"No need."

"Wait here."

I went out to the Volvo and retrieved my laptop. I set it up on its own bin and pulled up Eugenie's photo file.

"Did Eugenie take a lot of photos?" I asked.

"Oh, yeah, real shutterbug. I bought her a fancy digital camera a few years ago to replace her old Canon. She used some Web site to get her prints. Put 'em in a regular album. Nothin' arty. Just vacation stuff and get-togethers. You want to see it?"

"I would. In the meantime, I've got something to show you."

I first pulled up the cabin on the lake.

"Is this where you folks stayed?"

He looked at the shot and shook his head.

"Nope. Looks nice, though."

"Really," I said. "Never stayed there."

"Nope. We mostly went to a campground in Bennington, Vermont. Easy walking distance from an airfield cut right out of the woods. Great spot. Brought all the gear in the plane, got up there in two hops and a jump. Eugenie loved to camp."

"What about this?" I asked, clicking on the bar shot.

"Where'd you get that?" he asked. "That was Eugenie's birthday party a couple years ago at the Schooner. That's her dad and aunt. Them two are from the bike club Eugenie used to belong to." He pointed at the ones in the denim outfits. "Can almost remember their names. Ridin' that Harley was her second most fun thing to do, till she had to focus on the flying. Don't know the others. Not sure Eugenie did either. These're all people Birkson invited. That's my back over there." He pointed at himself, facing away, wearing a flannel shirt. "I had a good enough time, but a lot of Matt's buddies are ex-cons or still in the game. Not good for me, even bein' well past parole. Rather keep a low profile."

I moved on to the shot of Eugenie's Cessna.

"Please tell me that's her plane."

"Yep. Took that no more'n a few months ago. That's her baby. Not so easy to look at."

"Sorry," I said, and clicked on to the fund-raiser photo. "Know these people?"

He examined the photo carefully, then shook his head.

"I thought maybe they was movie stars I'd know, but I can't say I do. I never look at those magazines stacked around the sidewalks. Not my scene."

Brian approached, wiping his hands on the thighs of his mechanic's jumpsuit. He looked over his father's shoulder at the computer screen. I clicked back to the party at the Schooner.

"Know any of these people?" I asked. "Besides the Birksons, of course."

He studied the photo, then pointed at the couple in denim.

"That's Dutch and Sandy Andersen. Eugenie rode with them in the day. Dutch don't like me. Can't say I like him."

"When was the day?" I asked.

"Long time ago. Before she started working with my dad. Could tear down and rebuild that hog of hers like nothin' else. I saw her do it, right here in this hangar. Right before she sold it off. I was maybe twelve at the time. It was sittin' around for years. I was hoping to get my hands on it. Worth a lot more now than when she sold it."

"You don't happen to have a picture of the bike, do you?" I asked Ed.

"Sure. It's in the album. Had to get one to sell it. It was tough to give it up, but, to be honest, not as much as you'd think. By then, she was all airplane engines and airplanes."

I had another thought.

"Eugenie's photo album, does it have anything from her childhood? I'm thinking about her brother."

"Not in the album–that's just since our time together–but she's got black and whites of the brother and the mom before she took off," said Ed. "Showed them to me once. I'll see what I can dig out."

"What happened to him, anyway?" I asked.

"Who, the brother? Don't know," said Brian. "Long before my time. Nobody in the family wants to talk about it. I think just boltin' the scene pissed everybody off. Just like the old lady. Fucked-up family."

" 'Nuff of that," said Ed.

"Sorry, Dad. You're right. Didn't mean the disrespect."

I'd had some experience with people's names disappearing from family discourse, so it wasn't hard for me to understand.

"Do you mind if I send a courier over to pick up that album tonight?" I asked Ed. "How much time do you need to look for the old family shots?"

"Not much. Hour maybe. I can have it all ready by six o'clock."

Ordinarily, I do my own schlepping, but after Ed's late-night visit to my house, and his obvious tipsiness at the funeral, this seemed like the ideal time to have somebody make a run for me. As we sat there, I placed the call, then handed the phone to Ed so he could provide directions. As usual, the courier acted like I was his best and most valuable client, even though I gave him only a dozen or so gigs a year. I like to think it was because I saved his bacon from being fried in a big larceny case. Especially since he was actually innocent, a rarity among my defense clientele.

"I'll be at your office by six-thirty on the dot, Miss Jackie. With utmost pleasure."

"To both our pleasures. I will be awaiting."

Before I left, I showed Ed and Brian the final picture, the one of Delbert's Deli. Again, not much recognition.

"Looks familiar," said Ed. "Can't say more'n that."

"It used to be a little food store in North Sea called the Peconic Pantry where the shopkeeper was robbed and assaulted."

Ed looked a little closer.

"Oh, sure. Billy O'Dwyer. Met him at Sanger. He was coming in about the time I was coming out. He looked me up as soon as he arrived. A Hamptons boy, so I did what I could to look after him, get him set up. Didn't belong there."

I felt my face start to burn, and hoped it didn't show.

"What do you mean?" I asked.

"Just a kid, but not like the other kids that filled the place. College boy. Smart and polite. I was inside when the thing went down, so I didn't know the particulars, but what little I heard didn't fit with O'Dwyer. Didn't have the hot head, like I had, or the blood urge, or the killer's pride most of the young idiots seemed to have."

"So you didn't stay in touch," I said.

"Nah. I was out six months after he got there, and when I left he was in good hands. Meaning, protected by the ones who'd protected me for three years. Nobody survives outside a group, but it don't have to be shanks in the gut or pervo shit all the time. Just a little team play. Don't know what happened to him after that."

I wasn't sure how Brian felt hearing all this, but Ed seemed undeterred. I guessed by then, thirty years after the fact, this had been long talked out.

"So you think he might not have done it?" I asked, hoping like hell the little tremor I felt in my voice wasn't audible.

"He said he did it," said Ed, "so I guess he did. I just found it hard to believe."

"Did he ever say if he had accomplices?"

Conklin said no.

"Never came up. Though I can't say we talked about it much. Some of the guys loved to hash over what landed them in the joint. Usually to convince you how bad they were screwed by their lawyers, or the system, or whatever. Mostly, I kept that stuff to myself. No point. O'Dwyer was like that."

The Conklins might have been up for more difficult and emotionally challenging analysis, but by then, I sure as hell wasn't. The turn things had taken shouldn't have been entirely unexpected–I knew both Billy and Conklin had been at Sanger, though I hadn't checked for overlap. Whatever focus and deliberateness I'd had at the start of the conversation was completely blown.

Flummoxed though I was, I felt, or rather hoped, I'd learned some important information. I just needed some head space to sort it out, and that wasn't going to happen right then. What I really needed was fresh air, away from the gleam of polished steel and the smell of lubricating oil.

So I packed away the laptop, and was up off the bins and on my way to the hangar door when Ed said, "It's funny, though, now that I'm rememberin' all this."

I stopped.

"What's funny?'

"If it weren't for O'Dwyer, I probably wouldn't've met Eugenie."

"You wouldn't?"

He looked a bit in the thrall of reminiscence, so I gave him time to assemble his thoughts.

"That first time, she came in here to thank me," he said.

"For what?"

"For keeping Billy out of trouble on the inside. He was a friend of hers from high school, and he wrote her to say that me and my gang had probably saved his life, if not his virgin ass, though that's not how she put it."

Back in Water Mill I found a note stuck to my office door. It was from Makoto Sato, the guy who owns the Japanese restaurant on the first floor below my office. He asked me to come down and see him.

It was barely noon, and the restaurant only served dinner. But the back door was open, so I walked in. There were people working behind the bar and the sushi counter, but all the seats were empty. Except for one in a remote corner, far from the front windows.

"Well," I said. "What do you know."

"Hi, Jackie. Want some tea?"

I sat down and took in the awesome ingenuousness and precision that was Webster Ig. He still looked about twenty years old, though he was closer to my age, his soft brown hair just long enough to allow a part that looked drawn in with a razor and a straightedge. His blue eyes were far paler than mine, like a fresh spring day, clear of bad habits and burdened conscience. He was in his customary white shirt and plain, dark tie, his suit coat draped over a chair. In front of him was a folder with papers that he neatened up and put away.

"Needed something to do while I waited."

"How'd you know I was going to show up?" I asked.

"I didn't."

"I hope you didn't freak out Mr. Sato."

"You may remember I was stationed at Yokota Air Base for five years," he said, adding another line in Japanese as he bowed his head. "He thinks I'm merely an old friend paying a visit."

"You are, but not merely. Nice to see you."

"Ditto. How's the law practice? Still getting in trouble, obviously."

"What do you mean 'still'? When was I ever in trouble?"

He grinned.

"Would it surprise you to learn that inter-agency cooperation within the law-enforcement community is often less than thoroughly collegial?" he asked.

"Disturbingly, no."

"This isn't all bad."

"Really," I said.

He took another sip of tea and waited while a young Asian man in a yellow Yankees hat set a cup in front of me, which I filled from Webster's pot. It was green tea, slightly bitter but a lively change of pace.

"In the absence of reliable official communications, unofficial networks tend to form. These are based on mutual trust, or mutually assured destruction. It's like a black market, and the trade is information."

"Lovely. The American public would be so pleased to hear this."

" 'Unofficial' is the operative word here," he said. "The communications might not be sanctioned, but they're also unregulated."

"Not unlike the conversation we're having right now."

"In gangster movies they'd say, 'We're just talkin' here.' I also did some talkin' with a friend at Homeland Security."

"Please don't tell me you're dating Inspector Li."

He smiled. "I thought our social lives were off-limits."

"Sorry."

"My friend, forever nameless, knows quite a bit about you."

"I knew it. Goddammit, I'm being surveilled. What damn good is it to have a constitution if nobody pays any attention to it anymore? You can't just do that to an attorney, especially in the absence of cause, without a shred of due process. It's illegal, and–"

"Whoa, rein in the righteous ponies. You're not under surveillance, or investigation, or anything like that. They know you from the Windsong bombing. When you and Sam got plastered all over East Hampton. You might remember that was only a month after that bloody mess in D.C. Forgive us, but two big explosions in a row might just pique the curiosity of domestic security."

He was talking about the car bomb that mangled my face. He was also kind enough not to mention he was the first guy I went out with after the fact, while I was still pink from all the plastic surgeries.

"Oh," I said.

"My friend also knew that your phone had been used to text a code to a disposable cell phone. Your phone and several others, so you were never considered a suspect in any way."

"Cold comfort," I said.

"Do you know a woman named Janie Wilson?" he asked.

"The Plant Lady. She has a radio show. And is a very nice person. How can you not be, playing around with plants all day?"

"All my plants die within forty-eight hours of receipt," said Ig.

"Did they tell you about water?"

"Ms. Wilson had about a dozen calls with similar coded messages sent to almost the same number of disposable cells. Unlike you, she's under intense investigation. So far, nothing, according to my friend, who's close but not in the middle of it."

While he talked, Ig methodically straightened the corners of the papers extending past the edges of the manila folder. In another few minutes, they'd be as one. While still looking more boy than man, he'd fleshed out a little. Some heft around the jawline, rougher hands, more prominent veins, and dryer skin.

"So it's industrial espionage or something else?" I asked.

"If the receivers of the information have nothing to do with their country's defense apparatus, it's industrial espionage. If they do, it's a breach of our national security. Treason is an old-fashioned word, but that's what it is."

"So nobody at the DHS, FBI, or NTSB thinks it was drugs?" I asked.

"Nobody. The people on the receiving end of those messages are only interested in things that either fly through the air or blow things up, or both."

I fiddled with my tea, less than eager to siphon off the dregs that had settled like an aromatic wad of crud at the bottom of the cup.

"I don't suppose your friend knew much about the crash itself," I said. "The NTSB is calling it an accident."

"That's just a smoke screen. Those planes don't spontaneously self-destruct. The family maintained it, so the conjecture is sabotage committed in the course of her travels. There are any number of ways you could rig a failure. The favorite is replacing an oil line with something made of a material that breaks down in the presence of hydrocarbons, either aviation fuel or lubricating oil. Strong enough initially to get you in the air and fly for a while, but ultimately failing under heat and pressure. Segments of polyester tube saturated with oil were found in the wreckage, so it's the likely scenario."

I realized I was so thrust forward in my seat I was in danger of tipping over the table. I sat back and crossed my arms over my chest.

"You don't know how it feels to hear that, Web. It's so good to know I'm not crazy."

"You are crazy, but you can also be right."

"Why the hell don't the cops in Southampton have that same information? What can it hurt just to share a little? Aren't we on the same team?"

"We should be, but we're definitely not. For most of my colleagues, preserving the prerogatives of their organizational frame of reference is much more important than serving the interests of the nation as a whole."

"That's brilliant," I said.

Makoto came over and asked if we wanted more tea. He looked at me when he did this in a way I interpreted as protective. I told him yes, and thanked him for being so gracious to my old friend. He bowed and I bowed and that was that. As Makoto left I noticed two of his employees, who'd been standing a few feet away, moved away with him.

"I've changed my mind," said Ig.

"About what?"

"I told you when we broke up that I didn't want to be friends. That was foolish. I want to be friends."

"Enlightenment. That's what happens when you study literature."

"Self-preservation. You're going to call me periodically and make your presence felt no matter what I do. I might as well write you into the script and enjoy the play."

I told him how happy that made me, on a variety of levels, and also that I had a boyfriend that I was mostly sure about–to get that out of the way before I gave him a kiss on the cheek. The moment triggered a few memories, courtesy of the smell and taste of him, which I did a great job of suppressing.

There wasn't much else he could tell me about the domestic spying case beyond the fact that they hadn't fingered a perp for any of it, though they had a list of suspects. He encouraged me to come forward with anything I learned, and I assured him I would.

Back out in the daylight, he put on his suit jacket and sunglasses, hugged me, and disappeared back into the mists and shifting sands of American criminal justice and domestic security.

Bolted into my office once again, I set up the laptop and checked e-mail. There was a message from jjloveplants.com. I bit.

"Thank you for your complimentary messages regarding my botanical skills, which must come highly overrated," the message read. "I apologize for the delay in writing you back. I have been very busy grading student papers."

"Yeah, yeah," I said, "tough life."

"And the recent death of my mother caused me to return to California for several days," the message went on.

"Great. Nice one, Jackie."

"In regard to the photo you sent me, I'm afraid I can't pinpoint the exact location it was taken in."

"That's what I figured," I said to the screen.

"But it's either East Farmingville or Bedard, Vermont."

"Really."

"I'd start with Bedard. The *Picea mariana* (black spruce, or swamp spruce) likes swampy conditions, which are more prevalent there."

He went on to justify his analysis by listing about a hundred other species of flower and plant, with their Latin names, noting whether they were indigenous or imported, sturdy or endangered, welcome or invasive–along with possible remedies, including the introduction of benign insects. I read as much as I could bear, out of respect for his efforts, wrote him back to declare that he'd answered every question I could ever imagine asking, extended my sympathies on the death of his mother, hit Send, then clicked on MapQuest.

Bedard was a swampy, lake-infested town on the Canadian border about twenty-four miles northeast of Burlington. It had a few motels, lots of cabins to rent, a store a guy named Rajesh called The Indian Trading Post, which I appreciated, the usual car dealerships and repair shops, and a landing field called Three Creeks that claimed a smooth runway, a phone booth, and a wind sock. I e-mailed Rajesh and asked him if he could identify the cabin photographed in an attached jpeg, and if not, who in town might.

Then I roamed around online until my eyes started to blur. So I took a break and got out the manila envelope with Sam's boxes and arrows. Left to my own devices, I wouldn't have done these schematics, but now that I had them, what the heck. I started filling in the new pieces of information, using some of his abbreviations and some of my own invention, which were about three times longer. Then I added a bunch more boxes, which looked more like loose rectangles, or trapezoids, and drew in some arrows that were too curvy to be real arrows, so just to improve my artistic execution, I drew some more, which I then had to erase. This caused me to erase some of Sam's work as well, which I had a little trouble reconstituting. I did the best I could, until I was distracted by a squiggle I'd drawn that looked like the head of a French poodle, so I drew in the rest of the dog and had it say, "Look at all these chicken scratches. But where are the chickens? I love to chase those noisy chickens!" Then I tried to write that in French, but not sure of the translation, went online and spent an hour trying to divine the French equivalent of "chicken scratches." The best I could achieve was *coups de griffe de poulet,* which really didn't work as the right expression, so I spent another half hour on a site that compared French and English idioms, where the closest I could get to chicken scratches was *pattes de mouche,* which literally translated as "legs of the fly." This snapped me out of it, causing me to abandon the manila envelope entirely, stuffing it back into my briefcase before making a fresh cup of coffee and lighting a cigarette over which to enjoy the invigorating aroma.

That left me free to do what came more naturally, which was to sit and grind over whatever facts, feelings, and unsupported supposition happened to be churning away in my mind, without the aid of technical drawings. Unfortunately, what facts I had were highly unquestionable, and what feelings I had were totally compromised by underlying emotional storms that kept sloshing into the deliberations like boarding seas over the stern of a sinking ship.

That left unsupported supposition, one of my comfort zones.

I decided to build some support under my primary supposition by flopping on the sofa with the copy of Eugenie's log left by Ross and Sullivan. Not unlike Sam's boxes and arrows, it was filled with numbingly dry and lifeless information, data points that were supposed to tell you something if you were inclined to put in the necessary effort, which I couldn't immediately bring myself to do. There was no record of Bedard or East Farmingville, or any other towns north of Bennington, Vermont. I did notice on her passenger lists, however, the frequent presence of Benson MacAvoy, which wasn't a surprise, given what he'd told me.

Most of the trips with MacAvoy were to Connecticut, to places like Stratford and Brainard Field in Hartford, places I'd never been to but might have driven past. There was nothing odd about any of it. MacAvoy was a political consultant who worked out of the Hamptons, and Eugenie was the operator of an air taxi. They knew each other well.

Come on, Jackie, I said to myself. Connect the boxes.

Benson knew Eugenie, who knew Billy, who knew Benson. Ergo, Billy knew Eugenie, confirmed by Ed Conklin. So why hadn't he said so?

Because he's an ex-con who doesn't say anything he doesn't have to. Because his wife was there making sure he said as little as possible. I had no real leverage, and I hardly tried. I couldn't do it. He wasn't just another witness, another source. He was a specter out of the nightmare past.

I forced myself to think through what to do next.

I needed to know where Billy worked. His wife certainly wouldn't tell me. Sullivan could get it from Billy's parole records, but that would open a can of worms I couldn't afford right then. Maybe I was thinking too hard, so I wasn't thinking at all.

I booted up the laptop and brought up my last search for Billy O'Dwyer, which Randall's software had automatically saved. One of the features that made the software clearly extra-illegal was the ability to capture people's social security number, the key that unlocks your entire life. It took a few clicks to narrow in on Billy's number, and then I just requested the works.

Buried in the middle of the vital statistics, credit histories, prison records and parole check-ins, visits to the walk-in clinic in Port Jeff, car loans, college applications (pre-prison, which I passed over as quickly as I could), and voter registration was the name of a single employer, Harrison & Flynn TeleSales, Coram, Long Island.

It was only midday, so I encountered little traffic on the way up to Coram, a town just south of Port Jefferson. I drove with the radio off to aid concentration, which I found easier to achieve in the car than in most other places. I didn't know what this said about my driving habits. I hadn't run into anyone yet, though a few had run into me.

This was also a good way to keep my rational self sequestered from my emotional self, which had done nothing but undermine any clarity I might have had regarding my brother, and thus deserved to be banished. Instead, I set my mind on the plan, which like many of my plans extended only to the moment I knocked on someone's door or strode unheralded into their reception area, as I did that day at Harrison & Flynn TeleSales.

"My name is Jacqueline Swaitkowski. I'm an attorney and officer of the court," I told the receptionist, handing her my Officer of the Court card. "I need to speak with someone in management, and without delay."

This had the predictable effect. She took off her headset and immediately left her post to fetch someone. There was a small seating area with a coffee table covered in telemarketing trade journals. I stood and waited.

A little guy of indeterminate age, with thin curly hair encircling a bald crown, a polyester shirt, and pants that buckled over his bulging midriff, rushed into the reception area, followed by the receptionist. He held my card. I stuck out my hand and used his grip to move him out of the receptionist's earshot.

"I'm here to speak with William O'Dwyer," I said in soft, urgent tones. "He may be reluctant, but you must insist. He knows who I am. It would be in his and your company's best interest to cooperate."

"This is pretty out of the norm," he said.

"Do you have a conference room I can use?"

"We do. Should I be calling my lawyer?"

"This is a matter solely concerning Mr. O'Dwyer. If you want it to become the concern of Harrison and Flynn as well, that's your prerogative. Though let me warn you, it'll be far easier to engage with me now than to later un-engage with this situation down the line, which you will undoubtedly want to do."

I knew little of the art of telemarketing, but I was betting it involved a quick reading of a situation, snap decisions, and the ability to move on to more lucrative prospects without looking back.

"Follow me," he said, and I did.

The conference room was surprisingly well-appointed. It had a nice conference table and an original work of art over a sideboard where you could pour coffee from an elegant silver decanter. At the center of the table was a black phone that looked like a little flying saucer, with several smaller saucers connected by black wires placed on a leather blotter at each seat. There were no windows, but a big flat-screen monitor filled much of one wall, and a whiteboard was on the wall at the opposite end of the room. The carpet was deep pile, and fresh air flowed down from vents in the ceiling.

The chair I sat in was appropriately comfortable, which mattered little as the minutes ticked off. It wasn't hard to conjure the hundred bad things that could be happening on the other side of the closed door. But there was nothing to do but wait and feel my body go rigid with frustrated anticipation.

Then suddenly Billy was there, his pale cheeks slightly rosy, his eyes darker in the sockets than I remembered them, until I realized he wasn't wearing his glasses, but rather carried them in his hand. His red hair was slicked back with some type of product, and he wore a white shirt unbuttoned at the top and a tie loose around the collar.

"I can't talk to you without Ivan," he said, standing at the open door. "My lawyer. I promised Kathy."

I tapped the blotter next to me.

"Sit down, Billy. I'm your sister."

He stayed standing, but the rose on his cheeks turned a brilliant red. I wondered how often my own cheeks betrayed me in the same way.

"I actually wondered about that the last time," he said. "The hair and the name."

"I married a Swaitkowski. He's dead. Come on, sit down."

He pulled out the chair and sat down, and then put on his glasses.

"I can see it now," he said. "Why the lawyer act?"

"Not an act. I'm an attorney. I couldn't face you as just your sister. I meant to, but when I saw you, I choked. I apologize."

"I don't blame you. I might've done the same."

"I know a lot more now than I did before. I need to ask some tough questions. If you want Ivan present, that's your call. But he's liable to prevent you from saying things I need you to say. You just have to trust that it stops with me. Even though you have zero basis for that trust."

"I don't know. You're my sister. That should mean something. And I've got nothing to hide. I did my time and I've been the most law-abiding citizen in the country since then. Not even a parking ticket. And don't ever get stuck behind me on the road, because I always drive below the speed limit."

As I sat there with him, most of the thoughts I'd always imagined sharing with him evaporated. The cocky, unreachable boy wonder of my childhood memory was now a slightly overweight middle-aged guy with a soft handshake and the undeniable air of resignation.

"You knew Eugenie Birkson, didn't you? You wrote to her from prison."

He smiled and shook his head.

"I knew her brother, Matt. I tried to reach him, but she's the one who wrote me back, telling me she didn't know where to forward my letters. She apologized for opening his mail, but I was glad to have someone on the other end respond. She's the only one who did."

I remembered pulling letters from Sanger Prison out of the mailbox the first few years he was gone, but then they stopped. I felt my throat begin to tighten again, but I swallowed the lump and pressed on.

"Did you stay in touch?" I asked.

"I haven't heard from her since she hooked up with Ed Conklin, which wasn't her fault. I just didn't feel like writing anymore. Nothing to tell. But I was glad for how that all worked out. Conklin will never know how much he did for me."

As he spoke he fiddled with his glasses, which he'd taken off again and put on the conference room table. My father used to do the same thing, something I'd forgotten until that moment. I wondered how many other phantoms of my past knowing Billy better would reveal.

"I talked to Benson MacAvoy, another associate from the day, apparently," I said.

"Brazen Bennie, we called him, which he was."

"He said you were best buds."

"We were. When Bennie was around, girls were automatic."

"That was never a problem for you, either, as I recall."

"You were too little to know anything. He called you carrottop and you liked it. Though he pissed off Mom. Too much of a wiseass."

"I also talked to Clinton Andrews," I said, or rather blurted. Billy shut his eyes and let his head fall slightly to the side. I moved closer to him. "I'm terribly sorry to bring this up, but you should know the guy's a human marvel. He's fitter, healthier, more robust and frankly, randier than guys half his age."

He opened his eyes again and nodded.

"I know. Kathy told me. We met at group therapy, so I'd already told her everything I could think of. Before we got married she had me investigated, just to check my story. Isn't that beautiful? Trust but verify."

"Did she really know everything?" I asked.

He looked up from the table and nodded.

"It wouldn't work otherwise," he said. "Even a single secret could kill it off. Would kill me off."

"Even a secret that might exonerate you?" I asked.

He squinted at me as he had on the porch up in Port Jeff, searching with his eyes and his mind.

"Nothing can do that," he said.

"Clinton said there were two other guys there that night. He doesn't remember anything beyond that, but he's sure of it."

"He couldn't have remembered anything."

"That's what the cops told him, two years after you were convicted and imprisoned. So that's as far as the story went."

"Explains why I never heard it. Too bad it isn't true. I can take a lot of this, Jacqueline, but if you don't mind, I'd rather not live that night all over again. I cut a deal with the prosecutor–a guilty plea, but no allocution, so Mom and Dad wouldn't have to hear all the dirty details. That's how it was then, and that's how I want to keep it."

"Even from your wife?"

He shook his head.

"I told you. No secrets between Kathy and me. I don't owe the world the same deal."

Brother or no brother, I knew a hard line when I saw one. This was Billy's, uncrossed for thirty years. He wasn't crossing it now, even with me. Especially with me. More pressure would only harden his resolve.

"Anyway," he said, "this is all ancient history. Nothing to do with poor Eugenie."

"You're sure about that?" I asked, but he just looked at me with his moist, defeated eyes and I knew that was the end of the conversation.

So I left him with a handshake, and went back out into the sun and spring air, with Billy's words dashing madly around my mind, one word in particular repeating itself with audible clarity. My name, my full name. Jacqueline. The only name my parents ever used to address me, heard again–spoken as they would have spoken it–for the first time since my mother died, from the lips of the brother who may as well have.

17

Before leaving the office to go see Billy I'd looked up another name and address: Dutch Andersen, Hampton Bays, Long Island. Dutch was officially Wilbur Andersen, and his wife, Sandy, officially Sancha Maria, so I didn't get there immediately. What helped was the official Web site of the Sound Avengers, a motorcycle club whose social activities did little to substantiate the name.

Dutch had a plumbing business and installed boat toilets at a marina off the Shinnecock Canal. I reached Sandy at his office, and she told me that's where I could find him, working hard to get his boating customers launched for the season.

I was directed to a big powerboat with a double-decker flying bridge. Dutch was below, with his head and torso bent into a deep hold in the V berth that presumably contained the waste system. Always afraid of causing injury to workingmen caught in one of my surprise visits, I was forced to wait almost ten minutes for him to emerge. And I still startled him.

"Whoa, didn't know you was standin' there. Why didn't you say something?"

"Didn't want to startle you."

Dutch was tall, angular, and wide-shouldered, with yellow and white hair and blue eyes. The only denim he wore was a pair of jeans. His shirt was a smudge-covered checked cotton with the sleeves rolled up, exposing a tattoo of a stylized motorcycle—distilled to the essence of two wheels, handlebars, and an oversized chrome exhaust belching flames.

"What can I do you for?" he asked.

I handed him one of my cards and he confirmed that he was Dutch Andersen.

"I'm investigating Eugenie Birkson's plane crash. You knew her. I'd like to ask a couple questions."

He looked amenable.

"Sure, only I don't know anything about it. We go back a ways, but she hadn't rode with the 'Vengers for a lotta years. Only did a few years at that, but earned her patch."

"Good rider?"

"Fearless. And a freaking great mechanic. Had the gift. Do you want one of these?" he asked, pulling a dripping wet Corona out of a small cooler.

"Sure."

He opened both bottles with a pocketknife. We each took a swig.

I showed him the photo of him and Sandy at Eugenie's birthday party.

"So you know her father," I said.

"Sure. Known him since I was an aspiring delinquent. Fenced his boosted cigarettes around the neighborhood. Made good money till I sold a few cartons to a narc. I think the fucker turned in one carton as evidence and kept the rest. Earned my V patch. Prison time, even if it was only juvie hall. Long time ago. Water under the bridge."

I asked him if he knew the third couple in the shot, but he didn't.

"There were a lot of people there I didn't know. Friends of Matt's from Up Island. For an ornery son of a bitch, the guy knows a lot of people. I got the feeling that was Matt's party as much as Eugenie's. Payback to his crew. Some real hard cases there that night."

We took a few moments to drink the beer.

"So you know Ed Conklin, Eugenie's husband," I said, wiping my mouth with my sleeve.

"The Bubbie? Sure. That's him there." He pointed to Conklin where he stood turned away from the camera. "Him and his idiot albino."

"Idiot? How so?"

Forthcoming till then, Dutch looked sorry he'd said that. I helped him along.

"This is all confidential, Mr. Andersen. Nothing you tell me will get back to anyone you don't want it to get back to."

"Ed Conklin's a quiet dude, but he almost killed a man with his bare hands. He don't see what others see in Brian. Fathers usually don't."

I had to agree with him there.

"Ed will hear nothing about Brian from me," I said, hoping I could keep that promise.

Andersen thought some more, then said, "He's a hater. He was a probie in the club for a while. Got in on the strength of his parents' cred and her bike, which we heard he had, but never saw. Turned out she'd sold it a long time ago. Brian just had this crappy rice rocket. We're pretty flexible in the 'Vengers, but the sound of that thing. . . . Fuckin' sewing machine."

"What's the hater part?"

He polished off his beer.

"The Sound Avengers aren't what you'd call the most liberal group of people, but we're not a bunch of rednecks. Some get worked up over all the Hispanics and spout off some right-wing crap, but only a few. We got three black guys wearing patches, been with the club from the beginning. And we got our own don't-ask-don't-tell policy, if you know what I'm saying."

"I think I do."

"Not all the guys haul around an old lady. It's not that hard to figure out. Unless you're some dumb shit like Brian Conklin who gets drunk around the bonfire and starts talking about ridin' over to Fire Island and bustin' heads. Just for the sport of it. If it weren't for his old man, you know whose head would've been busted that night."

I'd forgotten what Brian had said at Eugenie's funeral. Or put it out of my mind, out of respect for his losing another mother. There wasn't that much to like or dislike about the guy, but in retrospect, he did seem a little off-center, maybe unbalanced by forces stirring just below the surface.

I'd seen it before. Hate cases were among the few I refused to accept, if I thought there was the remotest chance the defendant was guilty. I know that's not what defense attorneys are supposed to do, but I wouldn't do the work if I couldn't draw some lines.

I thanked Andersen for the beer and reassured him that his confidences would be preserved. We shook hands, but before I left I asked him about Matt Jr.

"Did you know him?" I asked.

"Not really. His dad would drive him around in his truck, but he never let him out of the cab. Probably didn't want him to know what was going on. Not that it did any good. The kid turned hellion anyway, and got out of Dodge at the first opportunity. Said to be another freak with a bike, like his sister. Never got a chance to ride with him."

I left after that. The chat with Dutch was going to make it harder to visit Ed in his repair hangar on the chance that I'd have to talk to Brian, and it had done little to advance progress on the Eugenie case. But as wiser people than me have said, all information means something to somebody, somewhere.

By the time I made it back to Southampton, the sun was sinking toward the horizon and I'd had about as much as I could take of ex-cons, errant children, biker chicks, and busted lives. I needed a dose of benevolence and decency, uncompromised by ill-concealed malice or reckless disregard for the welfare of innocents. And I needed it in a big package.

"Harry," I said when he answered the phone, "this is Jackie. Do you remember me?"

"I do. Reddish blond hair, or is it blondish red? With a figure cambered in all the right places and a pleasant natural fragrance."

"Nothing about my mind?"

"I was getting to that," he said.

"Don't bother. I've only got a few brain cells left."

"You want to finish them off?" he asked.

"Gin and tonic. Lots of ice. Lime. Tall glass. Start mixing. I'll be there in five minutes."

I got there in more like fifteen, which was par for the course. Harry had anticipated this, and was just dropping in the limes when I rang the doorbell.

Cool to my lips, the drink brought warmth to my heart and soul. As did the sight of Harry, in a white shirt big enough to use as a mainsail, baggy linen pants tied at the waist with a rope, and leather sandals. My hopes for that moment were utterly fulfilled.

"Throwing you out of my house was the best thing I ever did," I said.

"It didn't seem that way at the time," he said, rising to my offered toast.

"Since you moved back to town you've never once disappointed me, pissed me off, or hurt my feelings," I said. "Whatever isn't ideal about this relationship, from my point of view, is entirely my responsibility. I know that now for certain, so I wanted you to know it, too, before I get distracted by something and forget what I was going to say. This is very tasty. Blue Sapphire? Who won the Yankees opener? I remember the Yankees. They play a type of game, with a ball. What was your name again?"

"Tough day?"

"I went to see my brother."

"Oh."

"If in the next half hour I tell you everything I've recently learned, can we then talk about something slightly less terrifying and gut-wrenching? Like the economy or deforestation?"

He preserved his record of agreeableness so I could go through everything. It took more like an hour and a half, but as usual, he'd already adjusted for the time parameters. He asked a few questions and clarified a few details, but mostly he listened with keen attentiveness. Without me noticing what he was doing, he also made dinner and set the table, so just as I was wrapping up, he was lighting the candles.

"Where'd all that come from?" I asked, pointing at the spread on the table.

"The food fairies. I have them on retainer."

When we sat down to eat he asked, "So, no conclusions?"

"No, but I have a theory," I said.

"Good."

"A testable hypothesis."

"That's better than untestable," he said.

"Or detestable. I haven't figured out the test method yet, but that's what a succulent dinner and a good night's sleep is all about."

"We specialize here in restful sleep."

"I was thinking back at my office. With you," I quickly added. "I'm expecting a package, and besides, I have an alarm and video monitors. A bodyguard would nicely fill out the panoply."

I really didn't want to sleep alone, and I especially didn't want to go back to the office in the dark. I couldn't face that after such a lovely respite from disquiet and fear.

"The office it is," said Harry, continuing his winning streak.

We formed a Volvo station wagon motorcade of two, me in front, Harry bringing up the rear. The trip was uneventful, and the lack of drama continued at the office. I picked up the package delivered by the courier, punched in the alarm code at the door and in we went.

Harry's face fell a bit when he saw the pull-out bed, looking fairly petite in sofa mode. He had reason to be concerned, but there was nothing I could do but blithely pretend there wasn't a problem.

I fussed over Harry and ignored the package filled with Ed Conklin's family photos as long as I could bear it. Finally I said, "Hey, let's sit on the sofa and look at this thing together!"

It was pretty much a disappointment. As Conklin had said, pages of vacations and get-togethers with family and friends. Some aerials of New York City, Boston, wooded New England hills, and Long Island waterfront. No overlap with the photos on the memory card, which I didn't know was significant or coincidental.

Only two black-and-white photos stood out. One of a Harley-Davidson straddled by a teenage boy, and a shot labeled "Matty with Mom." It was easy to see the family resemblance between Eugenie and her brother, who I assumed was also the kid on the Harley, though camera shake had blurred his features somewhat.

"How much do photographs illuminate and how much do they misinform?" asked Harry.

"That's way too weighty for me right now," I said.

"But germane."

So I thought about it.

"You're right. We can't know without the context. I could argue either way with any given photograph."

I looked at the two black and whites of Matty with this thought in mind. Then I took them over to the printer/copier/scanner and scanned them in. I downloaded a set to my laptop, then sent the others to Randall with a note that said, "I hope these illuminate rather than misinform."

Harry quietly watched the whole procedure, which I only realized when I pushed the e-mail Send button.

"Obsession is one of your disappointments in me, isn't it," I said.

He shook his head.

"It used to be, but I've learned it's not a zero-sum game. Your maniacal devotions don't reduce your attention to me. They'd happen anyway. It's who you are. If you want to add me in, I'll take it."

That's when I shut down all the office equipment, including my cell phone, and shut down my mind as best I could so I could devote every watt of emotional energy to Harry, struck dumb as I was by his kindness and generosity, and feeling all other fleeting attractions disintegrate and disappear into nothingness.

Early the next morning I was beckoned by Randall Dodge.

"You killed my night when you sent those black and whites," he said. "I was about to go home and put cold compresses on my eyeballs. Now I think I've gone blind."

"You found something."

"Not sure. But it's worth a trip over here. You need to look on the big monitors. Bring coffee and glyceride-laden carbohydrates. Then I need to go to bed."

Harry and I caravanned back, stopping at the corner place for the requested provisions. The lady behind the counter said we must have a lot of hungry mouths to feed. I pointed at Harry and said, Just two of these.

Randall looked like hell. His face gleamed with dried sweat, and his eyes were as red as Rosemary's baby's. His clothes looked as slept-in as they were, the wrinkled mattress on the floor in a distant corner further proof. As was the aroma in the back room, never floral, now cutable with a dull knife.

"I feel bad," I said. "I didn't mean to put you through all this."

"Yes you did," said Randall. "That's okay. I love a challenge. Sort of. Gimme the coffee. Hi, Harry. She's sorry to put you through this, too."

"No I'm not," I said.

We let Randall go wash his face, put on a clean sweatshirt from a box of promotional logo wear–the words "I ate at Good to the Last Byte" on the front with a picture of a CD covered in cream cheese. We waited while he downed a large hazelnut coffee and two of the croissants we brought, enhanced by grape jelly and Grey Poupon mustard from the shop refrigerator.

"Okay," said Randall, licking a glob of mustard off his fingertips, "let's do it."

A single click brought up the images on his big LCD monitor. Several dozen thumbnail photos filled the screen. He clicked on the first one.

"Here's where I started. The photo with the two guys reflected in the deli window that you found on Eugenie's memory card. It took me a few hours, but I finally determined you were wrong," he said, looking up at me.

"Shit."

"It wasn't two guys. It was a guy and a gal."

"Really."

"Look," he said, clicking on the next thumbnail. It was a close-up of the reflection of the person who'd snapped the shot, processed through Randall's image-enhancement software. He pointed to a specific spot on the image. "See these bumps on her chest? In my culture we call them tits, or knockers, sometimes boobies. That makes her a girl."

He went back to the original photo, zoomed in on the shooter's chest, then switched back and forth with the enhanced image. It was obvious.

"This would stand up in federal court," said Randall. "For all the time it took me, I did relatively little manipulation. You got this flair at the hips. It's a female."

"Eugenie?"

"Maybe," said Randall. "But her face is completely obscured by the camera. Nothin' nobody can do about that."

"What about the guy?"

"That's the interesting part. Let's take a look at the *Chronicle*'s motorcycle rally series."

He opened and closed the sequence of news photos taken at the Peconic Pantry that Roberta and I had dug out of the *Chronicle*'s archives.

"I'm only doing this to simulate in tiny time increments the immensely tedious process I went through to study each of these photographs, driven as I was by the black and whites you sent over of the young guy sitting on the Harley, also as a little kid with his mother, who I could have sworn I saw at the motorcycle rally. And I did," he said, slowing the pace of the frames along with his words. "Right here."

He stopped on one of the news photos. Then he zoomed in on a particular bike and blew it up. The image softened dramatically, but then he brought up the motorcycle shot I'd sent him and put them side by side.

"What works best with these programs is to have a version of the thing you're trying to enhance. If this little cluster of pixels looks like this when fuzzy, it should look like this when clear."

He clicked back and forth between the shot I'd sent him and the one from the motorcycle rally, calling up a string of saved images that allowed us to see hours of labor unfold in seconds.

"This would not stand up in federal court because I'm making too many artistic assumptions. The wizards in intelligence would know it was a righteous enhancement, but any half-baked defense lawyer would tear my technique to shreds."

"Defense lawyers don't tear people to shreds," I said. "We peck them to death."

What we saw emerge was Eugenie's Harley. More important, with Matt Jr. sitting on it.

"So now we know where the Harley came from in the first place," I said. "It was probably Matt Jr.'s, and he left it in the garage when he split the scene."

"But that's still not the most interesting part," said Randall.

"You're taking a long time to get to the point," I said. "This is uncharacteristic."

He looked up from the screen.

"Much of the beauty is in the process, not just the outcome."

"He's right," said Harry, transfixed.

I sighed.

Randall went back to the screen and clicked his mouse.

"Let's go back to the original image of Matt Jr. and his Harley at the motorcycle rally. Notice this guy."

He used his cursor, which was a little arrow after all, to point at someone standing in front of Matt's bike. With another series of clicks he zoomed in on the figure, which quickly started to lose its definition. Randall fiddled with the clarity and contrast, then asked us to stand and move about ten feet away from the computer screen.

"Sometimes it's better to move back than to zoom in," he said. "Who do you see?"

We were all quiet as we stared at the screen.

"I have no idea," said Harry.

"I do," I said.

"I knew you would," said Randall.

"Who, who?" asked Harry.

Randall went back to the keyboard and brought up the photo of the fund-raiser from Eugenie's memory card. Then he cropped out one of the attendees and superimposed the image next to that of the figure at the motorcycle rally, who was grinning and holding up a beer. Then he cropped out the ghostly image from Eugenie's photo of Delbert's that I found on her memory card and put it alongside the others. All three cropped portraits, side by side.

"Benson MacAvoy," said Harry.

"Voilà," said Randall.

"It could all be just an illusion," I said. "Those are pretty fuzzy images."

Randall looked up at me.

"What do you think?" he asked.

"I think it's Benson MacAvoy and that it's inadmissible in county and state court, much less federal court, but who cares. Randall, you are indeed a samurai of the digital image."

"Thank you," he said, in that neutral, Native American way he had.

"Bastard lied to me," I said. "Implied he'd only known Eugenie as an adult, as the pilot of his air taxi. But here he is with Matt Jr., then Eugenie, when they were all basically kids."

Randall rose up from his chair. Though several inches shorter than Harry, he was still like a redwood tree standing next to me.

"Who wants Jolt and who's for Mountain Dew?" he said.

I climbed into his chair and took control of the mouse while he and Harry concocted some sort of evil brew out of available materials. I clicked around the thumbnails until I came to the original *Chronicle* photograph of the motorcycle rally from which Randall had extracted Matt Jr.'s and Benson's images. I created the little cropping box around the two of them, then expanded it to include a few more people standing by. I moved this image into a separate window, opened it up, and made it a little bigger. Then I did as Randall had instructed before. I stood up and moved away from the screen. Now well versed in the visual tricks of highly pixilated images, I saw him immediately, standing right behind Benson.

My brother, Billy O'Dwyer, also grinning and holding up a beer.

18

Joe Sullivan left a message on my office voice mail that they'd tracked down the sender of the death threat, and to call back as soon as I could. *There* was a dilemma. The cops rarely like you discovering things before they do. This is a lesson I never stop learning. On the other hand, they hate wasting time even more.

I decided to just face the music and call.

"It's the Great Khan, but you probably already know this," said Sullivan. "Assuming Randall Dodge is as good as he's supposed to be."

"He is."

"Does he have a close working relationship with the plainclothes division of the Nassau County seventh police precinct?"

"I don't believe he does."

"Then he's not as good as we are," said Sullivan.

"By that criteria, I'm in full agreement."

"You should be. My contacts told me they've been watching those skin joints for months, rotating undercover people through on a regular basis. There's all kinds of illegal shit going down there. And they know your boy Khan."

"Do they know who jumped on his open e-mail?"

"No. But now they're watching. No big deal. They're there anyway, and it's a good tip for them. If your perp could do it, so could anybody. We also passed word along to the feds to monitor the Khan's messages, but don't hold your breath on that one."

It was still morning, plenty of time to dash over to Massapequa. I printed out a map and checked the Khan's blog, which looked like any other blog, better than most, actually. The content was in English, with full sentences and decent spelling and punctuation, but it made no sense at all. Brilliantly so, because it read rather well.

Best of all, it had a picture of the Great Khan, who looked for all the world like a guy whose real name was Sid Kronenberg. I printed out that page as well, and the contact pages with maps of the two homeless shelters I could identify in Massapequa.

Technically, Long Island is bracketed by the Hamptons at one end and Brooklyn/Queens at the other. Although, if you live here, it's the part in the middle that you think of as the essential place, the one you mean when you say Long Island. It's Western Suffolk and Nassau Counties. This is the tractless land of single-family houses arranged in grids or along gentle curves that can easily snare the unwary, strip development so brilliantly lit you can see it from Jupiter, expressways and parkways, muscle shirts, comedic accents (only to those who live somewhere else), and some remarkably creative applications of ostentatious jewelry, by men and women alike.

Because you have to drive through acres of pine barrens that stand like a barrier reef between the Hamptons and the rest of Long Island, it's easy to feel like we live on our own island, which reinforces the sense of otherness as we drive west, crossing over to the mainland, an alien place.

Massapequa stood near the center of this universe. I'd been there a few times to depose witnesses for Burton's criminal cases, so I had a vague sense of how to get around. Since I'd navigated most of my life with a vague sense, I thought this shouldn't pose much of a problem. And, after all, I had a map and directions.

The worst part about getting lost, which I did anyway, was having to ask people on the street how to get to the Hot Spot. When I was pushed to describe the place, things got worse.

"Sure, sugar, now I know what you're talking about. You a dancer?"

This caused me to dispense a number of business cards, which I hoped wouldn't yield too much in the way of fresh trade.

As Randall had described, the Hot Spot was flanked on either side by a strip club and a porn shop, called, respectively, Salutations and The Gentleman's Place. I wondered if the gentlemen who frequented that place favored pipes, ascots, and the London *Times,* as one would assume from the name. "Salutations" I thought was self-explanatory. Hello, you patsy, you degenerate, you pathetic sexist lonely heart.

A single parking lot served the complex. I got as close as I could to the Hot Spot, but still had to walk past a corner of the club where some of the girls were leaning on a metal rail smoking cigarettes. They all wore long coats that on a different type of professional you'd think were out of season. I waved as I walked by, and they all waved back, one saying, "Hi, doll."

Compared to the inside of the Hot Spot, Randall's place was lit by Klieg lights. It took a while for my eyes to adjust well enough to locate the operator, who sat behind a counter just to the right of the door. I stumbled over to him and introduced myself.

"I'm looking for one of your regular customers. Sid Kronenberg, also known as–"

"The Khanster. No question. Here all the time. When he's not aligning the magnetic fields that contain the Universal Force."

As my pupils stretched to their maximum diameter, I was able to make out some of the guy's features, not happily. His face was a fleshy oval–high forehead, little nose, and no chin, a deficiency exaggerated by a penciled-on moustache and goatee. His voice came out through his nose, and was about three registers higher than Randall's, which explained why Randall had thought he was talking to a kid over the phone.

"Is he here now?"

"Are you from Social Services?" he asked.

"Not exactly."

"Tell them to get that son of a bitch into a bathtub. I don't mind the rants, but the stink is over the line."

"I will. Where do you think I can find him?"

I saw a shadowy shrug.

"No idea. Under a bridge somewhere, I guess. Or picking up bottles and cans. Gotta get the money somewhere for the online time."

"Does he have a favorite computer?" I asked, peering blindly into the room.

"Number three if he can get it."

He flicked on a tiny LED flashlight that lit up the number three on what I took to be the outside of a cubicle.

"Do other patrons ask for number two or number four whenever Sid's in three?" I asked.

"That's what everybody wants to know," he said.

"Everybody?"

"First some guy on the phone who was all over the Khan thing, then a couple cops from the seventh precinct who made me turn on the lights so they could do whatever nonsense they wanted to do back there. Freaked the hell out of the customers."

"So do they? Ask to sit next to Sid?"

"Not to my knowledge. Or if it happens, I don't remember the details," he said, instinctively following the advice I'd given Ross and Sullivan.

"Anyone in three now?"

"Nope."

"Mind if I take a look?"

"Knock yourself out. Take this," he said, handing me the flashlight, which turned out to be built into a pen. I shot it in the same general direction, and felt my way in the dark. At this point, I could see the outer walls of the room, reflecting the glow of computer screens, which helped establish my bearings. I reached number three and squeezed between it and number two and sat down in front of the screen. I looked around the near pitch black and thought, This is a ridiculous waste of time. But then I thought, This is also where the person who threatened me launched his poison. Who was likely the same person who attacked me, or at least was in cahoots with him. So it might have been a waste of time, but it wasn't ridiculous.

Right then a guy next to me moaned and said, "Oh, yeah," prompting me to work my way back to the front door. I handed over the mini-flashlight.

"Why's the Khan so popular all of a sudden?" the guy asked. "He's not like the Unabomber or some shit, is he?"

"If you see him, please give him my card. I just want to talk to him."

The guy acted like he could read the card in that light. Maybe he could. Maybe he'd already evolved the ability to perceive lettering in the dark, sensing the words through his fingertips.

"That's cop speak for 'The Khan knows something or did something he shouldn't have done,' " said the guy. "Any lame ass would know that."

"Mr. Kronenberg is actually more the victim in this case, in a manner of speaking. So yes, he might know something that would be helpful. Can you give him my card?"

"Sure. If you promise me you'll hose him down. With Clorox."

"I'll do my best."

Back outside, I was grateful to be out in the light, nearly blinded though I was. A man in a business suit brushed past me on his way in, caught between averting his face and looking at what sort of woman would be a Hot Spot customer. A frustrated woman, as it turned out, but not for reasons he might have imagined.

It took another tortured effort to find Hope Haven, one of two homeless men's shelters on my list, in terms of time spent wandering the streets of Massapequa, though not so much in asking directions. Everyone probably assumed I was Social Services, and I let them.

The guy manning this counter also had a goatee, but what a difference a chin makes. The goatee was black, and the man was tall, trim, and hard as a hickory branch. I could see this from his arms, exposed by his black T-shirt and covered in prison tats. On his head was a thin, black knit cap entirely disguising what was underneath. His handshake was a knucklebuster, not unlike Benson MacAvoy's.

"I'm looking for the Great Khan," I told him. "I'm a representative of the Universal Force, and we're concerned that we haven't heard from him in a few days."

"He'll be relieved," he said, in a coarse but calm voice. "It's not easy being the only archangel in North America. Sometimes you feel so alone."

"What're your special powers?" I asked.

"Seeing through the transparent contrivances of law enforcement," he said, using the tips of his fingers to tap out a rhythm on the surface of his desk.

We studied each other for a few moments. If we'd been a pair of dogs, tails would be wagging, but hackles slightly ruffled.

"You better polish up on the powers, friend," I said. "I work the other side." I handed him a card, the one that emphasized defense attorney.

"You Sid's lawyer?" he asked.

"It's not like that," I said. "It's a case I'm working on. Sid might know something that would help. Or he might not. That's all."

"The cops have been around saying the same thing."

"Nobody wants to hassle the guy. Trust is a hard thing to convey in just a few minutes, isn't it?" I added, suddenly struck by how true that was. I'd lied, or at least undersold the truth, so often that it got easy to believe any means were okay if the ends were pure. Yet for the people being lied to, does that really make a difference?

"It is," he said.

So I abandoned all technique and simply told him the truth, that someone had become aware that Sid frequently walked away from his computer while he was on his e-mail, and had jumped on that opportunity to create a new address on Sid's account so he could write a death threat. To me.

"That's it?" he asked.

"In a nutshell. Your local cops are on it because my local cops are trying to look after me, because even though we're usually on opposite sides of the contest, they like me, I think, sort of. Or they're operating under the principle that she might be a pain in the ass, but she's our pain in the ass."

The guy was wavering, so I sat on the edge of his desk and took a pen out of his shirt pocket. I used it to write in the margins of the official-looking form he'd been filling out: "A little trust won't kill you. Might even do you some good."

"Have we met?" he asked.

"I don't think so."

"You're acting like we have."

I stood up from the desk.

"You're right. I'm being presumptuous. And impetuous, which is a problem of mine. I'm working on it in my spare time. Meanwhile, I'd really like to have a sit-down with Sid Kronenberg. You can be there if you want. In fact, I'd prefer you were. For Sid's sake as well as mine."

The guy stuck out his hand.

"Marshall," he said.

"Jackie."

"Come with me."

I followed him out the back door of the storefront office to a small parking lot, where I got into his rusty GMC pickup with barely a hesitation. He said I could pick whatever I wanted on the radio, but I opted for nothing. The truck smelled floral; the exact type, a florist could have probably deciphered, but I hadn't a clue. So I asked.

"My sister uses the truck to bring lavender out from the North Fork," he said. "I don't know what she does with it after that, but I do like the meat loaf and gravy dinners she gives me in return."

"Where did you do your time?" I asked.

"Sanger first round. Hungerford second. About a nickel each. For the record, I was falsely accused on both occasions. But I did my civic duty and served my sentences without complaint."

"Do you know Matt Birkson?"

"I thought this was about Sid Kronenberg."

"It is. Just curious," I said.

"You might be curious, but not just. Yes. I know Matt. Checking my bona fides? Everybody knows Matt."

"Ever meet his kids?"

He looked at me with a strangely sympathetic look.

"You talking about little Matty? Man, that's a long time ago. Ball of fire, that kid. Only time I saw the old man soften up, the time I said he had a fine-looking boy. Put his arm around the kid and nearly smiled. Kid had the look of trouble in his eyes, despite all that. I remember it clear as a bell."

"What about the girl, Eugenie?" I asked.

He shook his head.

"Heard she had the same devil in her, but never had the pleasure."

"So what's the deal with Sid. Mental illness–wise."

"Schizophrenia. Pretty full blown. Has trouble separating reality from delusion, though he's pretty well organized even in that state. The Great Khan thing is pretty well developed, loopy though it is. I think there's also an underlay of bipolar disorder, mostly manifest in the manic state, though I've seen him dive into the dumps."

"You a shrink?" I asked.

"No, just thoroughly shrunk. And I do a little reading."

"Okay, so what can I expect?"

"How do you feel about bodily odors?"

I had an idea where he was going with that, but didn't fully appreciate the implications until we pulled into a little parking area next to a big pond, ostensibly a public recreation area but apparently co-opted by a ragged tent city–if a half dozen tents made of blue tarps, plywood, and corrugated sheets of fiberglass constituted a city. It looked like an active place–women hanging up laundry, or huddled in conversation, kids chasing one another with plastic bats and grubbing around in the dirt with happy-looking dogs, and men sitting together in beach chairs under the one shade tree, smoking and drinking beer out of an ice chest.

Sid's tent was off by itself, hard up against the tree line. It was an elaborate-looking thing, with triangular panels that I thought looked like a geodesic dome until I realized it was, in fact, a geodesic dome. The external frame was made of black anodized pipes, within which was stretched a silver material that was either plastic or fabric or a combination of the two. It gleamed in the sun. Around the dome was nothing but the gravel of the parking lot, scrub grass, and leaves, seemingly undisturbed as if an orbiting spacecraft had dropped the dome into place to provide a comfortable habitat for its envoy to the human race. Maybe one had.

Marshall stopped me when we were still about twenty feet away.

"Yo, Khan. You home?" he called.

Nothing happened, so he called again.

"Sid, it's me. Marshall. You got company."

A five-foot, two-inch guy in white boxers and undershirt hopped out of the dome like he'd been ejected by some mechanical device. He looked a little bewildered, as you would be too had this happened to you. He was pale and thin, with a head far too big for his body. His face, though filled with confusion, bordered on handsome, with a high forehead, a nice nose, and Paul Newman's blue eyes. I guessed his age at a bit over forty, or a bit less than that, but well worn.

"Sid, over here," said Marshall. "There's a lady who wants to talk to you."

"Lady?" said Sid, trying to focus on us. "That can't be bad. How do I look?"

"You need to put on a pair of pants and a shirt," said Marshall. "Shoes, too, so you don't cut your feet."

"So, formal is it? Be right back."

Even at twenty feet, I began to realize how Sid had earned his olfactory reputation.

"We're not meeting with him inside that tent, are we?" I asked Marshall.

He grinned.

"Squeamish are we?"

"Isn't that a park bench over there?" I asked, pointing toward the little beach that served the pond.

"Let's see what he says."

"Cool digs, anyway," I said.

"Sid's a physicist when he isn't a schizophrenic. He made that thing himself. I have no idea how. It just sort of grew there over time. He's a sweet guy. Not happy that the Universal Force picked him to be the Great Khan. He told me he'd much rather search for the Higgs boson or rot on the couch watching TV."

"He's got a TV in there?"

"Satellite."

Sid came out wearing a suit jacket, a pair of floral surfer baggies, and penny loafers. It looked good on him. He'd combed his hair back and was smoking a cigarette in a cigarette holder held between his teeth FDR-style. We shook hands. His smell was impressive, and not all bad, just stunningly strong. I suspected not all the ingredients were natural.

"Ms. Swaitkowski's an attorney," said Marshall. "She thinks you might be able to help her defend one of her clients."

Sid took the cigarette out of his mouth and held the tip of the holder an inch away from his lips.

"Lawyers come in two sizes," he said. "Evil and eviler. Which are you?"

"Neither," I said. "I'm a good lawyer. Good at craft and good in heart."

"A third size? Who knew?"

"Let's go over here and talk," I said, guiding him toward the park bench. "Love your dome, by the way."

"Fuller was a bit of a dick, if you want my opinion. Too fuller of himself, I like to say. Didn't even invent the damn thing, but took all the credit. Happens all the time. When you look at the great achievements of mankind, the guy who makes all the money isn't the one who comes up with the idea. Brunelleschi stole the Pantheon to make the Duomo, James Watt ripped off everybody in sight, Edison stole the movies, Ford stole the assembly line, Gates stole DOS, Jobs stole the GUI. They're all a bunch of thieves. Clever, though. You have to give 'em that. What have you stolen?"

"My lover's heart."

Sid winced.

"Oh, God, I hate that sentimental claptrap. Tell me the truth."

We reached the park bench and he sat down. I noticed the cigarette in his holder had gone out, so I lit it with a lighter.

"I steal people's willingness to help me to serve my own ends," I said, "like I'm trying to do with you. I'm hoping you can tell me something of immense value to me, without my giving back anything in return. Except my gratitude and respect."

"If you give me that, then it's not stealing," he said. "Technically."

Marshall had been standing back through all this, but once Sid was thoroughly settled on the park bench, he leaned in and looked closely into Sid's face. Sid sat immobile while he did this.

"In some places you can be ordered to take your meds," Marshall said to Sid.

"Meds schmeds. In some places they cut off your balls for spitting in the street. What is this, Nazi-pequa? What's your stake in this, doll?" he asked me. "You Social Services? Here for an assessment?" He broke that last word into each of its syllabic parts.

"No. I'm here to protect your privacy."

That took him a bit aback.

"Whoa, that's totally freaky. A government agency spends a billion dollars to send a babe out into the field to protect the privacy of a homeless mental patient who could care less whether he wears a veil or pulls his pecker out in Times Square."

I put my hand on his shoulder.

"First off, call me a babe again and I'll break your nose," I said, waiting a moment for that to sink in. "We talked about respect. This is what I get or your life as you know it disappears. Secondly, the government doesn't care about you. As a private citizen and legal defense attorney, I do. And if you want to pull out your pecker in Times Square, go ahead. Be good for the tourist trade."

As I spoke, Marshall started looking very unhappy, but settled down as he realized where I was going.

"Got it," said Sid, putting his hands in his lap and gently rocking back and forward. Marshall eased in closer, in what I took to be an involuntary act of compassion.

"You okay?" he asked Sid.

"I'm fa-bu-lous," he said, stretching the word to its limits.

"You like to go to the Hot Spot," I said. "The Internet café."

"I like to go online. That's the only place where they take cash.

Though I'm working on getting wireless at the pond. If I could get my pond mates to pitch in. They don't seem to care."

"Did you know you left your computer before signing out and somebody used your e-mail address to send a message?" I asked.

"That bastard Khan," he said. "I knew it."

"Has he done this before?" I asked. I noticed Marshall looking at me with disappointment.

"Done this before?" Sid half yelled. "The son of a bitch does it all the time. You don't think I'm in this situation voluntarily, do you? Is he here?" he said to Marshall.

Marshall shook his head. "I don't think so."

"Bastard."

"Do you think someone might have finished up the Khan's Internet session?" I asked.

"Oh sure, and suffer certain annihilation? Don't be ridiculous. The Khan's a bit of a dickhead, but he tolerates rip-off artists none too gladly."

"So you can't think how this could have happened?" I asked.

While he thought about that, he snapped his head side to side, as if trying to catch someone in the act.

"Might've been the pranksters," said Sid.

"The pranksters?"

"Oscar Wilde, Jacques Cousteau, and Casper the Friendly Ghost. Them's the pranksters. As if I don't know what they're up to. You a prankster?" he asked me. "Little Orphan Annie. With potatoes," he added, gesturing with the international sign for prominent breasts. I would have smacked him, but his tone of voice saved him; the description was purely informational, or so he made me believe.

"You'll have to forgive me, Sid, but I don't know what sort of pranks you're talking about," I said. "I'm not as enlightened as you."

"Don't try to manipulate me," he said. "I get that kind of crap all the time from highly trained psychiatric professionals."

One of the more enduring myths is that it's easy to get a defendant off the hook by reason of insanity. In fact, it's very difficult, and rarely invoked. Guys like Sid are one of the reasons why. Psychiatrists can say all they want about a clinical diagnosis, but if a judge can't tell from minute to minute whether a guy is really crazy or faking it, the judge is going to opt for sane so the proceedings can take place in the realm of logic and reason, a realm legal people understand and can function within.

"It's not fair," I said.

"What's not?" he said.

"You know everything about the world I live in, but I know nothing of yours. Do you do that on purpose, keep it exclusive so you can have all the power?"

Sid wasn't sure about that one.

"Wow, whoa, left-hand turn, no turn signal."

"What's a prank? Just one," I said. "So I know what you mean. Come on."

Sid held his hands up in front of my face and wiggled his fingers.

"Invisible hands that come into my house and take things. Steal, pilfer, snatch, and purloin."

"What kinds of things?"

"Things. Thoughts. Ideas. Discoveries. They're in my brain and then they're taken, just like that. And the occasional thing of some use, like a toaster or a single sock. Like, what good is a single sock that doesn't match any other in the drawer?"

"That I get," I said. "I totally have the same problem."

"Where else could they go?" he asked. "Who but Oscar Wilde would have the sense of humor to do such a thing?"

"You're right about that," I said.

"You know Oscar?"

"What does Jacques Cousteau take?"

Sid struggled with that, frowning and shaking his head in rapid little bursts.

"Don't remember. I think there might've been some tropical fish I was supposed to take care of. Somebody might've found them dead. Can't say why. Pissed off Cousteau, though I can't help liking the guy. Must be the French accent."

"All your pranksters are likeable," I said.

"You like Casper? Don't know why. Nasty bugger. Scares me."

"So not so friendly."

"Ghostly. Got that part down. Spooks me the fuck out."

I looked at Marshall, who shrugged, sympathy for both of us written on his face.

"Who do you think finished your session, Sid?" I asked. "Which one of the pranksters?"

He waved his hands in my face again, then abruptly stopped and pointed at me with his two index fingers.

"The one with the knife, if you really must know."

"One of the pranksters threatened you with a knife?" I asked.

"Commandeered the keyboard. Had a sharp-looking sticker. I think imported. Probably German. I wouldn't put it past them."

"Which one?" Marshall asked, surprising me that he was still tracking the conversation.

Sid put his two fists up against his forehead and made a growly sound.

"Which one? Which one indeed," he said. "Could have been any of them." He took away his fists and looked at me. "Could have been you."

"It wasn't me. I'm the one who got the e-mail. Even Einstein wouldn't let a person be in two places at once," I said.

"Even? Especially Einstein," he almost yelled at me. "Hated all that mumbo-jumbo quantum phantasmagoria. You're talking non-locality, and that was Einstein's biggest bugaboo, though unfortunately, some wise guys proved it a genuine phenomenon. Or so some think; I'm not convinced. I punch you in the nose in Massapequa and you feel it instantaneously while arm-wrestling Martians over shots and beers.

That's the idea, though I still don't buy it. Hello, speed of light? It's not just two hundred and eighty-two thousand miles a second, it's the law. Can't be done. Makes no sense to you? That's good, because it makes no sense to me, either, and I'm a theoretical physicist, though I've done the equations that unfortunately prove non-locality, as do a few important experiments that nobody knows about even though they could provide the foundation for interstellar space exploration and maybe win George Lucas the Oscar he deserves, if not the Nobel Prize, but will probably never get for reasons you'll have to torture out of me, if you care and have the time and proper equipment."

"So you really don't remember? Or you're just afraid to say?" I asked, as gently as I could.

Sid whipped his head over to look at me.

"Fear is a very useful emotion," he said. "We evolved it to keep from getting devoured by saber-toothed tigers or setting ourselves on fire. You try living on the streets for just one day, then tell me whether a healthy sense of fear is a good thing or not."

"Why be afraid to tell me who commandeered your computer? That can't hurt you. In fact, it'll remove a proven threat. You can't lose."

"When did we meet? How many minutes ago? How long have I dealt with the pranksters?"

He was right. As usual, I was running on my own frantic schedule, not a regular person's, or a paranoid schizophrenic's for that matter.

I gave him a card with my e-mail address and office and cell phone numbers.

"You're right. When you're ready, give me a call. I appreciate anything you can tell me. Or not."

He looked at the card, then back at me with gratitude.

"Haven't had anybody's card in a while. Pretty cool. I'll take care of it." He patted the shirt pocket into which he'd stuffed the card. "Safe with me."

"Don't worry about that, just tell me anything you remember. It's important."

We left him at the picnic table, and were halfway to the car when he called us back. Marshall stayed put and I walked back.

"What's up?" I asked.

Sid looked up at me from where he sat at the picnic table, my card back in his hand.

"I'm afraid," he said. "I'm afraid all the time. It's an awful way to live."

"I wish I could help you, Sid, but I'm a lawyer, not a psychiatrist. I think Marshall over there really cares about you. Give him the word, and he'll be right there."

Sid waved me closer.

"That's not Marshall," he said.

"Really."

He shook his head.

"That's Wild Bill Hickok, desperado."

"But he's on your side."

"Oh, absolutely. But you don't understand. No one can defy the Khan. He's the swingin' dick on campus. The big enchilada. The ultimate boss, no offense to Mr. Springsteen."

"Sorry," I said. "It must be a terrible thing for you."

He nodded in vigorous agreement, so much so that I thought he'd pitch forward off the bench seat.

"Casper reports directly to the Khan. He's like the Khan's messenger boy. You can't hide anything from that guy. One word out of me, and zap, I'm a dead man. You understand?"

"Not exactly, but I sympathize. You're not gonna get into trouble because of me."

"It's a terrible way to live," he said. "Having people talking to you inside your brain. Just the regular me is bad enough."

"That I understand, Mr. Kronenberg. I truly do."

That seemed to satisfy him, thin as my reassurance was. I sat with him for a bit on the bench, and even found it in myself to pat his shoulder, which was all bone and flabby flesh. He was quiet for a while, but then started talking to himself, and though I might have learned something from the conversation, I left, feeling it was rude to sit there and eavesdrop.

On the way back to my car, Marshall asked if I'd learned anything. A little bit, I told him, just enough to be worried about Sid.

"The illness isn't him. It's just something he has," said Marshall.

"That's not what I'm worried about," I said. "He knows something, and the wrong people know he knows. He didn't just wander away from his computer. He was forced. What're the chances of getting him off the streets and into a safe place?"

"Close to zero. And even if we could, he'd really hate it."

I know thoughts originate in the mind, but we all know some are first detected in the area around the heart. I can identify one of those heartfelt thoughts. It's a form of apprehension, spawned by what seems to be the approach of an intractable problem. My subconscious, which is frequently in direct contention with those cardiological impulses, has worked out all the possibilities, run the if/then scenarios, and decided on the low probability of a positive outcome, no matter what I try to do.

I hate that feeling, mostly because it can be a precursor to something even worse. Self-doubt, maybe, or defeatism. Ugly parts of me that crouch in the corners like Sid's demons, conspiring and cajoling, and striving to take command over those other, better parts.

I took out my cell phone and called Joe Sullivan.

"How good a relationship do you have with the seventh precinct?" I asked when he picked up the phone.

"Good. Twenty years working cross-island cases together."

"They need to bust the Great Khan," I said.

"Not gonna happen," said Marshall, shaking his head. I cupped my hand over the phone.

"If anything happens to him, I won't be the only one with a very bad conscience."

Marshall still looked unhappy, but he let me urge Sullivan to help get Sid off the streets. Sullivan gave in after minimum resistance, which was more reflex than genuine opposition. I knew how hard it was from a legal standpoint to impose protective custody, especially when the protected is unwilling. And from experience, these were the people most in need of protection.

"I can have Alicia Brimbeck represent him," I told Sullivan. "That'll go a long way with the judge."

It didn't go that far with Marshall, but he seemed willing to give up the fight. Maybe because I suggested Sid could move in with him, if that made him feel better.

"You could get the Universal Force to do the dishes."

By the time I was in my car and on the way back to the East End, Sullivan had called me to say it was all arranged. He said he'd cashed in a load of chips, implying that I was doing the same. I didn't care. I just drove along the highway, letting a little wind through the driver's side window and feeling my heart loosen that traitorous grip.

19

It surprises me that I don't travel very often, given how much I love to fly. I can understand why people are afraid of flying, but the first time I took off from JFK and felt those gigantic jet engines pinning me to my seat, and, as we conquered gravity, saw a detailed miniature of Manhattan laid out beneath me, I almost swooned from the excitement.

The subsequent month in France was fine, but every day I eagerly awaited liftoff from De Gaulle.

So when I got the e-mail from Bedard, Vermont, my heart soared in more ways than one.

> Attorney Swaitkowski:
>
> I am honored that you chose me to assist you in the pursuit of the information you are seeking. I have done my utmost to be worthy of your trust and have diligently investigated with thoroughness and energy. Thus, it is with considerable pleasure and pride that I report success.
>
> I have found your cabin.
>
> Sincerely,
>
> Rajesh

I wrote him back:

Rajesh:

You're the man. I'm coming up tomorrow. Expect an uptick in sales at the Indian Trading Post.

Thanks and best wishes,

Jackie

I called Ralph Toomey at the East Hampton Airport who put me in touch with Claude James, who not only ran his own air taxi business, but had been a good friend of Eugenie's. I went through the reservation process, which amounted to calling Claude on his cell phone and getting directions to his hangar, which was two doors down from the Conklins'.

That's where the similarity ended. Where Ed's hangar was a dark, oily cave, Claude's was like an auto showroom, bright and clean, with a painted floor and all the tools and equipment stored in drawers behind red cabinet doors. His Piper Saratoga dominated the middle of the room, like a gleaming chrome, blue, and white–painted piece of performance art. Claude gleamed as well, or at least his teeth did when he smiled and stuck out his hand.

I knew he had an accent from the phone call, but I realized which kind when he said, "Allo, mademoiselle. So we go to Canada?"

"Not all the way. Almost," I said to him in French.

"*Très bien.*"

Claude was short and broad all over–broad torso, big hands, and a wide, flat nose. A former pilot for Air Canada, he wore a flight jacket, not unlike the phony one I was wearing, and blue jeans over thick legs. He'd grown up in Montreal, but in his early thirties moved away, seduced by a few hundred layovers in New York. Subsequently downsized (maybe that's why he looked like someone had squashed a taller, thinner version of himself), he bought the Piper and moved to the East End.

I learned all this before we took off, his loquaciousness further contrasting with the laconic Ed Conklin. I made him switch to English partway through the story. Though I loved the way he spoke, the conversation was too involved for my Parisian French to follow his Canadian accent and vocabulary.

He let me sit in the copilot's seat while he used a lawn tractor to tow the Piper out of the hangar. The interior of the aircraft was just as clean and beautifully maintained as the exterior. The only distraction being the not-so-subtle smell of Gauloises, which always reminded me, in an oddly pleasant way, of horse shit. And even more pleasantly of dark wood and polished granite, *café noir,* and the steamy squeal of espresso machines.

I sat quietly while Claude flicked switches and turned dials on the instrument panel, watched the propellers spin up to the appropriate RPMs, and radioed on 122.7 that we were about to take off. Two other pilots in the vicinity rogered that, and after a quick taxi over to the runway, we were airborne.

This was maybe my third ride in a small prop, and again I kicked myself for not doing it more. I loved the way it swung up into the air, the dips and surges as we climbed, and the tight banking as he aimed the nose at Northern New England.

"Yippee," I said.

"You enjoying this?"

"Immensely."

"Good for me. Much better than the white-knucklers. I'm always afraid they don't get to the little bag in time."

It was even more fun to make out familiar landmarks on the South Fork and Shelter Island than to see the Empire State Building. The villages looked smaller than they should have in relation to the open and wooded terrain, and the bays looked bigger. White powerboats moved below us, their wakes drawing a white V on the calm surface. The sailboats threw far less of a wake, but their sails were luminous and elegantly tipped toward the east. Moments later we were crossing the vineyards of the North Fork and zinging out over Long Island Sound, which glistened in pale blue, like Webster Ig's eyes, reflecting the early morning sun.

"If I'd known about this earlier I might have skipped law school," I said. "I could have been the other notorious lady pilot of the Hamptons."

"Did you know Eugenie?" he asked.

"Unfortunately, no."

I told him I was the last person she saw, skipping gingerly over the details, which seemed appropriate given our current disposition. I also told him we were heading up to Burlington as part of an investigation into her crash. I apologized for not telling him more, but like everyone in the world, he didn't think I would, or necessarily should. I asked him to be accurate with his flight logs, but to keep our ultimate destination to himself.

"Consider it done. Anything to help the cause. I miss that nutty woman."

"You liked her."

"Oh, yes. I like anyone that cheerful. And a very good pilot. She flew that Cessna like an extension of her own body."

"Do you know anyone who didn't like her?" I asked.

He shook his head.

"Not among the pilots or ground people. I didn't know her other friends and acquaintances. Both Ed and her father had been in scrapes with the law, but I think a long time ago, yes?"

"Yes."

The contours of the Connecticut shoreline began to look like more than hazy gray lumps as we approached. The first identifiable structures were power stations, one to the west in New Haven, and the nuclear plant well to the east, near New London. We went between, over a lighthouse at the head of the Connecticut River, which we followed all the way to Hartford, where Claude veered to the east to stay clear of air traffic around Bradley Field, then readjusted our course to head straight for Burlington.

"Ever been to Three Creeks Field?" I asked him.

"No. But I've been to smaller and bumpier in tighter spaces. It looks like a nice little facility."

I was torn between grilling him more about Eugenie and just staring at the terrain below, which I was encouraged to see nearly completely covered in trees. I knew there were buildings down there as well, but it's astonishing how much of New England is forest. And not always so. It was nearly stripped bare for farming in the eighteenth century. I also loved to see the stone walls from that altitude, which in April were still fairly evident, betraying the fields, village streets, and foundations of an earlier time, back before the settlers knew America actually had some very rich soil to the west that you could farm without the pleasure of chopping down trees or digging up tons of stumps and boulders.

"Did you know any of Eugenie's customers?" I asked him.

"No. Names of customers is one thing we pilots don't eagerly share."

"How about Benson MacAvoy? He was a regular of hers."

"Not had the privilege."

A little short of two hours after leaving East Hampton, Claude pointed down at Three Creeks, which looked like someone had snipped off a piece of two-lane highway and dropped it into the middle of a big lawn. He circled a few times, then dusted off the bottom of the Saratoga with the tops of the encircling pine trees and set the plane down with hardly a tremor.

"*Bravo, capitaine,*" I said.

"*Merci beaucoup.*"

After the props stopped, we climbed out over the wings and I tried without success to use my cell phone, which explained the phone booth. I called Rajesh.

"Hello, sir. I'm here at the airfield," I said.

"And I am here at the Trading Post. I will be there in ten minutes."

While we waited, I educated Claude on the surrounding flora, in some cases using the Latin name, or what I thought I remembered it to be from Dr. Johnson's itemized description.

"Botany a hobby of yours?"

I shook my head.

"E-mailing."

Rajesh showed up in a tiny Toyota pickup truck, which made me wince. I owned one just like it that I'd inherited from Potato Pete, and like him, I managed to destroy it on Brick Kiln Road. The difference was mine wasn't an accident, and not my fault, and I lived to tell about. That's not why I winced. I imagined squeezing into the little passenger compartment with Claude and Rajesh and then suffering the charms of the little truck's suspension system as we drove over pitted dirt roads.

I was spared.

Rajesh jumped out of the truck and shook our hands. He was a tall guy with deep-set eyes and thick gray hair. He wore a black and yellow checked wool coat over a fire-engine-red flannel shirt, jeans, and hiking boots. I started the process of overthanking him, but he seemed more concerned about my sneakers and Claude's black shoes.

"How're you set for walking?" he asked. "It's not very far, but there are rocks."

"We're walking?" I asked, deeply relieved.

It turned out Claude's shoes were made to suit both boardroom and hiking trail, and my sneaks were more than up to the challenge. There were rocks, but the path we took was mostly dirt covered in leaves and the needles from the *Picea mariana.*

It was still morning, and the air was New England crisp and clear, which I noted to Claude.

"That's Québécois air you're referring to," said Claude. "We flew the whole way into a light but steady northwesterly breeze."

"You're awfully good to be doing this, Rajesh," I called ahead. "Can I call you Rajesh? I don't know if that's your first name or last."

"Please do," he said, looking back at me as we walked. "My last name you wouldn't be able to pronounce."

During our brief e-mail exchange, I'd told him I needed to find the cabin as part of an investigation into a fatal plane crash. I acknowledged the seemingly remote connection, and asked his forgiveness for not explaining further. He took it all remarkably in stride.

"And I like your shirt and jacket combo," I said. "It looks great."

"How else could I be your colorful native guide?"

I heard Claude chuckle, the way Frenchmen do, deep in his throat.

"How did you find this place?" I asked Rajesh, after we'd walked for a while.

"On the Internet."

"Get out of here."

"That is where I got the names of real estate agents in the area who sell or rent out cabins like this. Then I visit them and show them the picture. On the third try I hit pay dirt."

About ten minutes later, the trail lost its definition as we entered a crowded stand of hemlocks, which will notoriously kill off ground cover by creating a canopy light can barely penetrate. But through the dead lower branches it was easy to see the rear of the cabin where it stood next to a still pond.

We cleared the remaining distance in a few minutes. The three of us stood in a line and looked around.

"Was it a rental or a sale?" I asked.

"Rental."

"You don't happen to know the name of the renter?"

He reached in his front jeans pocket as he walked and pulled out a piece of paper, which he handed back to me. It was a Xerox copy of a real estate listing. Included was a black-and-white photo of the cabin, taken from a different angle but undeniably the same building. Someone, presumably Rajesh, had scribbled some notes and phone numbers in the margins. And a name.

Matthew Birkson Jr.

I sat down on the ground and stared at the paper in my hand. Claude asked me if I was all right, and I said I was just a little tired and needed a moment to rest. The two of them joined me on the ground, waiting for the next thing the crazy lady lawyer had in mind.

Whatever mind she had left.

I whispered the name Matthew Birkson Jr. over and over, as if that would tease the explanation out of my scattered thoughts.

"What the hell," I said out loud.

"Don't know, mademoiselle," said Claude. "You tell us."

I looked at them as if they were parties to every wild conjecture racing through my mind. They took it cheerfully, like Eugenie would probably do.

Then I stood up and walked over to the cabin. I looked in the window, waiting for my eyes to adjust to the change in light. All I could see was a bed and a chest of drawers. I moved to another window. More of the same. By then, Claude and Rajesh were there looking with me. We agreed that only bedrooms and probably a common bath occupied that part of the cabin. We went around to the front and repeated the process. To one side of the front door was a dining room. To the other, a seating area in front of a fireplace. Through partially drawn curtains, I could see a coffee table on which paperwork was stacked and some comfy-looking overstuffed chairs. That was about it. I knocked on the front door. Nothing. Then I tried the doorknob. Locked.

Moment of truth.

"Say, boys, why don't you take a little walk around the pond. Check out the wildflowers and compare notes on Montreal and Mumbai."

That confused them at first, understandably. So I did my best to explain.

"As a lawyer, I can advise you that if someone was, for example, going to break into a private dwelling without the authority of a warrant or the sanction of the local police, since she's been too busy to arrange all that, and you had no knowledge of this, you couldn't be held as an accomplice."

Then I did one of those exaggerated winks and shooed them off the front porch. They readily complied.

My friend Sam likes to think he isn't bragging when he tells me how he cracks locks with a bobby pin, a penlight, and tweezers pulled out of a Swiss Army knife. I could no sooner do that than fly to the moon. Instead I got a rock out of the woods and used it to break a window. A few moments later I was inside, after forcing my hands into a pair of surgical gloves I'd brought along in the faint hope of this very occasion.

The interior of the cabin was far more refined than the outside. Bordering on luxurious. The walls were Sheetrocked and painted, the trim a varnished hardwood, the floors dark-stained oak and the furnishings a type of Wild West chic favored by California billionaires and decorators in Telluride and Park City, Utah.

I found the kitchen and rifled through all the cabinets and drawers. Everything looked new and rarely used, and expensive. I knew this because everything in my kitchen was exactly the opposite. The oven was clean as a whistle, but the microwave showed a fair amount of splatter. The refrigerator held only individually wrapped slices of American cheese, half a quart of thoroughly decayed milk, pizza, and beer.

Men, I thought, as convinced as a tracker crouched over a pile of deer stool.

I checked the bedrooms and the first-floor bath, and found more of the same. Dirty shower, shaving cream, and the absence of face towels. Upstairs was nearly the same, though the shower had a bottle of expensive conditioner and a pink razor, another telltale. So, all boys downstairs, at least one girl on the second floor.

Back downstairs, I checked out the living room. I went right to the stack of paper on the coffee table. It was mostly printouts of PowerPoint presentations. Monotonous and jargon-filled pages of bullet points that made no sense to me whatsoever. But I persisted with one of them until it became clear that the presenters were describing a type of mini-surface-to-air missile that they claimed with barely restrained enthusiasm a child could carry in his school backpack and subsequently use to take down any low-flying aircraft in the dead of night.

I stuck the papers under my arm and searched the rest of the room, finding only a few cocktail glasses, one unwashed wineglass (with a lipstick smudge), and a stack of DVDs. So girl or girls were allowed on the first floor for social events.

There was a DVD player connected to a wide-screen TV, but no cable. Neither telephones nor computers, or even a place to plug them in. There was no basement, but I found a utility room that housed the HVAC and electrical panel. I'd put in my time as a real estate lawyer crawling around cobwebbed basements looking for proof of the mechanicals claimed in the listing, so I knew what a phone or cable hookup looked like. There weren't any.

I spent the rest of the time finding a screwdriver, some screws, and a piece of plywood I could attach to the outside of the windowpane I'd busted through. Then I went to find my international expeditionary force, which was sitting next to the pond, engaged in voluble commentary on the virtues of their respective homelands.

Both adroitly avoided noticing the stack of white paper clutched under my arm.

"Let's lose this joint," I said, which neither of them understood explicitly, but they got the inference.

A few hours later, after I'd salvaged the dubious opportunity to ride in the old pickup to the Indian Trading Post, where I bought a slightly oversized version of the black and yellow checked coat, we were on our way back to Long Island, stopping at Burlington International along the way to refuel.

"Did you get what you wanted?" Claude asked me once we were settled in.

"Sort of. Maybe I got more than I wanted. I can't tell."

"It sounds like you have a complicated life," he said. "I'm glad to be just the driver."

"Do you ever get lost up here in the sky? I can imagine you might, if you're innocently flying along and something throws you a curve."

He didn't answer right away, probably out of professional reserve.

"Every pilot has his or her moments. As when your eyes are telling you one thing and your instruments another. Or when you break out of a cloud and have no idea where the hell you are. But that doesn't happen very often these days, the technology is so good."

"So that's how I feel. Like I just broke out of a cloud and don't know where the hell I am," I said. "And no GPS."

We flew most of the way in silence, which must have been my fault, since Claude was such an effusive guy. I was trapped inside my head, wrangling facts, fears, and assumptions, none too successfully. Though I did have what Sam calls an operating theory. A logical construct that explains most, if not all, the factors on the table, even if it can't be proven empirically. Like blaming the loss of single socks on a prankster. Sid Kronenberg and I might buy it, but not an unbiased observer.

I was able to shake myself into consciousness as we crossed back over Long Island Sound and I saw the map of the East End drawn in beautiful greens and blues. I felt the weightless descent of the plane into East Hampton, where on landing I endured a tiny death, grieving over the fact that I hadn't flirted with the clouds like Eugenie Birkson, and a tiny celebration, since her death felt less a tragedy for having lived her life untethered by gravity or misbegotten dreams.

20

Back on the ground and safely in my office, I called Sam Acquillo on his cell phone.

"Aren't you glad you got one of these?" I asked when he answered.

"What?"

"Cell phone."

"I would be if people would stop calling," he said.

"I need company."

"Isn't that what Goodlander's for?"

"Not for this trip. He just looks intimidating. I need someone who actually is."

I told him I'd pick him up around dinnertime at his cottage, giving him time to get home, clean up, and feed Eddie. He didn't press me further about the assignment. He owed me a lot of favors. A few hundred, by rough estimate.

Sam often employs his three Adirondack chairs out on the breakwater above the pebble beach to drink with his girlfriend and dog, and one other guest, and watch the sunset over the Little Peconic Bay. I've spent both productive and entirely desultory hours out there, I thought as I approached, escorted to the shoreline by the bouncing, twirling mutt.

Sam's girlfriend, Amanda, was in her usual spot, turned slightly perpendicular to Sam so they could yak without straining their necks. Her ancestry was part Italian, which showed prominently in her deep olive complexion, which would have been her most striking feature if the rest of her hadn't been so striking. She was a little on the other side of forty, her face was clear and wrinkle-free, and her shape just shy of too thin. Her hair was a thick reddish brown, with crimson highlights and an excess of natural wave.

I didn't like her that much, and not because of how she looked. Though always polite, she didn't like me much either. Sam and I had never had the slightest romantic twinge for each other, which she knew, so it wasn't jealousy. It was something less easily defined, but components included suspicion and distrust, for me earned over years of observing her behavior. Sam, ordinarily the worst cynic at the party, didn't really trust her either, but he definitely loved her, so that was all he needed. Things were all or nothing with Sam, one of the least appealing aspects of his personality.

Though Amanda and I didn't like or trust each other, it never stopped us from having a pleasant time whenever we were thrust together.

"We've brought out wine for you," she said, hoisting a bottle out of an ice bucket, "though there's plenty of Sam's Absolut if you prefer."

"Wine's fine. Just one. I need to stay reasonably clearheaded."

"Sam told me you need to borrow him this evening. You will bring him back?"

"That's the plan," I said.

"Good. He's agreed to fix the latch on the cabinet above my stove. I can't go another day with crockery falling into the soufflé."

"I like a little ceramic in the soufflé," said Sam. "Gives you something to crunch on."

I was also depending on Sam being reasonably clearheaded, which he always seemed to be, no matter how much vodka he downed. I once asked him about that and he said, "Practice makes perfect."

"Tell that to your liver," I said.

"Already have. It's on board."

While I had my glass of wine we watched the sky light up in purply red and gold, which was reflected on the nearly still waters of the Little Peconic. I'd noticed that the best of the sunset, the finale, comes right after the sun dips completely below the horizon. That night was no exception. The show then gradually slid into denouement, the brilliance fading to a gentle glow. Sometimes I believe that's all the beauty God thinks we can take.

"Come on, Sam," I said. "Time to go. Thanks for the wine," I said to Amanda, who waved as if we were already halfway across the lawn.

I briefed Sam while we drove to Sag Harbor. I brought him up-to-date with what I'd learned, and gave him my hypothesis. I used that exact word, because that's the kind of word he liked to use.

"So we're going to his house?" Sam asked.

I pulled the printout from MapQuest off my dashboard and handed it to him.

"You navigate."

Sag Harbor is a densely packed old whaling town that people discovered about twenty years ago had more than its share of colonial charm, side by side with a certain artistic and bohemian attitude, disappointing the people who'd discovered twenty years before that it was also an unpretentious and affordable place to live in the Hamptons. No longer. Still loaded with charm, it had succumbed to the same tidal wave of urbanity and property inflation that had swept over the rest of the South Fork.

Just outside the village proper were bigger lots with bigger houses, a few on Sag Harbor Bay, a name that always seemed redundant to me. Benson MacAvoy owned one of those, just to the west before you crossed over a bridge and dropped into town. He also had a dock, he'd told me, with its very own seventy-foot Hinckley Sou'wester sloop, which might have cost about the same as the house.

Our timing was flawless. Just as we approached the head of his driveway he turned in front of us in a battered Mercedes station wagon. We followed him down the drive and up to a parking area paved with white pebbles. His house was classic modern, which sounds like an oxymoron, but people out here would likely know what I mean—houses designed in the 1950s and '60s to look like boxes so people living in them could feel superior to those stuck in the same old shingle-style colonials with big gables, deep eaves, handsome twelve-pitch roofs, and wraparound porches supported by ionic columns.

This was an enlarged version of the former, two stories with decks everywhere and a big slab of painted concrete that looked like Kubrick's 2001 monolith soaring above the boxes, presumably a chimney designed to serve multiple fireplaces.

Benson jumped out of his car and ran over to meet us.

"Hey, Jackie. Wassup? Who's your friend?" We got out of the Volvo and Sam walked around to shake hands. Benson said, "Benson MacAvoy, political adviser."

"Sam Acquillo. Carpenter."

"He's being modest," I said. "He also builds kitchen cabinets."

"Come on in."

We followed him through a flat-panel door and up a flight of stairs to a large open room that encompassed the kitchen, dining area, and living room, divided by the black slab, which in fact allowed for fireplaces facing several directions. The wall across the room was solid glass, not unlike the one in Benson's office, only there was a lot more of it. The view was better as well—Sag Harbor's town docks, marinas, the yacht club, and the mooring field directly outside, already filling up with boats for the season.

"Love going to work; love coming home," said Benson. "Bar's over there." He pointed to one end of the living room. "Help yourself while I shed the work duds." Sam complied without further prompting, pleased as punch to find a giant bottle of Grey Goose. I accepted a white wine with a single ice cube.

We soaked in the view until Benson reemerged wearing jeans, a Yale sweatshirt, and brown leather Top-Siders. He made himself a martini in the traditional glass, an approach I wanted to enjoy, though I always found it hard to take the first sip without feeling an icy rivulet stream down my forearm.

"What's the occasion?" he asked, waving us over to a set of squared-off, suede-covered couches that were surprisingly firm on the butt. "Not that I mind. Always good to see Jackie S. How did you find my house? Oh yeah, on the Internet. The end of privacy as we know it. Not that I don't take advantage myself when sniffing out political donors. I go on Google Earth and look for the biggest swimming pool, then cross-reference with the longest boat under registration and the frequency of outraged posts to the right blogs, and bingo. An invitation to personally impose on my candidate is in the mail."

"A search-and-impose operation," I said. "Sounds like what I spend half my life doing."

"So, Sam," said Benson, "are you friend or bodyguard?"

He said it with a smile, making a joke.

"Bodyguard," said Sam.

"So you're drinking on duty," he said, still in joke mode.

"It's in the contract."

Not sure where to go from there, he said to me, "Speaking of political donations, we're having an intimate get-together for you-know-who"—he held up a *Time* magazine lifted off the coffee table with one of our senators on the cover—"this weekend at you-know-who's house on Georgica Pond." He held up a copy of *People* magazine. "Would you like to come?"

"Who knows?" I said.

"Funny. No donation necessary. You'll be my date. Just supply the wit and good looks. For that I recommend what you were wearing at Eugenie's funeral."

"Can't do that," I said. "That's only for funerals."

"Now there's a waste."

"As for the date, I just got engaged to my boyfriend. Otherwise, I'd be all over it. Preening and grandiosity are my two favorite spectator sports."

"I'm not doing anything this weekend," said Sam.

"Too bad," said Benson, still trying to lock up my eyes. "But realize, never-say-never is my middle name."

"Names," said Sam. "They're your three middle names."

Benson gestured at Sam with his drink.

"So Jackie's not the only wit in the house. She brought along a supporting cast."

"Who's supporting whom?" said Sam.

"I was wondering why you said you didn't know Eugenie very well," I said, after sitting back on the hard couch and taking a sip of wine, "even though you've known her since you both were teenagers."

Benson's grin was truly a radiant and overpowering thing. When you had him in a room, even one this large, it felt like half room, half grin, so potent was its blinding glare. No wonder politicians and plutocrats paid so much to listen to his advice. The delivery alone was worth the price.

"Jackie, everybody who went to high school here in those days knew everybody else. There weren't that many of us. You assume it. I was one of the few whose fathers worked in the city. My mom wanted me to go to public school because she went to public school, even though her father could have bought all the private schools in town."

"You didn't just know her. You were good friends with her brother. And my brother, too. The three of you were, in your words, 'best buds.' None of which you thought worth sharing with me."

He bobbed his shoulders up and down and looked beseechingly around the room, as if petitioning an invisible audience.

"What, am I on *This Is Your Life*? We was kids." He said that last bit with a theatrical attempt at Jewish inflection. "I had some good friends. So the fuck what? They weren't my best buds, actually. I had some better buds. By the way, I like the played-down look, Jackie, but the outfit the other night? Much better." He used two hands to draw imaginary cleavage on his chest. "Don't tell Mr. Mountain," he added, looking at Sam.

"What's the cabin in Bedard for?" I asked.

Benson's grin flicked off.

"Bedard? Sounds like 'retard.' "

"It's a town in Vermont," I said.

"That explains it. Too much inbreeding up there."

"Why did Eugenie fly you up there?" I asked.

"She told you that? No, of course not. She's dead."

"She didn't tell me in words," I said. "But she told me. And it's admissible. That's legal talk, meaning I can prove it."

Benson kept up the bewildered, put-upon act.

"Prove what? What are we talking about here? This is nuts. Are you her adult supervisor?" he said to Sam. "What's this, inmates' night out? What's with you? Okay, it's the Inquisition. That's why you brought along the enforcer," he said, looking at Sam. "So you could intimidate me. Not happening."

"Not my intention," I said.

"You know where I got this scar?" said Benson, pointing at his lip and looking over at Sam, who said, "Badminton?"

"Middleweight intramural boxing champion, Yale. Actually happened when I slipped and slammed into the post. Took twenty stitches to sew her up."

Sam raised his hand without lifting his arm from the armrest.

"Light heavyweight contender, the Bronx and contiguous venues. Five years amateur, two professional. Don't even think about it."

Benson scowled, his political skills beginning to fray.

"So what's this all about, Jackie," he said, turning back to me. "Seriously, you're freaking me out."

"You first. Why didn't you tell me you knew Eugenie and her brother since high school? And why didn't you tell me you knew *my* brother? In any normal conversation, when people meet, these are the first things you bring up."

"I don't know. Who knows? Didn't seem important." Benson sat very still on his suede couch. "You need to tell me where you're going with this."

"To the FBI. I got 'em on speed dial," I said, holding up my cell phone. "Oh, and by the way," I said, flipping the phone open, "this little bugger keeps a record of every call, going back months. Date and time of day–or night, in this case. You weren't trying to get my phone number at that political event. You were sending what you thought was an untraceable signal. Just like you did at the Lavignes'. And I'll bet every other fund-raiser you've been to with Janie Wilson. Excellent ploy, sort of, since you're about to go down for it."

"For what?" he asked, his exasperation turning the word "what" into two syllables.

"Selling a corporation's proprietary technical information to another corporation," said Sam. "Few in law enforcement much care about that sort of thing usually, unless the information is thought to be vital to our national security. And then they care very much indeed."

"And you know this from making kitchen cabinets?" asked Benson.

"You'd be amazed," I said.

"You really think I'd do something like that? That is so bizarre," said Benson.

"You're a skill guy," I said. "You told me yourself. Sell to the highest bidder."

Benson took a sip of his martini, a trick made even more difficult by the slight tremor in his hand.

"If you actually believe all this blather, why am I talking to you and not the FBI?" he asked.

"Where is Matt Birkson Jr.?" I asked.

He used both hands to drum his fingers on the arms of his chair.

"Maybe you already know the answer to that and you're baiting me," he said. "You might be a lawyer, but I've been in politics my whole life. I know a sandbag when I see one about to drop on my head."

"You've got twenty-four hours to deliver Matt Jr."

I checked my wrist for dramatic emphasis, a gesture undermined somewhat by my not actually having a watch.

"Or what?" he asked.

"Twenty-four hours," I said.

I downed my wine, stood up, and gestured at Sam to do the same. Which he did, looking wistfully at his empty glass.

I led the way out of the house and over to my car. Sam lit a cigarette and handed it to me after we climbed aboard, then lit one for himself. I rolled down the windows and drove off.

"You implied that if he gave you what you wanted you wouldn't drop a dime on the industrial espionage," said Sam.

"I did. I lied. The Supreme Court has ruled that cops can lie their heads off in the course of an interrogation if the intention is to yield truthful testimony. I'm adopting that same privilege for myself. For naught, I'm sure, but I needed him to know I was on his ass. A little pressure can often squirt out some useful behavior."

"Like somebody killing you," he said, tactful as ever.

"What makes you think that?" I asked, slightly alarmed.

"Someone's already tried it; rape was just a bonus. If you're right about this guy, it could be him, or his agent. They'd likely ramp up the effort."

"Let him try. I'm ready."

"You should let me stay with you," said Sam.

"We've been over this already. Not gonna happen. Anyway, what good are you? Can't shoot for shit."

"Hate guns," he said.

"My point."

"Guns don't kill people. People with guns kill people."

"Not if you get there first."

I drove back to Oak Point, where I delivered Sam to Eddie and Amanda's considerable charms, then I went back to my office and fold-out couch, in the dark, like I'd sworn to myself I'd never do.

I eased into things by stopping at the Japanese restaurant and having another drink at the bar, a big-girl drink, not the watery white wine that Benson served. Makoto saw me and came over to say hello.

"Did you enjoy your visit with your old friend?" he asked.

"I did. Thanks."

He nodded in a half bow. I loved talking to Makoto, because so much of it involved those lovely little bows. It's pleasant to express respect for a person you actually respect, even knowing that's not the only reason you do it.

"Anytime. Happy to be your conference room," he said.

"I'll remember that. How're you at martial arts?"

"I can break an egg with one hand. Other than that, my ninety-eight-year-old mother would be a more effective fighter. Though you'd say she hardly looks ninety-two."

"One more of these, if you don't mind," I said, holding up the glass.

Before I went through the door leading up to my office, I took the Glock out of my purse. Then I put the purse strap over my head so I could hold the gun with two hands, the way you're trained to do. I went up the stairs and down the hall to my door. I partly wished one of the surveyors would come out so I could stuff the muzzle in his face, but instantly rejected the thought as unworthy and likely to screw up whatever good karma I had left. I punched in the alarm for my office door, opened it, and reached in to flick on the light, standing away from the door with the gun held next to my face, pointing at the ceiling.

Nothing happened, so I walked into the office with the Glock held straight out, finger inside the trigger guard. Nothing. I kicked the door closed and threw on the dead bolt. I pulled all the shades, then checked the bathroom and kitchenette, which were windowless, and the coat closet, my least favorite part. Nothing.

Still jittery, I rushed out of my clothes and into a sweat suit to allow for maximum freedom of movement, then spent an hour clearing a space into which I dragged my desk, so when I was on the computer I could face the door and have my back in a corner, away from both windows.

Then I flopped down onto the pull-out bed, in its upright and locked sofa position, and listened to my heart trying to thump its way out of my chest.

I can't do this much longer, I said to myself. I'll die of paranoia poisoning.

21

I felt the earth move all night. The same thing happens to me when I spend time on a sailboat. The random motion of the plane had transferred itself to some strange part of my mind that would replay the sensation for at least a day afterward.

I got up and put on my robe, sat down and turned on the computer. Then I got back up and made coffee so I'd have an excuse to light a cigarette. By then the computer had booted up and was ready for action.

I launched Randall's secret software and searched Matthew Birkson Jr. I got a birth notice from Southampton Hospital, June 10, 1960. Included were the parents, his weight, hand- and footprints. I continued the search, which yielded the usual things, like sports reports in local newspapers, and some less usual, like arrests for drunk and disorderly, speeding, and assault and battery. All raps he avoided doing time for by a hair's breadth, to the credit or discredit of my questionable profession.

I did the same for Eugenie Birkson, which added considerably to the stuff I'd already uncovered and downloaded. Then I did some cross-checking, going back to Matthew Birkson Jr. and looking up his Social Security number, something only Randall's software would be able to do. To my pleasant surprise, a scan of his application was in the file. I strained to read the blurred, handwritten information, though what I ultimately saw was clear enough. It was at the top of the form, after the request for the applicant's name.

Matthew Eugene Birkson Jr.

I skipped the shower, getting away with a splash of water on my face, brushed my teeth, and put on whatever clothes were within reach. I poured the rest of the coffee into a travel mug, slipped a small bag over my shoulder, and headed out.

When I was in the car I called Randall Dodge, waking him up.

"Oh, it's Jackie Swaitkowski," he said, his voice thick with exhaustion. "The person most responsible for this scourge of sleep deprivation."

I told him what I hoped he'd be able to do with his double-secret software, in purely theoretical terms, since as an officer of the court I could hardly ask someone to commit an illegal act.

"I'd do it myself, but I've never used that part of the application, and I can't afford the time to learn. And if I got caught, I could get disbarred. If you get caught you'll have me as your lawyer, so nothing to worry about."

"I won't get caught," he said. "They'll never know I was there."

"Right, the tracking mastery of the Native American warrior. Moving through the forest like a ghost. I can totally dig that."

He promised to call my cell if he had anything to report, assuming he could wake up enough to find the On button on the computer.

I was heading east toward Springs, so the rising sun was frequently in my face. The mist that often clothed the mornings out here in gray gauze moderated the effect. It also stuck to the windshield, forcing me to use the wipers and the defroster to see where I was going. Traffic was starting to build from the daily migration of tradesmen, waitstaff, retail clerks, and the rest of the working population priced out of the local real-estate market. It was nearly bumper-to-bumper through downtown East Hampton but eased up after I veered off Montauk Highway and headed toward Springs.

When I got to Matt Birkson's, Guthrie was out in the yard and, when I picked my way up the driveway, seemed pleased as punch to see me. I didn't have time to get all the way out of the car before he jumped up on me, leaving some impressive paw prints on my pants and the front of my shirt.

"Nice going, sport," I said, pushing him down with encouragement to stay there.

He accompanied me to the front door, which the more dangerous dog in the place opened only after some fairly persistent knocking.

"You again," said Birkson, answering the door in a gold-colored jumpsuit.

"I'm sorry to bug you, sir, but it's very important."

"Important to who?"

"To a lot of people, not least of all you," I said.

"I'll be the judge of that."

"Do we have to have all our conversations with me on the front stoop and you holding the door?"

He looked behind him into the house.

"I'm not exactly prepared for visitors," he said.

I looked around the property, spotting a pair of bent-up aluminum beach chairs.

"How 'bout over there?" I said, pointing. "It's warm enough."

"Jesus Christ," he said. He closed the door, and I didn't hear anything for about five minutes. I was about to start knocking again when the door opened and he came out with a blue goose-down vest over the jumpsuit. He walked past me and sat in one of the chairs. I sat in the other.

I'd rehearsed on the way over how I'd ease into this, as much as I rehearse anything, but looking at Birkson's hard-bit face and impatient eyes, I decided it wasn't worth it.

"I know about Eugenie," I said.

His squinted at me, not to see better, but to take stock.

"What's that supposed to mean."

"Any minute now I'm going to get a phone call that will confirm it beyond dispute. We could go through the motions of assertion and denial, but it's still going to come around to the same conclusion."

He sat silently, studying me.

"First make the assertion, then we'll see about the denial," he said.

Guthrie reestablished the relationship we'd begun by pressing up against my right leg. I dropped my hand down to pet him.

"She was Matt Jr., or Matt Jr. was Eugenie. However you want to put it. They were the same person."

He nodded slowly, not to affirm what I'd said, but more to acknowledge the topic of conversation.

"You say you got proof of that?" he asked.

I pulled out my cell and called Randall, apologizing for being a nudge, but he said it was okay, that he had what I wanted.

"Conclusively," he said.

I clicked the phone shut and nodded.

"Instead of graduating from high school, Matt left home. But not to ride the rails, or run away to sea, or any of that," I said. "He went and made the switch."

Birkson looked down at his hands, now clasped over his belly.

"Who else is making these accusations?" he asked.

"Right now, it's only me and people I work with," I said. "I can't promise it won't go any farther than that, but I'll do what I can. Depending on what you're willing to tell me."

He grinned a humorless grin.

"Plea bargain?" he said. "You can tell you're a lawyer."

"Come on. I came to you first."

He made a sigh that ended in a sort of growl.

"Most people are born equipped like a boy or a girl. But some others end up more or less in between," he said. "Some of these're more like girls, some more like boys, either in their heads or in the way they're put together. And sometimes they're all scrambled up. Matty's body kinda leaned toward boy, but in his head, he was all girl. You can imagine what kind of a torment that'd be."

"I can't imagine," I said.

"Matty was a wild one, that's for sure. Everybody figured it was because of my bad influence, but nobody knew the truth, except me and his mother, who really couldn't handle it. So she eventually left with her suitcase and her coke habit and I had to figure out what to do with him."

"But then you went to prison."

"Ida took him in, and I couldn't fairly keep it from her. Honestly, it was the best thing. You wouldn't think this, but I really wanted the kid to be whatever he wanted to be. I told him that more than once. But having a woman to talk to was the clincher. She helped him figure out how to be a girl, all the particulars, which he kind of took to, in a sort of transitionary way as this made-up sister, Eugenie. Then one day he decides, This is what I want to do, and I call him from the joint and say, Okay, I'll pay for it, and that was that. He leaves town for a few years, and by the time I'm done with my program, he's back as Eugenie, now a girl in every way, and nobody's the wiser."

"Is that true? That nobody's the wiser?" I asked.

He went back to studying me.

"That's what I believed. Never heard anything different."

"What about Ed?" I asked.

"I have no idea. That was between them. It wasn't the kind of thing I was going to discuss with my daughter."

I didn't know what to say to that, so I just sat there with my mouth shut, an unnatural state. Birkson saved me.

"Eugenie had a gift for all things mechanical. Always did. Hookin' up with Conklin made a life for her she could truly love. More than most people are able to say."

Guthrie must have noticed a disturbance in the emotional climate, because he left my side and went over to Birkson and shoved his muzzle into the old man's lap. I took it as a cue to let it go and just get out of there. There was more I wanted to know, but I couldn't bear to bring forth another ounce of sorrow.

"I'm sorry, Mr. Birkson," I said, and got up and walked over to my car and drove away. Through my rearview mirror I looked back at him scrunching around with Guthrie's muzzle and shaking his head, in disagreement or bewilderment. I was too far away to tell.

When I reached Bridgehampton, on the way back to Water Mill, I cut north and drove to my favorite horse pasture. The horses were out, and my favorite Certs addicts came galloping up with a great deal of excitement. I gave them a roll or two and apologized sincerely for my long absence.

In the middle of the pasture was a wide circle of fresh grass enclosed by a green wire fence. There was no other evidence of what had so recently happened there. I was glad the horses weren't thinking, Hey, remember the last time that woman showed up?

I looked at the sky and saw only the tiny, distant gleam of a commercial jet, safe in the air above, free from the corruption and duplicity down here on earth.

The last time I'd stood there I was confused about something, though now I couldn't remember what it was. I was still unsure about many things, but no longer confused over the essentials, at least as they related to the fate of Eugenie Birkson.

I peeled the wrapper off the last roll of Certs and chucked the little white disks out onto the grass. Then I got in my car and headed west toward Coram.

Harrison & Flynn TeleSales was still open for business when I got there. I had to go through the same receptionist gauntlet, and the chubby little nebbish put up the same feeble attempt at deterring me, which quickly withered in the face of my ferocious impatience, and soon enough I was waiting in the same comfy conference room with a cup of tea and a chest so tightened around my heart I wondered if I was about to stroke out.

Billy wasn't happy. He stormed into the room, his face red with exasperation.

"You can't keep doing this, Jacqueline," he said. "I need the work."

"I know," I said. "It's the last time. Just give me a few minutes."

He dropped like a bag of sand into one of the nice conference room chairs, unbuttoned his shirt collar and loosened his tie. I was sitting across from him. I put both forearms on the table and clasped my hands. I dipped my head toward the table surface, took a deep breath, then picked up my head and looked him right in the eye.

"Benson MacAvoy, Matty Birkson, and you were all there that night at the Peconic Pantry," I said, in as flat a voice as I could muster.

Billy sat in his chair like a lump, the implications of what I'd said pulling him downward, toward the earth.

"Says who?"

"I do. You were the Three Musketeers. Best buds. I don't know what happened, but I can guess. Matty was a wilding, an emotional powder keg. Angry, confused, who knows what. He loses it, gets into it with Clinton. Things get out of control. He hits Clinton with something. Maybe out of misconceived self-defense, maybe for the thrill of it. You all run, but not until after you dump out the register, grabbing the cash and the single check under the drawer, which you try to cash, to no good end. How am I doing so far?"

His face had that traitorous glow that comes with a ruddy complexion. Makes it hard for people like us to hide what we feel.

"You don't think I'm actually going to respond to that, do you?"

"I don't care if you do or not," I said. "You've been married to your story so long you might even believe it yourself.

"That's right. For twenty years I've kept it all buried underground. And you keep trying to dig it up. Why? I don't get the obsession."

I ignored that and pressed on.

"You're the one who gets busted, because you're the dumb ass who tries to cash the check. Now what? You could implicate your cohorts, but to what end? You're totally screwed, so why screw them, too? No point. I know that stubborn, Irish Catholic code of honor. You cleave to it even if nobody else does, because that's what you do."

He looked around the room, seeking escape. But I had him pinned to his chair with my eyes—my angry, inquisitional glare.

"It's ancient history," said Billy.

"Eugenie Birkson recently died over your so-called history. So no, it's anything but ancient."

"You're the one who thought there was virtue in stubbornness," said Billy. "I'd say black and your first thought was, How can I prove it's white?"

"Did you know?" I asked.

"Did I know what?"

"About Matty. That he was a girl in boy's clothing? You knew him all through childhood. You and Benson knew there wasn't a sister named Eugenie, until suddenly there was. Did you know Benson was selling industrial secrets, and that Eugenie was an accomplice, flying him up to Vermont, where they could spirit the goods over the Canadian border?"

I've made a study of interrogations, and concluded there are plenty of things that don't work, but no single technique that works every time. The only common denominator is the ability of the interrogator to interpret the facial expressions and body language of the interrogated. If you can read the cues, you can direct the flow.

Far less capable people than me would have read the shift in mood on Billy's face.

"I know nothing about that," he said.

"I think Benson knew the feds were closing in on him. He had to narrow his exposure, the greatest being Eugenie, who knew everything. I think he figured out a way to sabotage her plane so it would fail in flight. Take one variable out of the equation."

Billy pulled his head back as if I'd just reached across the table and slapped him.

"I think Brazen Bennie killed her," I said. "That's what ultimately became of the people you've protected all these years. Congratulations."

Billy shook his head with his whole body, like Stevie Wonder at the keyboard. Somewhere deep inside me sympathy tried to surface, but the rest of me, the animal on the hunt, slapped it out of the way.

"Eugenie's dead and you did the time. Only Benson gets away scot-free. It's time for the truth to come out," I said. "Come on; it'll be good for your soul."

I actually stood up and reached across the table and socked him gently in the chest, then sat down again. He looked at me as if he couldn't believe I'd just done that.

"Next time'll be the real thing," I said, smiling, like I didn't mean it, though part of me did.

"Bennie and I knew about Matty," said Billy, his face impassive, but with a tremor in his voice. "From the time we were kids. I think he needed to have someone know the truth, and for some stupid reason, he trusted us. It became a thing with me and Bennie to lock it down, to make it our life's work to protect Matty, who for all his crazy shit was wicked vulnerable, and afraid. Who wouldn't be. And I think he loved us, more than we could love him back, but that was all right. It worked out okay."

"Until he almost killed somebody," I said.

Billy closed his eyes and shook his head.

"You think you know so much, but you don't get it. That wasn't

Matty. He was a nutcase, but not like that. It was Benson. God forgive me, he's the one who beat on that store guy. We tried to stop him, but Bennie was always bigger and stronger. There was no way."

He put his head into his arms, which were folded on the table. I waited until he turned his head to the side so he could speak.

"The whole thing was Bennie's idea," he said. "Not for the money, for the thrills. He kept pushing us to do something radical. Something ultraviolent. We never thought he meant it till he was there whaling on that store guy with a steel pipe. It was Matty who pulled him off. I was too stupid and scared to do anything but stand there and watch. Matty pulled him out of the store, and I took all the stuff out of the register. It was just sitting there open and I thought why not? Don't ask me why, I just did it."

He burrowed his face back into his arms.

"So you took the whole rap because it was your fault you got caught," I said.

He nodded, without lifting his head.

"I didn't mind. If I hadn't tried to cash that check, I'd have gotten away, too. Clear of everything but my conscience. Like you said, what good would come from fuckin' up their lives as well? Bennie was the leader, but we followed. For Matty, it was a good motivation to get away and do what he'd always wanted to do. I was fine with that.

"To be honest, I did what I did because I was so fucking tired of doing everything the parents wanted me to do. It looks insanely stupid from where we are now, but at the time, you can't believe the pressure I was under to be what they needed me to be, with no regard whatsoever for what I actually wanted. The old man had this vision of me, this ideal. Bennie and Matt were my pressure valves, guys who saw me as just another guy, who I didn't have to impress, who I'd never disappoint. We created this little screwed-up separate reality and then convinced ourselves we could also live by a separate set of rules. Not such a bad thing as long as one of you isn't a sadistic thrill-freak."

There's nothing quieter than an office conference room. I think it's because it's always so filled with the noisy opinions of conference room occupants, so when they stop talking, it's like a tomb. That's how it was for the five minutes I sat there with my brother, him huddled into himself, me not knowing whether to hug his shoulders or rip out his heart.

"So you went away, but the two of them stayed in touch," I said.

"We all stayed in touch. Matty wired in protection for me in the joint through his old man–which is how Ed Conklin came into the picture. Matt ends up marrying my protector as Eugenie, which was too perfect when you think about it. Bennie becomes the superstar we always thought he'd be, and I get to live my life out as the piece of shit I truly am."

"A superstar clubs some guy nearly to death?" I said, my voice moving up a notch in volume. "Does a superstar sell industrial secrets to foreign agents? What's that, another reckless, immoral thrill? God knows what else he's done with the life you gave him."

"If I'd ratted out Benson he would've taken down Matty," said Billy, warming up himself. "Instead, he took care of her. Kept her secret. I know nothing about industrial espionage. I just know Eugenie was flying him all over the place, and from what I could tell, of her own free will."

A wave of grief came out of nowhere and washed over me. For Billy, for my parents. For me. Grief stirred in with fury. At reckless boys in general, but most especially at my brother and Benson MacAvoy.

"Eugenie's gone," I said. "Now there's nothing stopping you from taking Bennie down."

He smiled a crooked half smile.

"You're right. I hadn't even thought about that. Shows you how hard I work at repressing all that stuff. It's my full-time job. The work here is just a way to pass the time," he said, looking around the conference room.

"You didn't only take a hit in court, you took all the blame because you got caught. You wouldn't have been in that situation if it hadn't been for Benson MacAvoy. Christ, Billy, you're not in high school anymore. Why should that son of a bitch get away scot-free?"

He shook his head.

"I'm not doing it. I'm not putting myself and Kathy through all that. Not now. You don't know what we've been through."

This time I reached across the table and got a grip on his tie. I shook it hard.

"What if he killed her? Wouldn't that break the covenant–Bennie, you get to have your life, but you've got to look after Matty, or Eugenie, or whoever shows up next?"

He looked down at where I held his tie, then looked up at me with red, watery eyes.

"I'm not doing what you want. I can't. But I *am* going back to work, right now. And to hell with all of that," he said, though he made no effort to get up from the table.

He tried to hold eye contact, but then faltered and looked down at the table. I let go of his tie and wiped my hand off on my pants. Already standing, I slipped my pad back into my briefcase, which I slung over my shoulder.

"Fine," I said. "I'll do it without you."

I was nearly through the door when I heard him say, "She kept the pipe."

I stopped and looked back in the room.

"Say what?"

"Matty kept the pipe Bennie used to beat up the store guy. They were on Matty's motorcycle, so he was there when Bennie threw it in a Dumpster in the village. Matty went back and got it. He trusted Bennie well enough, but liked having an insurance policy."

22

It took less than an hour to get to Hampton Bays from Coram. I called Joe Sullivan on his cell phone to make sure he was at Town Police HQ. He wasn't, but he agreed to meet me there. Even though I wouldn't tell him what it was about, which he pointed out to me.

"Consider it the last favor you'll ever have to do for me," I told him.

"Done," he said, a little too promptly.

I then tried to focus on my driving so I wouldn't ruin the whole plan by killing myself on the highway. It wasn't easy. There was a lot on my mind.

When I knocked on Janet Orlovsky's bulletproof glass barricade it startled her. She almost looked happy to see me, then she caught herself. "Please tell Joe Sullivan I'm here," I said. "If that's okay. I have an appointment."

She broke new ground by simply calling him on the internal line.

Sullivan didn't look as compliant as I'd hoped when he opened the door to let me into the squad room. It wasn't the first time I'd asked to see him without telling him why, and not all of those meetings had gone particularly well.

"Welcome to HQ, counselor," he said. "Anything I can get you to make your visit more enjoyable? A little caviar? Cup of coffee?"

"Sure."

He took me into an interview room and then actually went to get us both coffee. I stayed standing till he got back in the room.

"We need Eugenie's camera case," I said. "Along with surgical gloves and a sharp knife."

He set the coffees down on the table.

"That's evidence."

"Thoroughly checked in, photographed, and logged. You should probably also get another witness, preferably whoever brings us the camera case from the evidence room so we maintain chain of possession."

That's when I sat down in a way I hoped conveyed I wasn't getting up again until he brought me the case. Respectfully.

Without taking his eyes off me he picked up the wall-mounted telephone and called the evidence room. Ten minutes later, a period filled with him asking me questions and me avoiding them, a young uniformed female cop showed up with the case, a handful of gloves, and an X-Acto knife. She brought along a yellow pad and a pen.

It was odd to see the case again, still dented and covered in dirt and grass stains. I put on the gloves, and after asking Joe's permission, opened it. All the contents had been removed, as separate pieces of evidence. Sullivan asked if we needed those, too, and I said no. The foam cutouts that held the camera, the extra lens, and unidentifiable accessories were thick and difficult to compress, so I really had to lean into the job.

"Hey, careful," said Sullivan.

I ignored him and continued to knead the foam until I found what I was looking for. I ran my hand along a seam between the foam and the front of the case.

"Cut here, and pull back the foam," I said to Sullivan.

"I can't tamper with evidence," he said.

"You're not tampering. You're investigating. That's what you do.

You're an investigator." A gloomy cloud was forming over his head. I leaned closer so the evidence room lady couldn't hear me. "If I'm right, there's a very serious collar on the way. You want to give that up?"

"If you're right? I've heard those words before," he said, but he went ahead and cut away the foam. The foam was too thick to fold, so he had to cut through three sides before he could access the inner surface of the case. Before he had a chance to do it himself, I reached in and pulled out the pipe.

It was a piece of galvanized steel, about fourteen inches long, wrapped in Saran wrap. At one end were the telltale reddish brown smudges of dried blood. At the other, I hoped, was an abundance of fingerprints and DNA.

I wished I'd had the sense to bring Burton or one of his criminal lawyers along for this moment. Ed Conklin was still my client, and Eugenie had been his wife, but I couldn't go after MacAvoy without connecting her to the pipe. Consequently, I was about to jump into shark-filled ethical waters, consoled only by the sure lack of precedence for the specific complications.

"This is the weapon used in the armed robbery and attempted murder of Clinton Andrews at the Peconic Pantry in North Sea, Southampton, on the night of May third, 1978. DNA will confirm that's his blood, and if there's a God, it'll also confirm that the assault was perpetrated by a man named Benson MacAvoy, eighteen at the time the crimes were committed. And as you know, crimes for which there are no statutes of limitation."

I looked over at the evidence room lady, waiting for her to catch up before I continued.

"Present at the scene were two other teenagers. One was William O'Dwyer, my brother," I said, causing Sullivan to arch an eyebrow. "Only O'Dwyer was convicted, as the result of trying to cash a check stolen from the store's register. He has remained silent on the presence of his accomplices, who are still unidentified, though the store owner,

Clinton Andrews, insisted there were three men involved in the robbery. To be fair to the prosecutors, this assertion came well after O'Dwyer was convicted, and given the severity of the injuries to Mr. Andrews, and the absence of corroboration, his testimony lacked credibility."

I waited again for the evidence lady to catch up. In a few moments, she nodded while still writing.

"In addition to William O'Dwyer and Benson MacAvoy, there was another teenager present during the crime. Eugenie Birkson came into possession of the assault weapon as a consequence of her relationship with this person, who had witnessed Mr. MacAvoy throw it in a Dumpster. This person later retrieved the pipe as a hedge against future betrayal by Mr. MacAvoy."

I held up the pipe.

"Tossing me the case wasn't about the camera or the photos on the memory card," I said to Sullivan. "She wanted me to have the pipe. She'd kept it close to her all those years, as an insurance policy against possible adverse behavior on the part of Benson MacAvoy, which unfortunately wasn't insurance enough."

Sullivan took the pipe out of my hand.

"So how did she get her hands on it?" he asked.

"That I'm not at liberty to discuss."

Sullivan frowned at me and I frowned back.

"Don't push me on this, Joe," I said. "I can't tell you. I'm so tangled up in personal, ethical, and professional conflicts I'll never get untangled. I just know that this bastard Benson MacAvoy almost killed Clinton Andrews and got away with it, and my brother, who just happened to be there, took the fall for the stupidest of reasons, thus smashing my family, and hence my childhood, into radioactive particles, such that it's likely I'm permanently scarred in a way that will compromise my emotional well-being for the rest of my life. Eugenie was no angel. She had a tough life in more ways than we can imagine, and that doesn't excuse everything she's done. But she didn't deserve to die."

"So you can prove MacAvoy caused the plane to crash," he said.

I shook my head.

"I don't know. I can build a case with lots of circumstantial evidence, but tangible proof will have to come from the feds, and we know how friendly they are to local prosecutions."

I dropped the file I'd taken out of the cabin in Vermont on the table.

"However," I said, "I've brought you a bargaining chip."

I told him about my trip north to the cabin, how I'd discovered the broken window and was astonished to find the door unlocked, and how I'd checked to make sure the place was secure and came upon this file folder. I described the contents, and suggested the papers be checked for prints and DNA, which I strongly believed would match those on the pipe.

"Even if the lab agrees to an expedited DNA test on this stuff and the pipe, it'll be three to four days before we get corroboration, if it exists," said Sullivan. "Ross isn't going to bring in a posh like MacAvoy on pure speculation. Your speculation, by the way."

Despite Sullivan's crummy innuendo, I knew he was right. And should the feds see any value in the files from Vermont, they'd start by checking out the cabin and go from there. No matter what, arresting MacAvoy was days, probably weeks, in the offing.

But there were things we could do in the interim. Beginning with briefing Ross Semple, always a wise course of action. Proven by the chief's glee as he thought about calling Fells and Li back for another visit, on his terms. I was glad to make him happy, something I'd surely have an opportunity to remind him of in the future, when a pleasant memory might overcome whatever inconvenient issue was then at hand.

I like to think of my ability to juggle conflicting emotions, and my dexterity with fuzzy logic in the service of rationalization, as a special power. One I used to connect the anger and remorse I felt for my brother to the joy of vindication over teasing out the truth about the Peconic Pantry attack, which morphed into shame over feeling even the tiniest ripple of sexual attraction for that monster Benson MacAvoy, leading to the sight of my high heels resting on his coffee table, a memory I followed back to Southampton, where Harry Goodlander opened the door of his converted garage, where he'd saved me yet again from the raging tempests in my mind, real and confabulated.

This was the antidote, the preventive care I needed to stave off the despair I knew was lying in wait, that inevitable reaction to witnessing the ugly truth of the past, made worse this time by being my own.

"Goodlander GeoTransit," said Harry, answering the phone as he always did, as if this was going to be the most exhilarating call he'd experience all week.

"If you ever need to dress up and go out to dinner and be indulged and preoccupied all night, I promise I'll take you," I said.

"I promise I'll let you."

"But you never ask. Not for yourself, anyway."

"I ask you out all the time," he said. "How do you know I don't need a little cheering up?" he asked.

Because I'm self-centered and moody? I thought. And then said out loud, "Because you always seem so cheerful on your own."

"That's stoicism masquerading as cheer," he said, his voice taking on a slightly lower pitch. "Inside I'm seething in agony, and you're the only one who cures the affliction."

"Now you're trying to make me feel better by pretending you feel worse than you really do. If that isn't love, what is?"

"I do love you, Jackie, even though you don't like me to say it."

I didn't, even if I'd just said it for him.

"So what do you want to do?" he asked.

"I want to break the curse of the funeral outfit."

"That sounds scary," he said.

"I can't condemn the one outfit that makes me feel the most

attractive and desirable to permanent funeral duty. Not when I'm feeling this lumpy and bedraggled."

"I can't think of a better way to break a curse. Slipping into a sexy outfit, then slipping out of it."

"Once again, you're reading my mind," I said, also pitching my voice to a lower register.

"I'll pick you up at seven. I need time to figure out what goes with black."

The only catch was that my funeral outfit was still hanging in a closet at my house on Brick Kiln Road. I checked the clock on the dashboard. There was still time to get there and back to my office with plenty of daylight to spare. Anyway, I'd pushed the sparse wardrobe I'd taken from my house that night about as far as I could, even for me. And it wouldn't hurt to see how everything was holding up.

On the way I distracted myself by listening to the overplayed songs on the local classic rock station, smoking cigarettes with all the windows open, and thinking of ways I could optimize the impending evening's fun. This almost crowded out all other thought, which was the idea.

As soon as I rolled down the long driveway to my house I felt a renewed affection for the place. Exile makes the heart grow fonder. It was a sunny day, and the profusion of new growth on the trees above almost glistened with replenished expectation.

I stood at the front door and dug my keys out of the muddled mess at the bottom of my purse. Inside, I slung the bag over my shoulder and did a quick sweep of all the rooms. It was more or less the way I remembered leaving it, with the exception of the lamp in the living room that'd been knocked over in the tussle and never restored to the side table. That creepy little note aside, it was pleasant to take in the sights and smells, made slightly less familiar by the brief passage of time.

Since I rarely kept much in the way of perishable food around, the kitchen was merely dank. I tossed a single bunch of rotten carrots in a plastic bag, scrubbed out the sink, and poured a cup of baking soda down the drain. I unplugged the coffeemaker, something I thought I'd already done, and headed back up the stairs to collect my clothes.

It took longer than I expected to select the right items to cover with plastic from the dry cleaner and haul down to the Volvo. I was on my final trip back to the second floor when my cell phone rang. I didn't recognize the number, which had a Nassau County area code. I answered anyway.

"So this is what you do for a living," said a woman's voice. "Ruin people's lives."

I climbed to the top of the stairs and went into the light of the front bedroom before answering.

"Who's this?"

"He's a good man. The best man I've ever known."

"Kathy?" I asked, finally placing the voice.

"He did one bad thing, and he's spent his entire life trying to rise above it."

"What did he tell you?" I asked.

"And you, his own sister, just want to drag him back down."

"He might be an even better man than you think," I said. "If you stop and actually think for a minute."

"You're the evil one in the family. Jealous Miss Priss."

Various parts of me fought to respond to that one, but luckily, the part that kept my head cool enough to practice criminal law, most of the time, prevailed.

"You need to tell me what Billy told you," I said.

"Do you have any idea what Benson MacAvoy has done for us? Do you think anyone else would've gotten Billy back on his feet, got him a place to stay, a job? Surely not his *family*."

Her emphasis on the word "family" was wet with contempt.

"You're obviously in no mood to be reasonable," I said. "But I can't have a conversation when I don't know what we're talking about."

"You know. Accusing Benson of attacking that man. You should also know that Billy confessed to everything. Not just in court, but to me. He opened his heart so he could heal. That was the night I fell in love with him. How dare you?"

"Where is Billy now?" I asked.

"None of your business. And if you don't stay away and stop harassing us, I'm calling the police. Even ex-convicts have rights, whether you believe it or not."

"Kathy, Billy's innocent. He didn't even know what Benson was planning to do."

"Go ahead, try twisting everything around," she said. "I've been warned."

I heard the sound of myself stopping on a breath and felt my face catch on fire.

"What do you mean, Kathy? Warned by who?"

"Who do you think? I'm not letting you slander Billy's best friend without him knowing about it."

"You didn't."

"Accusing people of crimes just because they won't go to bed with you? How low can you go?" she said, and she was about to say something else when I pushed the end button. I stood in the bedroom and waited for the screeching inside my head to quiet down enough for me to think.

That's when I heard the unmistakable sound of a car rolling down the gravel driveway and stopping below the window, the car door opening and then slamming shut.

23

I had my cell phone flipped open and my thumb poised over the buttons that would speed dial me into Southampton Town Police. I walked over to the window and looked down. All I saw was my Volvo, and no evidence of another car save for a cloud of gravel dust. I strained to look down the driveway from the awkward angle afforded by the bedroom window, to no avail. So I ran into the bedroom that faced that direction, pulled up the curtains, and looked down at Ed Conklin's pickup truck.

Relief, irritation, and a twinge of guilt swept over me in equal measure.

It was a devilish conundrum. Eugenie wanted the pipe's secrets revealed or she wouldn't have tossed the case out of the plane. Yet in so doing, she would be exposing her own involvement in the Peconic Pantry episode. Provided the authorities also learned her real identity. Compounding it all was my relationship with her husband, the guy who'd just arrived in his pickup, whose interests I was obliged to protect, even though they were often diametrically opposed to each other.

I'd tried like hell to keep Eugenie's big secret, but I wondered how long before the world knew what so few had held in confidence all these years. Ed undoubtedly knew he'd married a girl who'd once been a boy. Eugenie's social security number was still officially assigned to

Matthew Birkson Jr. It was unlikely she could hide that over all these years. Filing taxes, taking out loans, keeping up her pilot's license, renting a cabin in the woods of Vermont–there were just too many ways she'd be exposed without his cooperation.

Still, that didn't make me feel any better about the impending conversation.

"Goddammit," I said aloud. I put the phone back in my purse, which was still around my neck and over one shoulder, and walked back downstairs and out the front door. I looked over at the truck, down the drive, and across the lawn, but there was no one there.

"Yo, Ed," I called as I walked toward the pickup, which I then realized wasn't his, but one I'd seen parked at the hangar with the same decal promoting Conklin Maintenance and Repair on the side of the door. I moved closer and looked through the passenger-side window. Aside from the random flashlight, or socket wrench, all the junk on the seat and on top of the dashboard spoke of a young man–magazines devoted to heavy metal, half-naked women, and motorcycles, a pack of cigarettes, an iPod, an empty can of Red Bull, and a homemade flyer advertising a beach party featuring bitches, bonfires, and beer. Being the generally nosy person I am, I also looked in the voluminous area behind the seats, where pickup owners have been known to cram an impressive amount of crap.

Again, it was mostly tools and parts, baseball hats, more magazines, and in this case, a bashed-in Fred Flintstone mask peeking out from under a pair of greasy coveralls.

I heard the sound of him coming up behind me soon enough to spin around and jump away from the truck. Brian Conklin stood in the driveway with his hands in his pockets, a pale, slope-shouldered version of his father. He looked over my shoulder at the truck, then back at me, his skin glowing pinky white under the fading springtime sun.

Casper the Friendly Ghost.

I stepped toward the Volvo, but he moved almost lazily in front of me.

"You were looking in my truck," he said.

"Is this your truck?" I asked. "I thought it was your dad's. Looks just like it."

"You were looking. What did you see?"

"Nothing," I said, and started walking with greater authority toward my car. Brian stepped in front of me. I backed up.

"What did you see?" he said again.

"Nothing. What's the big deal?" I said. "You're not actually blocking my path, are you? That would be a very bad idea."

"I think it's bad to spy on people. That's what you're all about, isn't it? Creeping around spying on people. Is that what gets you off?"

"What are you doing at my house?" I asked. "Isn't that spying?"

"Watchin's not the same as spyin'," he said. "I knew you'd be back here some day. I just had to stop in once in a while."

What luck, I thought. I turned around and walked down the drive, away from the truck, where I had more room to maneuver. As he started to follow me, I turned back again and told him to stay where he was. He sauntered forward a few steps, then stopped.

"People know where I am," I said. "Don't do anything you'll regret."

He walked over to the bed of the pickup and reached in, pulling out a hammer with a long, thin handle and a tiny ball-shaped head.

"Should do the trick," he said, then ran directly at me.

I screamed, ducked my head down, and tried to dodge out of the way. I nearly made it, but he caught the upper sleeve of my jacket. I twisted away, but he held on.

"Not this time," he said, and whipped the little hammer into my shoulder.

I yelped again from the shock and pain, though the blow might have given the extra kick I needed to pull away. Rather than grab me again, he backed off, but in such a way that the path to my car was still effectively blocked.

"It was you," I said. "You killed her. Your own stepmother."

He tapped the hammer into his palm.

"Don't use the word 'mother' when talking about that fucking freak."

"You sabotaged the plane. You'd know how to do that. How to get it by your father."

"Not that hard if you know what you're doing," he said.

"The NTSB knows exactly how you did it," I said. "The question is why."

As I talked I eased my leather bag off my shoulder and unzipped it.

"What are you doing?" he said.

"I've got their report in here. I thought you should see how your name's all over it. You're days away from getting busted. You think hurting me is going to help your case?"

He tapped the hammer again, this time against his thigh.

"How're they going to know what I done with you?" he asked.

"I'll tell them."

"Not if I bash in your brains and feed your naked body to the sharks."

He took a step forward, and I asked him again if he didn't want to at least see what kind of evidence they had.

"I can read all I want when I'm done with you," he said as I reached inside my purse.

He lurched forward, and was only a few feet away when I cleared the Glock from my bag and leveled it at his chest.

"Maybe not," I said.

He stepped back a pace.

"Why'd you do it?" I asked.

He pointed at me with the hammer.

"Not impressed," he said.

"Why'd you kill Eugenie?" I asked again.

He smirked at me.

"I seen the name Matthew Birkson Jr. around the house my whole life, on mail and shit. She always said it was her brother's stuff that she had to forward on. Then I was in their basement looking for some shit from high school and found a whole stack of papers in a box. The dates don't hardly line up. I ask her about it, and she tells me the whole deal. I thought I was gonna die before I stopped puking my fucking guts out. My old man marries a fucking fag."

As he talked, his voice rose until he was nearly shouting, his Casper face turning more red then white.

"She kissed me good night when I was just an innocent kid and didn't know anything!" he yelled. "What kind of sick shit is that?"

"You're the one who's sick, Brian. Put the hammer down," I added, using the barrel of the Glock to gesture toward the ground.

"Fuck no. You're not gonna shoot me. No fuckin' woman has the balls to do that."

He threw the hammer at me. I flinched to the right and used my left hand to swat it away, keeping the other hand in control of the Glock, so when he rushed me I was still able to pull off a round, missing his heart but putting a tidy crease in his right side, which had an effect.

I stepped to the side to avoid his grasping hands as he collapsed to the ground, mewling in stunned disbelief.

"This fuckin' woman absolutely does," I told him, holding the gun to his head with one hand while I searched my purse for the cell phone with the other.

24

Burton Lewis sat on my pull-out sofa looking completely at ease. On his lap was a legal pad hooked to a clipboard made of exotic hardwood. He took notes as I recited the testimony I planned to give the next day in the attempted murder trial of Benson MacAvoy, occasionally flipping back through the pad to check for inconsistencies.

"So it wasn't until your brother revealed that Eugenie, as the former Mathew Birkson, had retrieved the assault weapon that you were convinced of MacAvoy's complicity in the crime," he said.

"That is correct. I purposely refrained from sharing my theories with the police until I knew I could support such a serious charge with incontrovertible evidence. Burton, you have a jillion lawyers who could be taking me through this. Don't you have better things to do?"

"I want to be sure you don't expose yourself to withholding. Nailing MacAvoy is priority one, I agree, but you can't be tarnished in the process."

"That isn't what I meant," I said.

"Fingerprinting and DNA tests have confirmed that the steel pipe was indeed the weapon used in the assault on Mr. Andrews, but traces belonging to both Mr. MacAvoy and Ms. Birkson were present on the pipe. Why should we believe Mr. MacAvoy was the only perpetrator?"

"Because Eugenie's prints were only on the bloody end, from when she picked the pipe out of the Dumpster. She kept it to have something over MacAvoy. Otherwise, she could have easily disposed of it in a thousand ways. She was a brilliant mechanic, for Pete's sake. With access to welding torches and lathes. To say nothing of small aircraft and the deep blue sea."

"Benson wasn't much of a criminal, for all his sadistic tendencies," said Burton.

"You think?" I said. "Trying to escape on his yacht after Billy's dopey wife told him I was onto him? Beating up on a convenience store owner is one thing. Selling composite technology critical to the American defense industry is another. Did he not know the Coast Guard works for Homeland Security? Tell me again why you're the one prepping me for trial?"

"You knew of the details of Mathew Birkson Jr.'s role in the robbery, and his subsequent transformation into Eugenie," said Burton, ignoring me. "Yet you failed to provide this information to the police when you and Detective Sullivan discovered the pipe. Why?"

"I felt constrained by client confidentiality since I was representing Eugenie's husband, Ed. I needed his permission to openly discuss his wife's complicated history, which I've subsequently received, hence my testimony today."

"Which entails?"

"Mathew Birkson Jr. was born with a condition known as intersex anatomy. Meaning his sexual equipment was ambiguous–somewhere between male and female. With any luck, people thus affected are spared surgical intervention until they reach an age where they're able to make a choice for themselves to remain as they are or be assigned to one gender or the other through surgery. Immediately following the robbery and assault, Matthew left for another city, where he lived for four years, during which time he elected to have the surgery that made him unambiguously female. He returned to East Hampton, where he'd grown up, as Eugenie Birkson, using a female variation of his middle name.

"Benson MacAvoy, who'd been Mathew Birkson Jr.'s childhood friend, was aware of this transition. At some point in their adult relationship, MacAvoy contracted with Eugenie to provide air taxi service for his frequent flights to various parts of New England. We've subsequently come to know these flights were part of an illegal enterprise that sold industrial secrets to foreign nationals. There is no evidence that Eugenie Birkson had any knowledge of illegal dealings, to which her murder was entirely unrelated. Consequently, there is no reason to suspect this was anything more than a simple chauffeuring arrangement between two old friends, as Mr. MacAvoy asserts."

Burton looked up from his pad to signal that he was suspending role-play for a moment.

"I understand Benson's phone calls to his customers won't be part of the evidence," he said.

"The NSA isn't about to discuss their methods in an open trial. It doesn't matter. The prosecutor doesn't need it to convict, and Benson's lawyers are just as happy to not go there. What we do know, unofficially, is that Benson favored the same crude but highly effective technique Brian Conklin used to evade electronic discovery–stealing other people's gear, whether computers and e-mail boxes or cell phones. But once again, Benson outsmarted himself. From what my source in the FBI tells me, NSA monitoring looks for exactly that kind of pattern: frequent calls to suspect parties made from stolen phones. Which is where Benson's thrill-seeking, master of the universe tendencies also caught up with him. Sneaking calls on the cell phones of his fellow partygoers is a classic ego trip for a narcissist like MacAvoy. And a bright red alert for the NSA. By the time people like Inspectors Fells and Li start circling, it's just a matter of time. My greatest fear was that they'd snatch him up and disappear him into the gulag before I could nail him for Eugenie's murder."

"Which is the only thing he wasn't guilty of," said Burton.

"Lucky for him for a lot of reasons. Matt Birkson Sr. and Ed Conklin are still plenty well connected at Sanger, where MacAvoy is most assuredly going to spend the bulk of his remaining life. Which wouldn't amount to much if he'd killed her."

"No it wouldn't," said Burton.

"I know you know this, but it's a tough goddamn world out there," I said.

"A world in which you've shown remarkable courage," said Burton.

"Remarkable stupidity. My instincts kept telling me there was something off about both MacAvoy and Brian Conklin. But did I listen? At least with Benson I can claim temporarily insane infatuation."

Burton took a flash drive tied to the end of a thin tether out of the inside pocket of his blue blazer and twirled it around his finger.

"I refuse to agree with you," he said. "I've always thought the world of you as a person, but now I see you for the crack defense lawyer you truly are. So you're hired. And that's that."

"Say that again?"

"You'll operate our new Suffolk County office. There's far too much activity out here for Alicia to handle alone, as she eloquently pointed out this week in her resignation letter, graciously withdrawn when I told her you were stepping up. She likes you, which is good, since you'll be working together closely."

"Now I know why you're really here."

"We'll match your current revenue, with regular increases unrelated to client load," he said. "We'll also cover an assistant, all out-of-pocket expenses, and reasonable T and E. All the necessary paperwork is on this flash drive. You just have to save the wretched refuse of the teeming East End, forego your existing base of real estate clients and the attendant charms of zoning appeals, title claims, and angry, disappointed buyers and sellers."

"I didn't specialize in criminal law."

"No, but you've had more than adequate on-the-job training. And the other attorneys will support you. Sam tells me you're selling your house. I bought this building. The lease is expiring this month for the parties across the hall. I thought that area would make a pleasant apartment, and you could turn this back into the airy, uncluttered office space I'm sure it once was," he said, looking about ingenuously.

The truth was, I'd been heading in that direction anyway. I just hadn't reconciled all the extra work for the lousy pay. Now there was Burton, like a genie out of the bottle, granting my wish. Better than a genie, a billionaire.

"If I'm not up to it I could always go back to real estate," I said.

"You could. No contracts. Just a handshake and a stack of case folders," he said, resting his arm on the banker's box he'd brought upstairs with him. "You could resist this in that habitual way of yours, but it would be such a waste of time, given that we both know you're going to accept."

Instead of shaking on the deal, I kissed him smack on the mouth. Gay as he was, he seemed to like it.

When he left, I booted up the laptop, stuck in the flash drive, and lit up a joint so I had something else to do while I stared out at the windmill and pondered the wonder of random happenstance, the bounty of unexpected deliverance.

Chris Knopf is author of *Short Squeeze*, the first novel in the Jackie Swaitkowski series; *Elysiana*; and the Sam Acquillo mystery series, including *The Last Refuge*, *Two Time*, *Head Wounds* (which won the Benjamin Franklin Award for Best Mystery) and *Hard Stop*. A copywriter by trade, Chris is a principal of Mintz & Hoke Communications Group. He lives with his wife, Mary, in Avon, Connecticut and Southampton, New York, where he sets sail on the sacred Little Peconic Bay.